# HARBINGER

KEN LOZITO

Published by Acoustical Books, LLC

KenLozito.com

Cover design by Jeff Brown

If you would like to be notified when my next book is released visit

www.kenlozito.com

ISBN: 978-1-945223-33-4

# 1

THICK DROPS of rain pelted the rover as a sudden thunderstorm rolled in, and rivulets of water streamed across the windshield before a low-powered shield engaged. As the shield pulsed, clearing Connor's view, a notification chimed and then popped into existence on the rover's holoscreen. Connor glanced over and then quickly dismissed it.

He heard Samson clear his throat from the passenger seat. "I don't think you're going to make that Security Council meeting," Samson said.

"Nathan will be there," Connor replied.

They were driving along a rough path thirty kilometers from Sanctuary. The rover was more than up to the task of navigating the rugged terrain, but Samson was right; they weren't going to get anywhere quickly.

Samson arched a thick eyebrow and remained quiet. Connor was glad his friend had rejoined the colony, but he'd noticed that Samson was still prone to long bouts of silence.

The only exception to that was when he was commanding his own Spec Ops platoon on a mission; however, when not on task, he was quietly reserved.

"This is just as important," Connor replied.

Samson made a show of glancing out the windows at the surrounding forest, looking unconvinced. "What are we doing way out here, and why take a rover?"

"I thought you of all people could appreciate a short trip away from the hustle and bustle of city life, even one like Sanctuary."

"Yeah, right," Samson said and shook his head. "Don't tell me then."

"Will anybody who's grumpy today please raise their hand? You didn't have to come, you know."

"Right now, I'm wishing I didn't," Samson said and glanced at the HUD overlay that refreshed with a flashing waypoint. "Since when is there a Recovery Institute building way out here?"

"Only the past few months. It's just one HAB unit and a bit of a work area."

"Who's it for?"

"His name is John Rollins," Connor said, and Samson frowned. "You've never met him. He was left behind in an alternate universe and became a prisoner of the Krake. When we found him, he was starving and on the verge of losing his mind."

"I've heard the name before and read the mission reports."

Connor gripped the rover steering wheel firmly. "It was bad. The atmosphere was slowly poisoning him, and I don't know how he survived. We all thought he was dead."

Samson nodded. He was a career soldier from Connor's old

Ghost Platoon before they'd been shanghaied into the colony. "What's he doing way out here?"

"Hopefully, getting better."

"Are you telling me the doctors recommended seclusion as some kind of therapy to deal with what this guy went through?"

"Rollins asked for this. He had a rough time during the Vemus War and . . . let's just say he's not a people person. He's being monitored and has regular visits from the staff at the Recovery Institute, but he prefers to be alone. Part of this arrangement requires him to return to Sanctuary at least once a month."

They were both quiet for a few minutes.

"Why do you do this?" Samson asked.

"What do you mean?"

"You make it personal."

"I left him behind."

"You just said you thought he was dead."

Connor was quiet. "I'm just checking up on an old friend."

"Were you friends?"

"What's with the third degree? What's your problem?" Connor asked.

"My problem is that you're allowing yourself to be pulled in a bunch of different directions, and we can't afford that right now. This is a distraction. You brought me back to help you prepare for the Krake, and I'm just doing my job by pointing that out."

Connor kept driving. Samson could believe whatever he wanted. The truth was that Connor did sometimes make things personal, and he cared about what had happened to Rollins, but that wasn't the only reason he was there.

Connor gave Samson a flat look, and Samson blew out a breath. “You almost had me going.”

“I knew you’d get there eventually. Rollins has had the most interaction with the Krake. I’m hoping he’ll remember something we can use,” Connor said.

He felt terrible about leaving Rollins behind, but they'd thought he was dead and hadn't had any time to do a thorough check. They'd had to flee the Krake military base and were lucky to get out alive. This was before Connor had rejoined the Colonial Defense Force, ending his early retirement.

They entered the campsite amid a few HAB units intended for long-term use away from any of the colonial cities. They were popular with the forward operating research bases that were still in use. Connor powered off the rover, and they stepped outside.

Rollins had been a combat engineer and liked to work with his hands, so Connor wasn't surprised to find a small warehouse with its doors open and lights on inside. Off to one side was a line of agricultural-type robots that were either in need of repair or just a basic maintenance cycle. Rollins had agreed to provide this service to help offset the resources required to maintain his living space way out here.

Connor called out for Rollins, and some of the machinery he could hear running from around the corner stopped. A lean man stepped out. He was wearing an apron with several tools in the pockets. His hands were dirty, and he had a few smudges on his cheeks, but Rollins looked much healthier than he used to. He’d regained some of the weight he’d lost from almost starving to death, but he was a long way from healed.

Rollins jutted his chin up once in an acknowledgment, glancing at Samson and then back at Connor. “I see you brought company this time." He turned back around the corner to the work area and put down the piece he'd been cleaning.

"I can have him wait with the rover if you want," Connor offered. The thunderstorm continued to rage outside. They were in the middle of a downpour, but it was a short walk to the rover and Connor knew the rain wouldn't bother Samson at all.

Rollins returned without the apron or the part he'd been carrying and glanced at the ground. "I know it shouldn't bother me," he said and then gritted his teeth. He looked at Connor. "He can stay."

"Thanks," Connor replied.

Rollins walked over to one of the workbenches and leaned back against it. Connor recognized that it was a strategic location that wouldn't allow anyone to approach Rollins from behind, as well as giving him a view of the entire area.

"I heard you were in trouble," Rollins said.

Connor's face reflected his surprise. "Is that so?"

"It's been all over the newsfeeds. I do check on them from time to time. The doctors are afraid I'll lose touch," Rollins said, shaking his head.

Connor glanced around the workshop. "It looks like you're keeping busy out here."

"It helps if I keep moving," Rollins replied.

"Well, you don't need to stop on my account. What are you working on?"

Rollins glanced toward his work area, and Connor followed his gaze. A standard Field Ops motion scanner was disassembled, the parts strewn across the workbench.

Rollins pressed his lips together, looking as if he was deciding whether to let Connor in on a secret he'd been keeping. Then he shrugged. “I was tweaking the detection capability of the scanner assembly.”

Connor approached the workbench. “What are you trying to do with it?”

“They’re preconfigured to look for things like ryklars or berwolves or any other predators we have in the area. I wanted to rotate the profiler to scan for something different. Almost like a general predator profile.”

Connor pursed his lips in thought for a moment. “Easier said than done. Are you getting inundated with false-positive readings?”

“I was, but I was able to get around that by having it use a standard field survey set of protocols—you know, the ones Field Ops uses to survey the region. Instead of just flagging a species as unknown and waiting for someone to catalog it, I’m having it make a guess as to whether it's a predator or not,” Rollins said.

What Rollins was describing was no easy feat. There was no way he could do this on his own, which meant he was working with somebody. This was a good thing.

“I had some help,” Rollins said, rubbing at an imaginary piece of dirt on his workbench.

“Who’s helping you?”

“Lockwood. He’s been sending me software updates based on the changes I’ve been making to the drone. And don’t look so surprised. The kid sent me a message a month ago asking how I was doing. He’s grown up a lot,” Rollins said.

Connor nodded. Rollins had an abrasive personality, and Connor remembered Rollins first meeting Lockwood almost two years ago when they’d stumbled upon the Ovarrow stasis pods. It was hard to believe it had been that long.

"He's one of the good ones," Connor agreed. "I'm glad you're keeping busy."

He could see why Rollins would take on a project like this. He'd spent months surviving, not knowing whether he was going to live or die in one of the harshest environments imaginable.

Rollins looked away from him and his shoulders rounded. "You want to know if I remember anything else."

Connor knew Rollins's recovery had been extremely difficult. The doctors had described his condition as an almost complete breakdown of conscious thought, more or less as if the man had been in a permanent mode of fight or flight. Connor had seen this behavior before in other soldiers he'd known—the ones who were broken inside but wouldn't let themselves quit.

"I wish I didn't have to," Connor said.

"You certainly gave me enough time. The Krake really didn't know what to do with me. After the bomb went off, things just fell apart. I managed to escape with the help of the other prisoners. They either let us go or they just didn't care anymore. Hell, they knew we were going to die anyway, so why waste the ammo?" Rollins said.

Connor grimaced. He planted that bomb when they'd gone back through the archway. It had been intended as a trap for the Krake.

"Now, don't go being like that. I'm glad you bombed those bastards. I would've done the same thing. They left some of their own behind."

Connor frowned. "They left other Krake behind?"

Rollins's bushy eyebrows pulled together and he nodded. "They all just killed themselves once the ships were gone.

There were eight or nine of them, and they just . . ." Rollins said and squeezed his eyes shut. "They could have survived. I don't understand why they did that. Several of the Ovarrow did the same thing later on, and they might've been the lucky ones. There was a lot of fighting for resources. I stayed alive by staying away from the group and moving around at night, at least before those creatures started showing up."

Connor remembered the strange predators they'd fought. Their bioluminescent fur glowed red when they were about to attack. They were fearsome creatures whose claws could tear through CDF combat suits.

"I tried to make my way to where we'd come through the archway, but it was too dangerous. It took me . . . I don't know how long for sure. Maybe a week or two to gather the components to transmit a distress signal. I had to cannibalize my own PDA to make it work. Everything after that was just . . . surviving, scavenging for something to eat. Nothing tasted right, and the air burned my lungs. They have me sleeping with a regulator now, which is supposed to help with the pain, but it still hurts to breathe sometimes, especially if I work too hard. I wish there was more I could tell you. I wish I could tell you something so you could go hit them where they live. They knew we were alive down there, trying to survive, and they sent those creatures down. Who does that to prisoners? If I knew something that could help you hurt them, I'd tell you. Hell, I'd volunteer to help you."

"I know you would, but you've done enough, John. Let someone else do it."

Rollins inhaled deeply and sighed. "The sleep regulators are supposed to help me rest. I wish they could stop me from dreaming, but they don't make medicine for that."

"Are you sure you're all right out here? I know you want to be alone, but sometimes it might help to be around people," Connor said.

Rollins shook his head. "Based on what I'm reading in the newsfeeds, there's been quite the upheaval. Government officials are being arrested. A rogue group was torturing the Ovarrow. Then there *you* are, front and center. They're claiming you abused your power as a CDF general."

"I did what had to be done. Now I'll need to answer for it," Connor replied.

Rollins snorted bitterly. "Sometimes people don't like to take their medicine. Sure, they're upset with what you did, but I bet the alternative would've been worse. I suppose you'll tell them to learn from it, but what's to stop them from making you their scapegoat?"

Connor could always count on rigid honesty from Rollins. "They need me, and they know it. At least, the right people know it."

Rollins nodded and then his eyes glittered as if he'd just remembered something. "The Krake came back to the planet two times. First, they were assessing the damage. Then the second time, they unleashed those creatures on us. After that, they never returned. The question you can ask the Security Council is: what happens if the Krake were to come here and start dumping those creatures on New Earth, wreaking havoc in the cities?"

Connor nodded grimly. "That's exactly what I intend to tell them. If you need anything at all, Rollins, you know how to contact me. If I'm not around, you can contact Diaz. He's pretty much at Sanctuary all the time."

Rollins shook his head. "That guy hated me."

"He didn't hate you. He thought you were a pain in the ass, which is the truth. You *are* a pain in the ass," Connor said, and Rollins nodded. "Seriously, he'd help you if you needed it."

Connor and Samson went back to the rover, and Samson was quiet as they drove away.

"I brought you along because you're the only one I know who's lived on his own away from everyone else for that long," Connor said.

"I lived away from the colony, but I was here on New Earth. I didn't survive on some kind of prison planet. I don't know if I could help him at all," Samson said.

Connor doubted that. Samson had lived apart from the colony for about eight years. The man had had that long to explore the continent, contending with all the creatures that called New Earth home, using only the barest survival skills. Connor knew Samson would think about Rollins and come up with some way to help the man in the future, even if he didn't think he could now. Connor couldn't do everything himself, and maybe he could hit two birds with one stone.

## 2

Connor looked out the window of the combat shuttle as it sped across the continent. New Earth's rings stretched from horizon to horizon in pale marble ribbons. He'd gotten used to the view and sometimes had trouble remembering the view of the sky back on what was now referred to as Old Earth. The colonists kept the memory of Old Earth alive through museums and tributes to the fallen, but Connor doubted they'd ever forget the birthplace of humanity, although because the colonial population had doubled, there was a significant increase in the younger generation who would only know New Earth as their home. They'd either been born here or were brought out of stasis at such a young age that they might as well have been born here.

He remembered the first time he'd seen New Earth and its rings. He'd been aboard the *Ark* and had just been brought out of stasis. He'd thought the whole thing was an elaborate hoax, but he'd been wrong. Ending up here wasn't anything he could've imagined. The journey to New Earth had taken over two hundred years, and everything he'd known before was gone.

The combat shuttle didn't actually have any windows since they were structural weaknesses that didn't belong on a combat ship. Sensors and cameras created the images that appeared on the holoscreens. The New Earth landscape stretched out away from them, and he realized that even though he'd explored a large portion of the area they were flying over, no one had explored all of it. They'd been on the planet for almost fourteen years, but there hadn't been time to search the entire continent.

The New Earth landscape was similar to Old Earth. There were mountain ranges, vibrantly colored forests, wide-open plains, and the ruins of alien cities. Some of it reminded him of Old Earth. He'd grown up on military bases on both Earth and space stations. Most of his childhood had been spent in the heart of the North American Alliance, which was comprised of old nation-states, with its core being the United States, Canada, and Mexico, but also included Great Britain and Spain. The NA Alliance had been around for over a century before Connor was born, and most of the culture and individual societies that stemmed from the nation-states had merged by then. However, the Ark Project had been funded by more than just the NA Alliance. The Asia Pac Alliance, containing parts of Europe and individualist nation-states, had also contributed. Over three hundred thousand colonists had gone to sleep on the *Ark* and awakened two hundred years later on a planet they hadn't been heading for. And even though it hadn't been their destination, they'd made a home here.

Connor inhaled deeply and sighed. Now, they had a population of over six hundred thousand. The Vemus—

believed to have wiped out all mammalian life on Earth—had followed them to New Earth. Connor and the rest of the Colonial Defense Force had been able to stop them, but it had nearly cost them everything. The Vemus was an alien symbiotic virus combined with bacterial infectious agents that had been targeted at mammalian life. The scientists who'd worked to cure it had also used it to target humans in order to consolidate power. It was that genetic modification that had made the Vemus hunt humans to the exclusion of all else and also what had driven the virus to find New Earth.

Sometimes Connor wondered what Old Earth looked like now, but maybe not knowing was a blessing. He imagined it was a place of devastation—cities destroyed and all the people gone, new animals rising up to fulfill a niche in the absence of humans. And the Vemus might still be there as well. The New Earth colony had sent probes back to Earth, but Connor would be an old man before those probes transmitted data back to them. Earth was sixty light-years away from the colony, and the probes they'd sent back, even traveling at relativistic speeds, would take at least sixty years to get there, but it was probably closer to seventy years. The probes needed time to slow down and assess the situation before moving into the system. Then, after that assessment, they'd begin transmitting data back to the colony.

Until recently, Connor had assumed that any data would take at least sixty years to reach New Earth. Given those timetables, the soonest they could learn about what had happened to the people of Earth would be about a hundred and forty years from now. He was sure the scientists could narrow it down to specifics, but his calculations were good enough for him. However, those calculations had been hypothesized before they'd been able to use subspace communication. Even in its limited form, they could potentially learn about Earth much sooner than they'd originally anticipated. The probes were not only equipped with scanners and powerful communication devices, but they also had an auto-factory with 3D printers capable of producing what the probes needed, including a subspace communication transceiver.

"Attention. We'll be approaching the landing pad in ten minutes. General Gates, transport has been arranged to bring you straight to the Colonial Administration Building," the pilot said.

Connor switched the viewpoint on the holoscreen and could see their approach to Sierra, one of New Earth's major cities. Construction of the pylons had begun for the regional maglev trains that would connect all the cities, and one of those branches would be coming to Sanctuary. He'd been aware of the project but hadn't thought it'd gained so much traction. It had been over six months since it was first proposed. *Well, that's not exactly right,* Connor thought, silently correcting himself. It had been proposed when they'd first established colonial cities, but it had been delayed because of the imperative to reallocate resources to the Colonial Defense Force. There'd been a need for sacrifice at the time, but now, many of the projects that had been put on hold were getting the green light.

Connor understood the reasoning for this, but at the same time, they needed to prepare for the possibility of a Krake invasion. Something else they couldn't have been prepared for when the *Ark* arrived was the fact that New Earth hadn't been as unoccupied as they'd originally thought. There was an intelligent alien species living there who called themselves

Ovarrow. When the colonists first started exploring New Earth, they'd found remnants of a vast civilization—abandoned cities and alien structures but also impact craters, which indicated signs of an orbital bombardment. Connor had had plenty of opportunity to study the alien ruins because his wife, Lenora, was an archaeologist.

He didn't know much about establishing a colony. He knew about space stations, military installations, and hunting shadow organizations. What he didn't know about was making a new world a home and who would be best qualified to help achieve that. There were the obvious choices of biologists, chemists, and engineers, but he'd never thought about an archaeologist. It seemed foolish to him now that this would be overlooked, and Lenora had more or less shoved him into that realization very quickly. How else would they learn about the world they were going to make a home on?

New Earth had layers upon layers of discoveries waiting to unfold—from the intelligent species like the Ovarrow to the animal life that lived here. Even the plant life was strangely familiar and yet quite exotic. Lenora had often said to Connor that they could spend the next century here and still wouldn't have unlocked all of New Earth's secrets. She liked to think of mysteries as secret stories yet to be unlocked. However, the more they learned about New Earth and the Ovarrow, the more that gave way to a general unrest that was felt by most colonists.

The Ovarrow were bipedal, with various shades of brown, pebbled skin like that of a reptile. Pointy protrusions stemmed from their shoulders and elbows. They had long arms and large hands with four long fingers, from which stubby black claws protruded. Their severe brow lines stretched to the backs of their wedge-shaped heads. They were lean and strong but had a bit of a stoop that made their heads bob when they walked.

Lenora and hordes of other scientists were working to put together the Ovarrow's history. Connor had stumbled onto another secret of New Earth when he'd discovered that the Ovarrow had hidden in bunkers, using a primitive form of stasis. The Ovarrow had fought wars among themselves, and it was later learned that they were defending themselves against an invader they called the Krake.

Connor remembered the NA Alliance first-contact protocols that had been refined for hundreds of years in the event that aliens came to visit Old Earth. They'd never had to use them. It had always been assumed that aliens would cross vast distances between stars, but that hadn't been the case with the Krake and New Earth. The Krake were a species that lived in another universe and had the technology to cross between universes. They explored and cataloged, but at some point in their history, they'd decided to experiment on and manipulate the Ovarrow they found. Based on appearance alone, the Krake and Ovarrow seemed to share a common ancestor, or maybe they were different branches on the same evolutionary tree. The colonists lacked DNA evidence to support it, but Connor knew it was only a matter of time. The Krake were going to return to New Earth one day, and Connor was determined to find a way to stop them.

He'd found evidence of the Ovarrow's attempt to reverse-engineer the technology that allowed the Krake to traverse between universes. The Krake had built a massive arch, and even though colonial physicists and engineers hated the phrase, Connor thought of it as an "open gateway" to another universe. Colonial scientists had had even more success with making the Krake technology work for them, and that had led to discoveries Connor suspected the Krake weren't aware of, but they still didn't know much about the Krake themselves. So far, their best intelligence about the Krake was that they were a highly advanced civilization that exploited societies from alternate universes for scientific gain. They practiced a strange form of ruthless scientific pragmatism, looking to predict the outcome of everything.

Learning about the existence of the Krake had given Connor many sleepless nights. He didn't require the standard seven to eight hours of sleep civilians needed because of his specialized implants. Most nights, he only required a few hours' sleep. The only reason most colonists didn't utilize his particular type of implant was a lack of long-term studies of the effects of fooling the brain into thinking it had gotten the required amount of rest that evolution had decided the human body needed. Connor had already had the prototype implants in him when he'd gone into stasis. They'd since been studied by colonial scientists, and a variant of them had been engineered for use by select colonists, mostly those in the CDF.

The combat shuttle landed on the CDF base at Sierra, and Connor got off. He was then transferred to a civilian aerial transport vehicle, commonly referred to as a C-cat, which was smaller and meant to carry only four or five people. He was soon heading toward the Colonial Administration Building. He'd been there only a few days before and hadn't expected to be summoned back quite so soon.

The flight to the administration building only took about fifteen minutes, and after they landed, Connor walked off the landing platform and headed inside the building. The last time he'd been there was when Meredith Cain, the former head of the Colonial Intelligence Bureau, had been arrested. This was in no small part due to Connor hunting down a rogue group that was terrorizing the Ovarrow. They'd made the mistake of bringing civilians into their crosshairs, including his wife. Connor had organized operations using unarmed Spec Ops soldiers to monitor and coordinate with Field Ops, but they were also ordered to detain key suspects until Field Ops could arrive. Many government officials viewed Connor's actions as an extreme abuse of power. The result was a political crap storm, and he was still waiting to see where the pieces would fall. His actions had been necessary, but he knew there'd be a cost. There was always a cost.

Connor walked through the halls of the Colonial Administration Building. There was always an influx of people walking the halls, either going to or coming from various meetings, often speaking with people over their personal comlinks. At four inches over six feet, Connor's broad shoulders often commanded a natural pathway through groups of people. He was difficult to miss in a crowd unless Samson was with him, who was the human version of a Nexstar combat suit heavy. Connor wasn't heavily muscled, but he was extremely strong and maintained a high level of fitness. It was just a natural part of who he was and was also necessary for his overall strategy to do things like keep breathing. On more than a few occasions, he'd needed all his strength just to survive. He'd seen soldiers who let their fitness go, to their own demise. This was something the Colonial Defense Force could not afford, whereas the militaries of Old Earth could indulge when they had populations numbering over fourteen billion people to draw from. There was plenty of fat to trim with a population that large, but not on New Earth. The CDF was lean, and so were its soldiers. Most colonists were physically fit. He wondered if that would wane as the years went on and people chose to stay in the cities they'd built rather than roam the countryside.

"Excuse me, General Gates," a woman said.

Connor turned toward the woman, and she smiled. "Hi, I'm Rebecca Kent. I'm one of Governor Wolf's aides. I was sent to inform you that the meeting has been moved to her office."

Connor nodded and gestured for Rebecca to lead the way. There were clusters of people gathered outside the governor's office. A few people glanced in his direction as he approached, and conversations became hushed remnants of what they'd once been. Connor ignored them as he walked by.

Rebecca waved at the receptionist/gatekeeper to the wing of offices where the governor and her staff worked.

"Seems a bit busier than normal," Connor said.

"This is the new *normal*," Rebecca replied, voicing the first hint of weariness at all the activity.

Given the extent of how many people had been implicated in the rogue group's activities, he shouldn't have been surprised, but he was.

"I know the way from here. You can move on to whatever else you have to do," Connor offered.

Rebecca checked her wrist computer and regarded Connor for few moments. "Good luck," she said.

She turned and left, and Connor frowned. Why would she wish him luck? He strode to Dana Wolf's office and unceremoniously opened the door, walking inside.

Connor saw Nathan standing off to the side. He gave Connor a crisp nod, but his brow was furrowed in concentration. Dana Wolf stood off to the other side, speaking with Bob Mullins. Connor's neck stiffened with a flash of annoyance. Mullins's short-cropped, curly hair had an oily shine to it. He stopped speaking, and his piggish eyes narrowed a little as he looked at Connor.

Dana smiled warmly and waved him over. "Connor, thank you for coming down here again on such short notice."

"Nathan said it was important."

"He was right. We just finished meeting with the Security Council," Dana said and gestured for them all to sit on the couches on the other side of her office.

Dana and Mullins sat on one side, while Nathan sat in one of the plush chairs. He didn't look happy. Nathan was as even-tempered as they came. This was one of the reasons Connor had recruited him into the CDF and also one of the things that made him an excellent leader. He wasn't prone to impulsive actions, and it took a lot to get under his skin.

"Did I miss anything important? I know the meeting today dealt particularly with the prosecution of everyone involved in the rogue group's activities," Connor said, then sat down and waited.

"It did, and Rex Coleman and his team are working on interviewing all the detainees," Dana answered.

Connor nodded. They were detainees until they were proven guilty.

Nathan cleared his throat, and Connor glanced at him for a moment, but Nathan kept his gaze on the governor.

Connor looked back at Dana and saw that Mullins was watching him with the focused intensity of a hungry wolf.

"This is about me, isn't it?" Connor asked.

"We are implementing changes in the CDF," Dana said. "These changes will affect you specifically, Connor."

Connor had been expecting something and kept his gaze on Governor Wolf. “I understand.”

“I’m not going to beat around the bush about this. We’re making Nathan the head of the CDF. The Security Council has voted.”

His first thought was that they were taking the CDF away from him. He glanced at Nathan, who didn’t look happy about the situation.

“I didn’t want this,” Nathan said.

Connor softened his gaze and nodded. He’d created the Colonial Defense Force for the purpose of defending the colony from the threat of invasion. He’d been involved in every aspect from its first inception until he'd retired after the Vemus War, although "retired" was a bit of a misnomer because his exposure to the Vemus meant he might’ve been compromised. When he rejoined the CDF, he and Nathan had split their duties, but Connor knew there needed to be one person in charge.

“All right, what else?” Connor said.

“It’s all right to take a few moments to take this in. We’re all aware of the sacrifices you've made to create our defenses,” Dana replied.

Connor felt a spike of irritation at feeling like he was being jerked around. “I don’t need a moment. I need to know what you intend to do with me. Is my commission canceled?”

“No,” Nathan said firmly.

“It’s undecided at this time,” Bob Mullins said.

Connor swung his gaze toward the man and then looked back at Governor Wolf.

“For the time being, you're still part of the Colonial Defense Force,” Dana said.

Connor leaned back in his chair and gauged the room. He

felt like he was attending the aftermath of an all-day debriefing that had probably been all about him and his actions.

"The CDF is more than just me."

Bob Mullins inhaled explosively. "You say that, but do you really mean it? We spent most of the day discussing the very actions that brought us into this situation. You treated the CDF as if it was your own personal army to do with as you saw fit without checking with colonial leadership. This makes you almost as bad as Meredith Cain. I know you think what you did was necessary, but it was no less damaging, and the repercussions will be felt for a long time."

"Bob," Connor said, "if you were any good at your job, you would've known what Meredith was doing and you would've stopped her. It's people like you who let a situation get to a point where someone like me has to do something to stop it. I don't regret anything I've done. Not one bit. I'd do it all again. You allowed that group to fester and infect the entire colony. What would you have done if I hadn't been here?"

Mullins leaned forward. "If it was up to me, you *wouldn't* be here. You'd be out of the CDF."

Connor smiled wolfishly. "At least now I know what *you* want, but you haven't answered my question. You're still looking to lay blame. You don't like how what I did made you feel. Or is it that you looked incompetent?"

"Maybe you're just too foolish to understand what your abuse of power has done," Mullins replied with a snarl.

"Bob," Dana said sternly, "you're out of line."

Mullins shook his head. "Fine."

Connor leaned forward. He was moments from springing to his feet. "No, keep going with it. Maybe there's something else you'd like to say. Take your best shot."

"Gentlemen, that's enough," Dana said. "Bob, I want you to leave, now."

Mullins glared at the governor, and she met his gaze with an unyielding one of her own. He stood up and stormed out of the room.

"Nathan," Governor Wolf said, "would you please give us a few moments? If you wouldn't mind waiting just outside."

"Very well," Nathan said and left the room.

They were quiet for a few moments while Connor slowly got his anger under control. He glanced at Dana Wolf, who was waiting for him to say something.

"I don't know why you have Mullins as one of your advisors," Connor said.

Dana smiled and grinned a little. "That's funny. Bob doesn't understand why I keep you around either. You're both very good at your jobs, even if you don't like each other."

Connor couldn't imagine what Mullins was good at other than being one giant pain in the ass, and said so.

"He gets things done. Sometimes he rubs people the wrong way, but so do a few other people I know. We're working for the same thing here, Connor."

"Really? I'm having trouble believing that. Honestly, I was shocked that Mullins wasn't implicated with Kurt Johnson or Meredith Cain."

Governor Wolf twitched one of her eyebrows. "He fits your profile of everything that's wrong, does he?"

"Yeah, sometimes."

"Do I, then?" Dana asked and immediately held up her hand. "Don't answer that. I already know the answer."

"If it's any consolation, I was glad you weren't implicated with the others," Connor said.

"I appreciate that, but it could also mean I'm just better at hiding my activity than the others were," Dana said, giving him a challenging look. "Look, we need to be honest with each other."

"I thought we already were."

"All right, then. I'm three years into my five-year term as governor. There's a significant chance that I either won't choose to run for a second term or that I might lose the election."

Connor's eyebrows knitted together into a thoughtful frown. "You wouldn't run again?"

"I haven't decided. Regardless, you need to start thinking about longevity."

"I don't understand."

"You managed to spot a massive conspiracy and root it out, but don't you realize there's a pretty significant chance that someone like Bob Mullins will be the next governor?" Dana said.

Connor shook his head. There was no way that guy could get enough votes.

"I can tell you don't believe me. Do you remember Stanton Parish? He won his election based on telling people what they wanted to hear. Like it or not, what you did is a hot topic. That's all that was really revealed in that Security Council meeting. People are afraid of you, but . . ." she said, pausing for a moment.

"They're letting it blind them to the actual problem," Connor said. "Which is the fact that I had to do what I did in order to solve the problem. I exposed the vulnerability, Dana. They don't have to like me for it, but they should damn well solve the problem so someone like me doesn't have to step in and do it next time."

Dana licked her lips and considered her next words for a few moments. "One of the things I admire about you is that when you see a problem you just go at it. You're good at working the problem, but sometimes you're a bit of a brute about it, and please know I say that with the highest affection. There's a time and a place for it, but it can also make people do foolish things. Honestly, I'm just waiting for them to start pointing fingers at me as being responsible for the entire situation."

"That's absurd."

"You're too kind."

"Fine. That's bat-shit crazy."

Dana chuckled softly. "You're a leader. It's evident in everything you do. Ultimately, we're responsible for what happens under our watches. Wouldn't you agree?"

"We are, but there are things out of our control. There's always something we can't plan for or anticipate. I think this will blow over. I knew there would be repercussions for my actions. And I knew I was risking being discharged from the CDF, but does that change what we're facing?" Connor asked.

Dana's acorn-colored eyes gleamed with amusement. "I do wonder what kind of governor *you'd* make."

Connor shook his head. "No way would I want that job. No offense."

Dana smiled. "I guess this is where I'm supposed to say you'd be perfect for the job *because* you don't want it, but I don't agree with that, at least not wholeheartedly. However, I think our motivations are quite similar. We both want what's best for the colony."

Connor nodded and was silent for a few moments. "So, you don't know what to do with me?"

"On the contrary, I know exactly what to do with you. Do you?"

Connor felt as if his thoughts had skipped a beat. Of all the responses he'd expected to hear, that wasn't one of them. "I want to—"

"Hold that thought. I'm going to get Nathan back in because I think the two of you need to talk. We're not finished, Connor, but I really do have to go," Dana said.

She left her office and Connor watched as Nathan walked back in. He walked over to Connor and watched him for a few moments.

"This is one of those moments where your old boss is now your new employee," Connor said, chuckling.

Nathan's eyes widened and then he grinned. "And here I thought this was going to be awkward."

"I've had commanding officers before, and for a lot longer than I've been the head of the CDF."

"Yeah, but did any of them recruit you and train you?"

"In that case, I can vouch for your qualifications."

Nathan smiled, and then the smile slipped away from his face. "This is serious, Connor. Mullins wasn't the only one who wanted you dishonorably discharged from the CDF."

"So, why wasn't I?"

"Because I wouldn't do it. They can make a recommendation, but that doesn't mean I have to follow through with it. So, the compromise was a demotion. A lot of bureaucracy if you ask me."

"I appreciate it."

"You'd do the same for me, and I happen to agree with everything you did. I don't know if I would've done the same thing, but I understand why it was necessary."

Connor pressed his lips together for a moment. "What would you have done differently?"

Nathan smiled wryly and pointed a finger at him. "I'm not gonna let you do that to me—make you sit there and second-guess your actions. I honestly don't know what I would've done differently. Everything happened pretty fast, and if proper channels had been used, there would've been a greater risk of losing the evidence."

Connor nodded. "What happens now, then?"

"I think they expect me to keep you in line. If I can't do that, they'll dismiss me."

Connor noted the undertones of Nathan's statement. He'd said it lightheartedly, but the CDF was just as important to Nathan as it was to Connor. "It won't come to that."

"I'm glad you didn't promise."

"You don't think I could keep that kind of promise?"

"I don't know if either one of us could keep that kind of promise."

That was a sobering thought. "So, what's next, *sir*."

Nathan shook his head. "Give me a break. Nothing's changed as far as I'm concerned. Our goal is to define the Krake threat. I want you to focus on that."

"I'm relieved. I was prepared to make a big speech about why we need to keep doing exactly that."

Nathan laughed. "You don't need to convince me, and Governor Wolf is also in agreement. As far as your status in the CDF, that could take months to work out, and I'm not going to sit by and do nothing while they figure out a way to get rid of you and me. So, what's your next move?"

"On the highest level, we need to gather more intelligence about the Krake. Right now . . ." Connor paused for a moment.

"I want to find the Ovarrow we ran into while getting components for the arch—the ones who slipped away from us."

Nathan nodded. "It makes me wonder how many Ovarrow bunkers are out there with stasis pods that we didn't find. They could have awakened earlier than the rest, or perhaps they didn't go into stasis at all."

"We're not sure. They're certainly good at hiding."

"How do you intend to find them?"

"I was planning on getting some help."

# 3

TRIDENT BATTLE GROUP had been conducting inner-system reconnaissance of the enemy star system for the past seventy-two hours. Colonel Sean Quinn sat in his ready room just off the *Vigilant*'s bridge, reviewing the latest status reports.

"Colonel Quinn," Gabriel, the *Vigilant*'s AI, said in a naturally modulated baritone, "there has been a reported decrease in efficiency aboard the *Babylon*, the *Acheron*, and the *Diligent*."

Sean grimaced at the mention of those ships' names. The senior officers serving aboard those ships had been part of the mutiny, and now he had junior officers filling the shoes of much more experienced officers in enemy territory.

"How bad is it?" Sean asked.

"Colonel, engineering and maintenance report standard efficiency, but it's the reaction times in combat readiness drills that have decreased seventeen percent."

*Seventeen percent*, Sean repeated to himself and shook his

head. If the Krake were to attack them now, they might be in real trouble. "Gabriel, is that an average percentage across the combat readiness drills, or is that the most recent measure?"

"That is the most recent measure. The average—"

"Never mind the average unless it's getting worse. Can you open a comlink to Major Shelton?"

"Certainly, sir. A moment, please," Gabriel replied.

A window appeared on the personal holoscreen above his desk, and Major Vanessa Shelton greeted him. She was a dark-skinned woman who was now in command of the *Yorktown*, a carrier vessel that held Talon-V fighter groups.

"I've just been reviewing the latest reports of the combat readiness drills," Sean said.

"I have, as well. I figured we'd discuss that at our next all-hands meeting."

"Ordinarily, I'd bring down the hammer on the non-performers, but given the circumstances, I don't think that's quite fair. At the same time, I can't accept that kind of performance. Do you have any suggestions?" Sean asked.

"We knew we were going to have to change our tactics if we had to engage the Krake, and these performance scores just prove that fact. I think we should move forward with your idea, which is to pair off the less experienced commanding officers with the more experienced ones."

Sean drummed his fingers on his desk for a moment while he considered. "I know it was my suggestion, but I'm not a huge fan of it. The risk will be handicapping the more experienced warships, and the captains of those ships have enough on their plates with commanding their own ships."

They'd been in this star system for almost three days, having used the space gate and the coordinates provided by a mysterious Krake fifth column faction that had come to their aid. The Krake had transmitted a set of coordinates, which was an invitation Sean had no choice but to explore. Since arriving, they hadn't received any broadcast greeting. Trident Battle Group had transitioned into this universe at a point where their entry would be among the outer planets, which reduced the risk of them being discovered by enemy ships in case this was a trap.

"I still think this is our best option, sir. We pair them off, but we'll need to convey to the junior officers that they're still responsible for commanding their ships. We don't have time for them to spend weeks developing their tactical awareness. Most of them *were* tactical officers, after all."

"I'm going to meet with them individually to see if we can work out some of the kinks," Sean said.

"I think that would be a good idea for more than the obvious reasons," Vanessa said.

It had only been three days since Sean had executed the mutineers and ended the first-ever mutiny in Colonial Defense Force history. He knew there were several officers who felt he'd gone too far, but the majority had accepted the outcome of the mutiny. Sean had been well within his rights to execute the mutineers. He'd also required all the officers to file their own reports about those events, holding nothing back. Sean wouldn't hide from his decision. The facts were there, and they supported him. In spite of all that, he regretted that he'd had to take the action at all. He was still furious with Lester Brody for sparking the mutiny, and he was angry with himself for allowing it to happen under his watch.

"There *is* an alternative," Sean said. "We could move the

XOs of the *Dutchman*, the *Albany*, and the *Burroughs* to command the other ships."

Vanessa frowned in thought. "If it was just a matter of rank, it really wouldn't make much difference. That might be a shortcoming in our overall rank structure, but the risk in doing this now is bringing our overall combat readiness down in efficiency."

"That's true, but we might not have much of a choice. If it comes to a fight, the crews of those ships deserve better," Sean said.

"Understood, sir. I do think we need to keep an eye on the *Babylon* and, in particular, Lieutenant Richard Pitts," Vanessa said.

Richard had been close friends with Ryan Ward, who'd been captain of the *Babylon*. He'd been among the mutineers and had come dangerously close to opening fire on the *Vigilant*.

"He doesn't have to like or approve of what I've done, but he's doing his job," Sean replied.

"Understood, sir," Vanessa replied.

"The *Dutchman* is due to report in soon. We'll speak again then," Sean said. "Oh, and thanks for being my sounding board."

Vanessa's lips lifted a little. "That's what I'm here for, sir."

The comlink went dark, and a short while later there was a knock at Sean's door. The door opened, and Lieutenant Jane Russo entered his office.

"You asked to see me, Colonel."

She'd been his lead technical officer on the *Vigilant*.

Sean invited her to sit down. "I need an XO on this ship, and you're my first choice."

Lieutenant Russo's eyebrows raised in surprise. "Sir?"

"I've talked about it with Major Shelton, and she has also recommended you. I realize that this is a bit of a surprise, and given the circumstances, I need you to rise to the occasion. That's why I'm going to give you a field promotion to captain, which will address any issues concerning rank when dealing with engineers and maintenance."

Russo smiled. "Thank you, Colonel. I won't let you down."

"I know you won't," Sean said. He approved of her choice of words. A lesser officer would have inserted a less direct statement along the lines of, "I'll *try* not to let you down." The way a person spoke was often indicative of their attitudes and whether or not they'd achieve their goals.

"There's more," Sean continued. He brought up a tactical recording of their last battle with Krake ships. "I know this is familiar to you, but we need to come up with a better strategy for dealing with Krake attack drones, in particular. We can't afford to keep hurling HADES V heavy missiles to blind them and then destroy them. We don't have enough missiles to sustain that level of use in an engagement."

"I understand, sir. We've been trying to think of ways to achieve more with less, but the only time we come into contact with Krake attack drones is in the middle of an actual attack."

Sean nodded. "I understand, but we'll need some out-of-the-box thinking."

Russo pursed her lips in thought for a moment. "If that's the case, then could I request clearance to show this to people who aren't in tactical, such as non-bridge crew and possibly maybe even some of the scientists? If we want out-of-the-box thinking, we might have to actually look elsewhere."

Sean smiled and twitched his head to the side with a slight nod. "Permission granted, Captain."

They both stood up and Captain Russo saluted Sean before leaving his office. Sean glanced at the holoscreen. He looked at it so much that he could see it with his eyes closed. When they'd first entered the system, he'd decided to do as much reconnaissance from the outer system as he could. But if he was going to get a good look at their target destination, which was the inner planets within the Goldilocks zone, without using any of his active scans, he needed to send a ship in.

Oliver Martinez commanded the *Dutchman.* He was an outstanding officer and a friend, but it was his affinity for playing "cat and mouse" that made him the best choice for a recon mission before Sean would commit the entire battlegroup to go to the waypoint.

They were able to use subspace communication, which allowed them to communicate instantaneously over vast distances. The theory posited that subspace communication would allow them to connect over dozens of light-years and not merely across a single star system. They hadn't tested the theory yet, for obvious reasons. Sean was grateful to be able to communicate across one star system and had utilized it in his tactics against the Krake. What they didn't know was whether the Krake were able to detect subspace comms or even use it themselves. There was so much they didn't know about the Krake, but that was why they were here. Even though there seemed to be a rebellious Krake faction that had assisted them, Sean had to be cautious, and that took time.

# 4

A FEW HOURS LATER, Sean sat in the command chair amid a phalanx of workstations on the bridge of the *Vigilant*. Newly promoted, Captain Russo sat at the XO's workstation to his left, and Oriana sat at the science officer's workstation to his right.

"Colonel Quinn," Specialist Irina Sansky said, "I have a subspace communications link from Captain Martinez on the *Dutchman*."

"Good. Put him on the main holoscreen," Sean said.

A few moments later, Captain Martinez's chiseled face and powerful neck appeared on the main holoscreen.

"Right on time, Captain," Sean said.

"The *Dutchman* aims to please, Colonel. I heard that we can now talk for longer than five-minute intervals," Martinez said.

"That's the claim, although there might be a moment while we reestablish the link. What do you have to report?"

Martinez glanced at someone off-screen. "Upload the report," he said and then looked at Sean. "It looks like a dead planet, sir. Our high-res images show a landscape that is scarred by bombardment craters. There are significant particulates in the atmosphere that are indicative of either a massive asteroid impact or a super volcano, but my guess is that somebody nuked this planet. We were able to see traces of what might be orbital bombardment platforms and possibly a derelict ship. We haven't done any active scans, but passive scans don't indicate any power signatures from known Krake ship types. You should have the images now."

A series of images appeared on the main holoscreen, which showed a distant view of the planet. Either the planet had been the victim of a massive meteor shower that pelted the surface, essentially scouring it to oblivion, or Martinez's estimation was correct. But the question remained as to why the Krake fifth column would send them here, especially given the time constraint.

"Colonel, I'd like your permission to take a closer look at those bombardment platforms and the derelict ship," Martinez said.

"Have there been any space gates detected?"

"Negative, sir."

"I want you to hold your position, Captain," Sean said. "We'll organize our timing so we arrive at the planet at the same time. That way, if we have an uninvited guest we'll be able to deal with it together."

"Understood, sir," Martinez said.

"Good work, Captain. We'll send you our intercept course in just a few minutes," Sean said, and the comlink severed. "Helm, plot a course to the NEC, best speed."

"Yes, Colonel, best speed to the NEC," Lieutenant Edwards said.

"Ops, send a briefing packet to the rest of the battle group, and I want us underway ASAP," Sean said.

"Aye, sir," Lieutenant Katherine Burrows said.

Sean looked at Russo. "Thoughts?"

"Either it's an elaborate trap for us, or they want us to find something, sir," Russo said.

Sean nodded. "That's what I was thinking."

"Sir, why didn't you have the *Dutchman* fly closer and do more reconnaissance?"

"If they'd gotten into trouble, we'd have been too far away to help. When we get closer, I'll have them move in to do more reconnaissance. We'll need to prep the away teams."

"Understood, Colonel," Russo said.

Sean brought the images up on his personal holoscreen and began swiping through them.

"Colonel," Oriana said, addressing him professionally when on the bridge, "have you thought of showing the Krake prisoners these images? Maybe they'll have something to say about it."

Sean rubbed his chin in thought for a few moments. "It's a good idea, but they haven't exactly been forthcoming with any information. They're still convinced that they should be dead," he said and shook his head. He stood up. "Do you want to observe while I ask them?"

"I'm not sure I can contribute anything," Oriana replied.

"You might see something the rest of us miss," Sean said.

"Lead the way, sir."

Sean smiled and then looked at Russo. "XO, you have the con."

Sean and Oriana left the bridge. Once they were in the

corridor, she glanced at him. "Is there something else you wanted to discuss with me?"

"There's plenty I'd like to discuss with you, but none of it's relevant to what we're doing now," Sean said and then pressed the button for the elevator. "Well, there is *one* thing. Something Russo said to me earlier. We need to come up with a way to defend ourselves against the Krake attack drones."

Oriana frowned. "Again, I don't think I have much to offer there."

Sean arched an eyebrow. "For a scientist, I thought you'd be more open to tackling this particular issue."

Oriana's eyes flashed. "These are the drones that, when armed, can melt through the hull of our ship?"

"They also fly pretty fast, are extremely agile, and are resistant to direct energy countermeasures. Point defense systems with mag cannons can stop them, but they can also be overwhelmed, and we don't have an endless supply of ammunition. One of the things that's been effective is utilizing the fusion warhead of a HADES V missile. It seems to overwhelm their sensors, and they lose formation. What we've done is detonate a few missiles in their vicinity and then mop up as many drones as we can before they go active again."

They rode the elevator down several decks. Oriana was quiet for a few moments while she considered the problem.

"So, the attack drone is vulnerable to either densely solid metals or a powerful fusion warhead?"

Sean nodded. "We can slow them down, but if enough of them are fired at us, it will overwhelm our defenses. We've run the numbers, and Gabriel has done the analysis. So far, I've used clever tactics to avoid a direct confrontation, or I've at least given us an escape so we didn't end up in a shooting match. At least I tried not to."

Oriana looked as though she was about to say something a couple of times, and Sean waited her out, but she just looked at him regretfully. "I don't think this is something I can really think about while we walk down a corridor, but I'll try and work it with my team. In order to generate the heat required to quickly melt through not only the hull of the ship but the decks in between would mean . . ." she said and paused for a moment.

"They're as hot as a yellow dwarf star burning at five thousand kelvins."

"I wonder what they use to fuel those combat drones."

Sean considered it for a few moments. "That's not a bad question, and I think that given enough time, we could actually build one of these drones. The other thing is that the Krake seem to have limited themselves to combat drones as their main weapon of war, at least as far as we've seen. So, if we can come up with a way to beat their offensive, we'd gain a significant advantage over them."

"This isn't the first time we've talked about their attack drones."

"I've been banging my head against it, and so have a lot of the other senior officers. I'll make the data available to you and your team, and if you think there's anyone else who can help come up with a way to defend against them, let me know and I'll clear them as well. And if you can have that to me by tomorrow morning, that would be really great," Sean said dryly and smiled.

Oriana grinned. "No problem. I'll get right on that for you. If you want, I can also invent an instantaneous FTL engine as well."

"Teleportation would be good too."

Oriana shook her head in exasperation. "There's a reason the mysteries of the universe are mysteries. They're not so easy to solve."

"And yet we utilize the space gate to transition between universes, which makes me wonder how many of these universes there are."

"More than a little and less than too much."

"Is that an exact number?" Sean asked, feigning seriousness.

"It's not infinite," she said and paused for a moment. "Sean, I don't know if I'll be able to help with the attack drones. It's like they're flinging miniature stars at us. About the only thing they react to aside from a solid piece of metal is an even bigger, more powerful star, and then only for a little bit."

"That's because once the warhead is detonated, it quickly disperses in space," Sean said.

Oriana's brows knitted together in intense concentration, and Sean didn't want to interrupt her thoughts. After a few moments, she looked at him.

"What?" he asked.

"I'm just thinking about stars. I'm going to need time with this, but I'll let you know if I come up with something."

Sean suspected she'd just thought of something but wouldn't discuss it until she'd given it a thorough analysis. He'd worked with other scientists who were the direct opposite, sharing every single thought they had whether or not it panned out. Over time, he'd come to prefer Oriana's approach. Life didn't always give a person what they wanted, but sometimes it did give them what they had to have. He just hoped they could come up with a solution sooner rather than later.

# 5

A PAIR of brilliant cerulean eyes regarded Connor from the holoscreen. Her long, auburn hair had a natural curl that seemed to complement her delicate cheekbones, although delicate was the furthest word from how Connor would describe his wife. Lenora was among the most beautiful women he'd ever seen. He hadn't sputtered incoherent sentences when they'd first met—he wasn't a foolish boy after all—but sometimes he was foolish when it came to her.

"I dare you," Lenora said.

"It's not like that at all."

"Connor," Lenora said, cramming volumes of meanings into that one word.

"You're sick, remember?"

Lenora narrowed her gaze. "I have a cold. I'm not dying."

"Colds don't normally come with nausea," Connor replied.

Lenora's slightly pink nose leaned closer to the screen. "I'm not pregnant either."

"I didn't—"

Lenora shook her head. "Ever since that whole bridge incident, you've slipped back into some old habits. I don't need your permission to see the Ovarrow."

"I never said you did."

"No, of course not. You just engineer events that make doing so incredibly inconvenient."

"Lenora, you're sick. Take a few days to get better and then go. I don't like it any more than you do."

Connor knew she wasn't really angry with him. He'd seen her angry before, and this was just mild frustration in comparison. Sometimes people just needed to rant, even if there wasn't much anyone could do about it. "I wish I could be home with you right now, but I have to do this."

Lenora inhaled deeply and sighed. "How bad is it?"

"They put Nathan in charge of the CDF."

"How does that change anything?"

"It's hard to say, really. I'm still focusing on finding out as much as I can about the Krake. And getting the Ovarrow to help is still our best shot at that."

Lenora was quiet for a few moments. "So, they demoted you and put Nathan in charge. You don't think it's going to simply stop at that, do you?"

Connor shook his head. "No," he admitted. "But Dana is still behind what we're trying to do."

"Okay, I forgive you for not being here to take care of me in my time of need. I'll just have to tough it out on my own without you," she said, her eyes narrowing playfully.

"Thanks," Connor said, smiling. "I'll make it up to you."

"Oh, I know you will. With interest," Lenora said, smiling, but then the smile seemed to disappear. "Be careful."

"I will, I promise," he answered.

Lenora looked away for a moment, pursing her lips in thought. "I know how you get. Just hurry up and get back here."

The holoscreen flickered off as she severed the connection, and Connor stared at it for a few moments. He was sitting in an isolated alcove on a troop carrier alpha. He heard the heavy stomp of footsteps approaching the area, and Samson leaned around the corner. Connor stood up.

"You sure you don't want to bring more men? The rest of the 7th will meet us at the waypoint, but we only have two squads with us here," Samson said.

"I just want to talk to them. If we bring too many soldiers with us, they probably won't talk to us at all," Connor said.

A few weeks earlier, diplomatic relations had been stretched thin between the CDF and the Ovarrow. A decisive show of force had been called for, and some lives had been lost. The Ovarrow needed to be shown that the CDF wasn't weak. Connor would've preferred a more diplomatic solution, but at the time and with colonial lives in danger, he couldn't afford it.

While in an Ovarrow city, Lenora had been trapped under the wreckage of a large bridge that had been sabotaged by a rogue colonial group. However, there was evidence showing that the support structures had already been eroded by a group of Ovarrow who lived in the city. As far as Connor knew, they hadn't received any updates about whether the Ovarrow had tracked down who the saboteurs were.

"If you say so," Samson said.

"I do."

"The Security Council is going to have kittens when they find out that you didn't bring a diplomatic envoy with you."

"We have Dash. He's done enough work with them in the past two years to fill that role for us."

Samson chuckled, and his deep voice sounded like it was coming from the base of his barrel chest. "That's thin, and you know it."

"I like to run a lean operation," Connor replied.

Dash DeWitt walked over to them. He was the only noncombatant among them, but he was in excellent shape due to the rigors of working outdoors, either exploring archaeological sites or just being active. Though he wasn't a soldier, he was weapons qualified for basic hunting rifles and powerful sidearms.

"I thought I heard someone mention my name," Dash said.

Samson merely looked at him, but Connor waved him over. A moment later, Samson left with a grunt. Connor watched Dash go a little pale as the much larger man stomped past him.

"That's one guy I don't ever want to make angry," Dash said.

"You should trust those instincts. He's a little rough around the edges, but in a fight, he'll keep you safe. I trust him."

Dash nodded. "That's good enough for me. So, what exactly do you want me to do once we get to the city?"

"I want to see if they'll help us find that other group of Ovarrow on the far side of the continent."

"I know that seems straightforward to you, but for them, it's actually quite complicated."

"I know," Connor said. "That's why you're here."

"I'll do whatever I can, but are you sure you don't want to bring in someone like Darius Cohen?"

Connor shook his head. "I can work with Darius, but for this mission, I'd much rather work with you. You know what we're up against and how important it is. You've seen it firsthand. Darius might not be any less dedicated than you are, but he hasn't seen it like you have."

"I understand. At least I think I do," Dash said with a half-smile.

The young man had certainly grown up quite a bit since he'd been Lenora's student. They'd bumped heads over the years, but growing up wasn't easy.

"Noah sent me a message saying he's been trying to get in contact with you."

Noah had been recovering from a severe head injury that left him in a coma for almost a year. Connor had previously brought him along on a short mission to deal with the rogue group, and Noah had more or less negotiated aggressively that he should also be there this time, but Connor didn't want to tempt fate twice. "Thanks for the message. I'll be in touch with Noah."

"He thinks he's been left behind," Dash said.

"He needs time to recover. I don't want to bring him on a mission like this. He still needs time to heal, regardless of what he thinks."

Dash nodded. "No, I get it. Believe me, I understand. But still, maybe you could just send him a short message just to acknowledge . . . him."

All the kids were growing up, it seemed. "I will, but after. We're almost there."

The troop carrier flew to what had been the colonial diplomatic LZ outside the Ovarrow city. The camp had been shut down, but there were still several communication terminals left for the Ovarrow to use.

The pilot flew at an altitude that didn't hide their approach while at the same time giving them a high vantage point from which to survey the Ovarrow city. Only about thirty percent of the city was occupied by the indigenous species, the ones the colonists had brought out of stasis.

Connor peered at the holoscreen image of the Ovarrow city. There was a wide expanse where the Ovarrow looked to be restoring vehicles—land crawlers. It was nothing that could be done quickly, but the Ovarrow certainly built things to last.

"We've given them time to see us. Take us to the LZ," Connor said.

The troop carrier banked into a shallow turn and landed at the abandoned camp. The loading ramp lowered to the ground, and Samson led three squads of soldiers off the aircraft. Connor and Dash followed.

Connor stepped off the ramp and circled around the troop carrier to view the city. The Ovarrow had bolstered their defenses, and he could see multiple places where Ovarrow soldiers, known as Mekaal, were patrolling. They were being watched, and Connor made no move to approach. Instead, he went to one of the consoles and Dash opened the interface.

"Send a message to both the high commissioner and the warlord that I'd like to speak with them," Connor said.

He watched Dash use the holo-interface to send the message to the terminal that was located inside the city.

"Message has been sent," Dash said.

"Excellent. Thank you. Now, we wait," Connor said.

They restricted their movements to stay near the camp, and six hours passed without any kind of reply from the Ovarrow. A few soldiers complained about the lack of acknowledgment. Connor glanced over at the diplomatic consoles and saw that there was no change. It was early in the afternoon, and he was getting a bit tired of waiting. He understood that he wasn't the

Ovarrow's favorite colonist, but there was something to be said for courtesy, and the lack of it was getting on his nerves.

Connor walked out of the camp and came to a stop in plain view. They were about two hundred meters from the entrance of the city. Dash and Samson walked over to him.

"I can try sending the message again," Dash offered.

Connor shook his head. "I'm not going to play games with them," he said and looked at Dash. "Let's take a walk, you and me."

"I have to advise against that, General," Samson said.

Three squads of soldiers began standing to approach the edge of the camp.

"Understood, Captain. I'm going to try a different tactic this time around. I want you to maintain this position."

The skin around Samson's eyes tightened. "How about you take two of my men in with you? Or better yet, I'll go with you."

"Negative. If we get neck deep in it, I'll need you to come get us," Connor replied, and Dash's eyes widened.

Samson glanced at Dash. "I hope you can handle that sidearm, kid."

Connor started walking toward the city, and Dash quickly caught up with him.

"You don't really expect any trouble, do you?"

Connor wanted to dismiss Dash's concerns, but he couldn't. The last time he'd been in that city, he'd had an army with him. He'd also called the warlord's bluff and threatened him. If the Ovarrow wanted to kill him, this would be a perfect opportunity.

"I taught you better than that. Always expect trouble," Connor said.

"I'm pretty sure I'll be okay. They like me," Dash replied.

He was right, and Connor knew it. He'd sent the message and tried to be patient, but he wasn't going to wait all day. Sometimes doors needed to be knocked open.

The entry to the Ovarrow city didn't have gates per se. They were more like improvised barricades. It wasn't the only entrance into the city, but this was where the diplomatic envoys used to come, and Connor wasn't about to try and sneak into the back door for this meeting. He doubted the Ovarrow would appreciate that. It was probably too soon to even make this request, but he didn't have the luxury of time for the Ovarrow to feel ready to work with him again. The Krake could already be making their way to this planet, and they needed to be prepared. Preparedness overrode the Ovarrow's finicky feelings about the human colonists living on their planet, who, incidentally, had brought them out of stasis.

He'd seen the Ovarrow stasis pods. He'd been there when they were first discovered and accidentally triggered the "end stasis" protocols. Connor looked at the Ovarrow, who clustered together behind the barricades, watching him suspiciously as he approached. The fact that there had been a massive colonial effort to bring over ten thousand Ovarrow out of stasis couldn't be missed, given that most of the tools the Ovarrow now used had been made by the colonists. Connor had helped organize the delivery of the supply caches found in the hidden bunkers where many of the stasis pods had been found. There were still thousands of Ovarrow in stasis, and these numbers were only based on the known bunker locations that Connor and many others had mapped out.

New Earth had one massive supercontinent that was similar in size to Earth's Pangea before millions of years of continental drift had separated them. Colonial geologists had found no evidence to support the same events occurring on New Earth. The supercontinent was home to massive lakes, long, powerful rivers, and a nearly extinct species of intelligent aliens who called themselves Ovarrow.

Over the past twelve years, people like his wife had tried to piece together the history associated with the alien ruins they'd found. No one could ever think of New Earth as a dull place to live. It had taken every bit of human ingenuity to not only make a life on this planet but to learn about its history—the calamities that had occurred. There'd been an impromptu ice age that only lasted for two hundred years. They'd since learned that the ice age had been triggered by the Ovarrow in a last-ditch effort to drive the Krake away. At the time humanity loaded three hundred thousand people aboard the *Ark* and began a voyage beyond Earth's solar system, the Ovarrow had been fighting a long war both with the Krake and among themselves.

Connor had thought that all the Ovarrow had gone into stasis pods, but he'd been wrong. Only mature Ovarrow could survive going into stasis, which was why the colonists had never found Ovarrow children in the pods.

He wondered why the Ovarrow they'd discovered on the other side of the continent had never tried to contact them. They must have known the colonists were living there. They hadn't tried to hide their presence on this world. Even with colonists restricting their activities to the western side of the continent, there was no way they could have missed the Vemus War. Battles had been fought on the ground but also in low orbit and even on New Earth's moons. So, the question that tugged at Connor the most was: why wouldn't they try to contact the colonists? The colonial government had decided to keep the presence of these other Ovarrow from the ones they'd brought out of stasis, but that was about to change.

The Mekaal soldiers standing atop the barricade said something in the Ovarrow language. Dash had the translator interface ready, but Connor could guess the meaning. The soldiers' weapons were quarterstaff-sized and were able to fire powerful energy blasts. They didn't point their weapons at them, but they were held at the ready and it wouldn't take much to make use of them.

"I'm here to speak with Warlord Vitory or High Commissioner Senleon. Can you tell them we're here?" Connor asked.

Dash made his personal holoscreen spread as far as it could go so Connor could see the Ovarrow translation. The Ovarrow spoke among themselves while keeping a careful watch on Connor and Dash.

"This isn't the warmest reception I've gotten from them," Dash said quietly.

"They didn't shoot at us, so that's something," Connor replied. But he hadn't expected the Ovarrow to shoot at them. They knew who he was, and they also knew who Dash was.

Connor looked up at the Mekaal, trying to figure out which one was their leader. The Ovarrow stuck to an almost rigid form of hierarchy, and he'd have the most luck gaining entry to the city by dealing with whoever was at the top of the pecking order.

Connor raised his hand and pointed his finger at the Mekaal soldier the others seemed to defer to. "I'm General Connor Gates of the Colonial Defense Force. I know you have your orders, but if someone doesn't get here in the next few minutes, I'm going to walk into your city. Whether you shoot me or not is up to you, but I am going to speak to your leaders."

The Mekaal soldiers read the message, and the one Connor had guessed was the leader regarded him. The dark, sunken eyes with brow ridges that went to the back of his head made him look as if he were constantly glaring. After a few moments, he touched the side of his helmet, which apparently was the universal signal for speaking over the comlink. The Ovarrow communications capabilities included shortwave radio signals, which could broadcast at distances of several thousand kilometers. The Mekaal uttered a short, decisive sentence and gestured for them to follow.

"We're in," Dash said.

Connor nodded and walked toward the barricade. He only carried a sidearm, but the Mekaal hardly paid it any notice. He'd expected that they'd want him to disarm, but then he recalled that the diplomatic envoys had been allowed a squad of armed soldiers.

They weren't entirely defenseless. Both Connor and Dash wore military-grade multi-protection suits made of nanorobotic material, which mimicked the clothing the colonists wore while providing a lot of protection.

The fact that they were walking into the city was a small victory unto itself. Nathan hadn't thought he'd be able to get inside or that the Ovarrow would speak with them. But getting inside had been the easy part; convincing the Ovarrow to help them would be slightly more difficult.

Connor glanced toward a cloaked recon drone flying overhead. Samson was keeping watch, but if the Ovarrow actually intended to harm them, Connor doubted that the CDF soldiers outside the city would be able to reach them in time.

Connor and Dash were on their own, but he'd faced worse odds.

Significant progress had been made with the cleanup efforts in the city, which Connor attributed to the use of the machines they'd found. This part of the city was slowly coming back to life, but Connor didn't have to look far to see the haunting remnants of a battle fought here hundreds of years ago.

He glanced down one of the side streets and stopped. A large section of the building on the corner had been torn away. Blackened, scorched remains marred what was left, with bits of jagged bronze, metallic alloy glittering in the sun. The Ovarrow preferred a rounded architecture that flared at the top, which made them defensible. There must have been an explosion. Connor glanced at the other side of the street and saw where huge chunks had lodged themselves into the nearby structures. He narrowed his gaze and peered into the building, his enhanced vision easily piercing the darkened interior.

"That was someone's home," Connor said to Dash.

"What the hell happened?"

They both looked at their Mekaal escorts, and the leader made an impatient gesture for them to follow.

Connor opened a comlink to Samson. "Scorched building southeast of us. Have the drone scout for more of the same, and look for a cause of the explosion."

"Acknowledged. Not a warm welcome, then?"

"It's too soon to tell," Connor said and closed the comlink.

As they walked farther into the city, Connor tried to get a feel for the mood of the Ovarrow they passed. Ovarrow didn't really show emotion the way humans did, or perhaps the Ovarrow were always in a near-constant state of dedicated focus on the task at hand. None of them were standing idly by.

Some of them stopped for a few seconds to look at Connor and Dash as they went by, but they quickly returned to what they were doing. More than a few of them seemed to recognize them.

Dash looked at Connor. "It looks like they remember you."

"Or were warned about me," he countered, and Dash frowned. "That's just the way it is."

Connor had tried to be civil. Frowning in thought, he tried to think of the term Nathan liked to use—diplomatic. Sometimes diplomacy took too damn long, and the Ovarrow seemed to respond to the use of force. It had been a dangerous precedent to set, but lives had been on the line. In particular, Lenora's life had been on the line.

Connor had been a professional soldier for most of his life. Even when he'd awakened on the *Ark*, he'd found a niche in the colony leading Search and Rescue. His skills had been well-utilized there, but then they'd formed the CDF. In the meeting rooms with the Security Council, he'd emphasized that the primary motivating factor for the military response to the terrorist act in the Ovarrow city had been that colonial lives had been at risk. He'd sent in the CDF and threatened the warlord. If the Ovarrow had kept attacking the soldiers who were securing the collapsed bridge, he'd have hit them hard. He wouldn't have wanted to do it, but he wouldn't have hesitated either. Connor suspected that more information had been conveyed in those few moments than in most of the diplomatic envoys put together. Now Connor would learn how the warlord had internalized such a lesson. Would he and the rest of the Ovarrow resent the colonists to the point that there would be no chance of forming an alliance, or would they acknowledge the truth and accept the fact that they needed each other?

Their escorts quickened the pace, and about ten minutes later, they were brought to a large building where the thick, russet-colored walls had been drawn to the side, leaving a vast atrium opened to fresh air. Connor had been to a number of Ovarrow ruins over the years, but he hadn't known that the buildings could actually do something like this. There was some kind of mechanism on the floor and along the ceiling that allowed sections of the walls to be collapsed into each other like an accordion. Inside were several work areas where groups of Ovarrow spoke to each other.

Connor saw the warlord. He wore armor similar to the rest of the soldiers. It was deep purple and had a power cord on the back, which also was used for some of the Ovarrow's weapons. He was older, with more lines to his face, but lean and muscular. He'd been speaking with the high commissioner, as well as other faction leaders. Their conversations abruptly ceased, and they turned to look at Connor and Dash.

Their escorts came to a stop, and Connor waited for the Ovarrow leadership to acknowledge them. This was a gesture of respect, since they were guests. Off to one side, a soldier brought in the colonial translator and activated it.

The warlord regarded Connor with a hint of malice in his gaze. The Warlord's First was standing by his side, his second-in-command. Cerot watched Connor curiously. Connor looked at the high commissioner.

There seemed to be so much tension in the room that Connor began to wonder whether it was purely due to his presence, as well as the CDF soldiers outside the city. He got the feeling that there was something else going on.

Connor activated his own translator and spoke. "Thank you

for seeing me, High Commissioner," he said, and his gaze flicked to the warlord. "Vitory."

The high commissioner regarded Connor for a few moments. When he spoke, another Ovarrow used the holo-interface to enter his words.

"Your presence here is surprising. It was my understanding that if the colonial government wanted to reopen communications, they'd send us a message through this console."

"You are correct, but I'm here of my own volition."

The warlord came to stand by the high commissioner's side. "Have you returned to make war?"

"No, I haven't," Connor answered.

"Then why are your soldiers outside our city walls? And there have been reports of a large force gathered some distance northeast of the city," Vitory said.

The Mekaal were scouting the area outside the city, having learned from their previous experience when they clashed with the CDF. Connor approved. "They're waiting for me. I'd like to speak with you peacefully, if you'll allow it."

Vitory glanced at High Commissioner Senleon and spoke a few words that weren't entered into the translator.

Senleon looked at Connor. "We appreciate the delicacy with which you handled coming here, but you must know we haven't changed our stance regarding an alliance with your colony."

"I understand that, and I'm not here to speak about those things," Connor said, waiting a few moments before continuing. "A short while ago, we found more Ovarrow living far away from here. We don't know much about them. Our initial contact with them was strained. It wasn't peaceful."

Connor used his neural implants to bring up a holographic

map of the continent that showed their current position and then the general location of where they'd found the other Ovarrow settlement.

Vitory studied the map for a few moments. "Did you attack them?"

"No, we didn't, but we did defend ourselves."

"This place is known to us, but nobody here has ever been there. Before we slept, there were limits to where we could travel in the open. This was one of our capitals," Senleon said.

Connor wondered which faction's capital it was but was reluctant to bring the question up at this point. The Ovarrow were sensitive to accusations, and certain questions might stop them communicating altogether because it implied that they were holding back information.

"Why did you go there?" Vitory asked.

"We found records that indicated there was an arch there, and we went there to study it to help us get our own arch working. Some of my people were trapped on the other side of the gateway, and we needed our arch to work. We think they were surprised by our presence, but we never actually spoke to them. We found Ovarrow dressed in ryklar skins, and they attacked us alongside them. These ryklars were different from the others we've seen. There are auditory systems . . ." Connor paused because the translator failed at that point. Connor gestured toward his ears. "These ryklars had had their ears removed. They were controlled by spectrums of light."

The Ovarrow translator did its best to convey what Connor had said, but he wondered how much was getting lost in translation. Mention of the arch had sparked several side conversations by the Ovarrow, but Vitory studied the holoscreen for a few moments. They knew the archway was

Krake technology used to traverse between universes. They also knew they were dangerous, and they were afraid.

"We've searched for the city and haven't found any stasis pods. Some of us believe that perhaps these Ovarrow didn't go into stasis. They weathered the long winter," Connor said.

"That theory may be correct. There weren't enough stasis pods for everyone," Senleon said.

A sobering silence settled on the Ovarrow. The memory of their time before stasis was still fresh in their minds. Their stasis technology had been flawed and they were lucky to be alive, but they retained their memories from before, and it had been a brutal time of survival.

"I'm here for two reasons," Connor continued. "The first is that we intend to go search for those Ovarrow, and I wanted to know if anyone here would like to come with us. I think it might help open communication between us. The reason I'm looking for them is to find out how they survived for so long. I also want to know what they know about the Krake. If they didn't go into stasis, they must've successfully hidden from the Krake. Perhaps they know something about them that will help us find where they live."

This brought another wave of scattered conversations among the Ovarrow, some of which involved both the warlord and the high commissioner, and Connor waited for them to finish.

Vitory turned to address Connor again. "You are only bringing soldiers to find them and not a diplomatic envoy?"

"That is correct. We expect there'll be significant danger, given what happened before. We've helped you, and now we seek your help in return," Connor replied.

"When do you plan to leave?" Senleon asked.

"As soon as I'm done here. We have troop carrier transports that will bring us to the city where we can begin our reconnaissance," Connor said.

Vitory stepped forward. "You expect us to send Ovarrow with you into a dangerous situation?"

"We would protect them."

"We are rebuilding and need all available Ovarrow to work toward that effort. Our answer is no," Vitory said.

Connor was about to reply when he received a comlink request from Samson.

"Go ahead," he said.

"We found four buildings in the same state. The burn marks are consistent with an overloaded Ovarrow power cell. Sergeant Ellison believes this is sabotage, and I'm inclined to agree with her."

Connor glanced at Vitory and brought up an image of the building that had been destroyed. "I've noticed that there are several buildings like this. Is there anything I can help you with?"

The warlord bared his teeth and Connor knew he'd struck a nerve. It seemed that the Ovarrow were dealing with a struggle of their own.

"We don't need your help."

"Maybe not, but you certainly didn't repay the help that's already been given to you. I think some of you would come with us, if given the chance," Connor said and glanced at the warlord's First. Cerot looked away. "We'll camp outside the city for one night and then leave in the morning. If any of your people would like to join us, they would be welcome."

Connor waited for the translator to finish and then turned and walked away. Dash quickly followed him, and after a few moments, their soldier escorts caught up to them and took up positions surrounding them.

"Dammit," Connor said. "You'd think they'd want to know about this other group. Why wouldn't they want to communicate with their own people?"

"I agree with you, but the Ovarrow are stubborn, and they're not like us. What makes sense to us is foreign to them."

Connor told Dash about the other buildings that had been destroyed. "They could be in the middle of some kind of rebellion, or perhaps the factions are striving for dominance."

"Did you notice their reaction to the mention of the Ovarrow who hadn't gone into stasis?"

Connor shook his head. "I was too busy watching them freak out about the Krake and the fact that we use an arch."

"I noticed that, too, but they looked ashamed."

Connor frowned in thought for a moment. "Why would they be ashamed?"

Dash shrugged. "Well, think about it. The world is ending around you and you have a way to weather out the storm, but not everyone can be saved. Then you wake up hundreds of years later and find out there's a group that was supposed to have died but instead they found a way to survive. Everyone who went into stasis left somebody behind. How would you feel if you woke up from all that? Maybe they just need a little bit of time."

Connor had to admit that there was some validity to Dash's argument. "I still feel like I'm wasting my time with them, and I don't know why they won't help us. Why can't they understand what's at stake?"

Dash remained quiet as they walked, and Connor sent a message to Samson that they were on their way back. Connor remembered the early days when the colonists had been building their colony, and he understood that the Ovarrow were also working hard to make this settlement work for them; but surely they could spare a few of their kind to come with them and contribute as delegates of some sort. Even if they were ashamed or were suffering from some kind of survivor's guilt, it didn't change the fact that sooner or later they'd cross paths with these other Ovarrow.

"Vitory seemed to regard that other group of Ovarrow as a threat," Connor said.

Dash pursed his lips and shrugged.

Maybe it was better that they didn't come with him. With or without the Ovarrow's help, he needed to keep pushing forward. But if all the Ovarrow reacted with an instant roadblock to any type of effort that involved learning more about the Krake, he wasn't sure how much help they were going to be. Why did it seem that the Ovarrow just wanted to pretend the Krake didn't exist, or was it that they had a different plan for dealing with the Krake when they arrived? Connor had no doubt that at some point the Krake were going to find their world. He glanced at the Ovarrow soldiers with them, and they kept their eyes forward. They were escorting them to the barricade, but he wished he could tell what they were thinking.

He felt his shoulders become tight with a very dark thought. What if when the Krake arrived, the Ovarrow chose to form an alliance with *them*? The Colonial Security Council assumed that since they'd brought them out of stasis and helped them reestablish themselves, the Ovarrow would naturally align with the colony, but could they be wrong? If the Ovarrow perceived that their survival was better served with the Krake, then they'd do what they thought was best for their people.

Connor clenched his teeth on those thoughts. He'd rather die on his feet than live on his knees, and he would've thought that anyone who'd gone to such lengths to survive would feel the same way. They couldn't form an alliance with the Krake. Connor pressed his lips together. Lars Mallory was convinced that the Ovarrow couldn't be trusted. What if Lars had been right? But he couldn't make sweeping judgments like that. If the Ovarrow chose to side with the Krake, then the colony would deal with that, too, but Connor refused to count them out until they made their intentions known.

# 6

THE OVARROW SOLDIERS escorted them as far as the barricades, and then Connor and Dash returned to the CDF camp.

Dash looked at Connor. “Do you mind if I write up a report to send back to Darius? I just want to tell him what we observed in the city.”

“That’s fine with me,” Connor answered, regarding the young man for a moment. “I have nothing to hide, Dash.”

“I know that, but sometimes . . .” he let the thought go unfinished for a few seconds. “I just learned that sometimes the timing of when reports are filed also has its place. It's just that this is a new development where the Ovarrow are concerned and, uh . . . Darius should know about it. I mean, they’ve been trying to keep tabs on them, but there's only so much you can see through the video feed from the occasional reconnaissance drone.”

Dash walked away and began recording his thoughts into a log.

Samson came and found Connor. "I'd like a word in private, General."

They walked a short distance away from the others, and Connor looked at his friend. "What's on your mind?"

"Off the record?" Samson said, and Connor nodded. "You're playing this a little fast and loose, aren't you?"

"I know you didn't like that I went into the city alone, but I don't think they would've let us in otherwise."

"We could've waited for them to allow it. It was reckless, and it's my job to point that out to you."

Connor had just wanted to get to the city and speak to the Ovarrow. "I acknowledge that there was some risk involved, but that's to be expected."

"Is that so? You expected the sabotaged buildings we found in there? There's something going on with the Ovarrow. If this was some kind of stronghold, I'd say they had an insurgency problem, but this is the Ovarrow. I know we're not supposed to associate their behaviors with ours, but I don't know what else it can be."

"You're right; I wasn't expecting that. Next time, I'll insist that a squad comes with me," Connor said.

"I'll hold you to that," Samson said. He rested his hands on his hips and arched his back in a stretch. "So, none of them are going to help us?"

Samson didn't come right out and say it, but the fact that the Ovarrow had once again refused to help them was becoming an issue.

"I know they have some very real challenges, but I'm getting kinda tired of this," Connor admitted. "But I can't do much about it unless we start abducting them."

Samson tilted his head to the side and pursed his lips as if the idea had merit. He shrugged. "If things are so bad that they can't even send a small squad with us, this might be a blessing in disguise. We have enough to worry about without bringing an Ovarrow squad to the table."

"It's not that simple," Connor said. "The Ovarrow don't rush to make decisions. That's why I told them I'd wait around until tomorrow."

Samson grunted. "Want to make a wager?"

Connor shook his head.

They made camp, posted sentries, and programmed a few recon drones to patrol the area. Connor didn't want anyone sneaking up on them. As the evening settled in, they could see lights coming from the city. Connor kept mulling over the day's events in his mind. He'd expected the Ovarrow to want to seek out others of their own kind, but that hadn't been the case. They were so guarded. Wouldn't they be interested in seeking out these others and *then* deciding whether or not they were enemies?

Frustrated with that line of thinking, he turned his attention to planning how they were going to look for the other Ovarrow. Sometime later, Private Colson came to seek him out, saying there was a group of Mekaal soldiers requesting to see him.

Connor walked to the middle of the camp where he saw six Ovarrow soldiers wearing dark armor. They were armed, but CDF soldiers nearby nullified any threat. An Ovarrow translation station was already set up, and Connor saw the warlord's First walk to the console.

Lenora had saved Cerot's life, and the Ovarrow knew that Lenora and Connor were married, which had been translated from "union" in Ovarrow nomenclature. The translators were based on the Ovarrow machine language used in their computers.

"General Gates, we would like to come with you to search for more of our people," Cerot said.

Connor read the message and regarded the young Ovarrow for a few moments. The warlord's First was related to the warlord. Connor wasn't exactly sure how the two were related, but there was definitely a family resemblance. He also understood that there was a rigid hierarchy among the Ovarrow.

"Does the warlord or high commissioner know you're here?" Connor asked.

The question appeared on the holoscreen, and all six Ovarrow glanced at each other for a brief moment before waiting for Cerot to answer.

"I am here to repay a debt. These Mekaal are here with me to also repay a debt," Cerot said.

Connor frowned in thought and gestured for Dash join him. "What do you make of this?"

"I think that at least three of them were trapped on the bridge with Lenora."

The Mekaal soldiers looked a bit on the young side, and Connor began to think this was some kind of a "rebellious youth" thing, but he needed the help. He glanced at Samson.

"You need to utilize the resources you've got. We need help, and they're here to help. Do you really want to send them back?" Samson said.

"Why the hesitation?" Dash asked.

"When someone is telling you something that's too good to be true, then it usually is," Connor said and turned back to

Cerot. "I'll let you come as long as you understand that you will do exactly as I say. Is this understood?"

Cerot read the message and didn't look at the other soldiers. "We will obey your commands, General."

Connor glanced back at the city. There were some colonists who thought they were too accommodating with the Ovarrow. In this case, he doubted Cerot had gotten permission to join them, but he didn't care anymore.

He began issuing orders to break camp. They'd be leaving as soon as possible. Then he drafted a message to both the warlord and the high commissioner, informing them of the situation. He timed the message to be sent after they left the camp. They would be well away by the time it was received.

# 7

CONNOR WALKED up the loading ramp of the troop carrier alpha, which was a beast of a ship. Calling it a mere troop carrier was a bit of a disservice. It could also haul equipment and had heavy armor but minimal weapons. It was an endurance vehicle meant to take damage. He walked over to Dash, who'd become the self-appointed liaison with the Ovarrow. Samson joined him.

"I was just trying to give them an idea about what to expect. I'm pretty sure none of the Ovarrow have flown above the atmosphere before," Dash said.

The quickest way to reach a city that was over twelve thousand kilometers away was to breach the atmosphere and then reenter. Connor also wanted to educate the Ovarrow on what their capabilities were. He expected that they'd report these events back to their leadership.

"Are these names correct?" Samson asked.

Connor frowned for a moment and then brought up his

own internal heads-up display. A jumble of letters appeared next to each of the Ovarrow soldiers. Cerot was easily pronounced, but the others were a mouthful. He looked at Dash. “Is that the best we can do?”

“It’s just an approximation based on the translator.”

Samson shook his head. “I can’t even pronounce that,” he said and gave Connor a look.

“I think we can do better,” Connor said and accessed the translator interface. He gestured toward the nearest Ovarrow and worked his way around, pointing at each one as he did. “Now you’re Joe, Felix, Luca.” He paused for a moment, frowning in thought. “Esteban.”

“*Esteban*? Are you serious?” Samson asked.

Connor shrugged and turned his attention back to the Ovarrow. There was one left. “Wesley,” he said. Samson gave him a monstrous glare but didn’t say anything. “That should work. I updated the translator interface to associate with the new names.”

One of the Ovarrow made a sound that almost sounded like "Joe," but he could have been clearing his throat.

“I should’ve thought of something like that. I was just trying to accurately translate what they were saying,” Dash said.

Samson stormed off, muttering under his breath.

“What’s wrong with him?” Dash asked.

“He doesn’t approve of one of the names.”

Dash glanced in the direction the big man had gone. “Why? What does he care?” Dash asked, and then his eyes widened. “One of those is *his* first name, isn’t it?”

Connor feigned indifference. “I can neither confirm nor deny. I invite you to ask him, but just make sure you wait awhile. I wouldn't ask him here. Leave yourself plenty of room to run."

Dash shook his head with a bit of a nervous grin. "That's all right. I don't really want to know that badly."

Looking at Cerot and the others, Connor activated the translator. "Enjoy the ride and listen to Dash," he said, giving Dash a companionable pat on the shoulder.

Cerot gave him an awkward nod, which he must've picked up from being around humans. The Ovarrow rested his large, four-fingered hands in his lap. His forearms were heavily muscled, giving them incredibly strong grip strength.

Connor glanced at the others, who all appeared a bit nervous, except for Esteban. He seemed to be focused on taking in his surroundings. Connor walked toward the front of the troop carrier and sat down next to Samson. The Spec Ops captain didn't look up.

"You couldn't just leave well enough alone, could you?"

"Do you know what the betting pool is for your first name? I gave him a one-in-five chance of getting it right, and it's only Dash who knows."

Samson snorted.

"You could've changed it at any time. Do you know how many times I get asked about it? You should pay me a monthly stipend just for keeping it from everyone else."

"What's with the name Esteban?"

Connor smiled. "It's just something Diaz used to do. When he couldn't remember somebody's name, he just called them Esteban."

Connor missed his friend but understood why he'd chosen to step away from the CDF for a while. Diaz had come dangerously close to dying. He had five kids—four daughters and a son—and Connor knew them all. A former Marine who had worked in law enforcement back on Old Earth, Diaz had been one of Connor's first friends in the colony and was definitely someone who'd watch your back. Connor was thankful he hadn't had to inform his friend's wife that her husband wouldn't be coming home. That scared him more than he cared to admit.

Since rejoining the CDF, Connor was determined to balance his personal life with his work. It had been simpler when it was just him and Lenora, but when Lauren was born, things had changed. *He* had changed. He found that he didn't like leaving home so much because he wanted to be around his daughter. Before rejoining the CDF, he'd imagined that he'd be able to do things with whatever family he had because he wasn't a soldier anymore. Lenora had hinted at wanting to get back to fieldwork, which Connor also enjoyed. He liked exploring New Earth, but learning about the Krake had changed all that. It was something he couldn't ignore. Sometimes he thought about letting someone else take the reins and deal with the Krake. He'd trained a lot of people when they created the Colonial Defense Force. It wasn't like when they'd first arrived on this planet. The CDF had been created out of necessity by people who weren't soldiers in their previous lives back on Old Earth. They could do their jobs very well, but no one had the experience Connor had. He'd been a soldier most of his life.

"The other three troop carriers are en route," Samson said.

"The best way for us to cover the most ground is to split up into three groups. One of the groups can do aerial reconnaissance while the rest of us explore the city," Connor said.

He activated the nearest holoscreen and brought up an image of the city, highlighting the areas the previous CDF team had already explored. "They weren't able to find them after our initial encounter. We left recon drones there for a few days, which gave us a map of the city, but we need both boots on the ground and eyes in the sky if we're going to find them."

"No one has been back since?" Samson asked.

Connor shook his head. "No time. We're the first."

"All right, so how do you want to do this?"

Connor leaned back in his chair and pressed his lips together in thought. "I think we should do several flyovers of the city, looking for signs of recent use and ryklar activity. Also, see if Cerot and the others spot anything worth investigating."

"Were there a lot of ryklars the last time you went there?"

"There was a large pack, but they don't seem to stay very long. There are most likely different packs that rotate from place to place, and they vary in size. So the ryklars that were there a few months ago might not be there anymore. However, the ones that were used as watchdogs in the attack were under Ovarrow control. We don't know where those are or how many of them there are," Connor said.

Samson studied the map of the city for a few moments. "If they were breeding ryklars, we should be able to find some evidence of that. They'd have to feed them, dispose of their waste, things like that. They'd also have to go out for supplies."

The troop carrier accelerated to breakaway speeds, but the inertia dampeners prevented them from feeling the acceleration.

"I don't remember seeing anything like farmland, but you're right. We should look for evidence of someone actually living in the city. I just don't think they did," Connor said.

"Then what were they doing there?"

"We weren't even aware of them until we started salvaging parts from the arch. In fact, there were no remnant power cores in standby anywhere. That can't be a coincidence. So, the real question is: where do they live and why maintain a watch on an arch that didn't have any power anyway?"

Several of the Ovarrow made surprised noises and gestured toward a wallscreen that showed a low-orbit view of New Earth. They were beyond the atmosphere, which gleamed with a shimmering blue glow. The ring that encircled New Earth was made up of the shattered remains of a third moon and was maintained by a smaller moon orbiting closer to the planet and a larger moon farther away. The gravitational pull had spread the remains of the third moon so thin that the vertical height was typically seven meters.

The Ovarrow continued to gasp in surprise, speaking with multi-toned sounds from their intricate vocal cords. They had two distinct vocal cords, which allowed them to communicate in such a way that there was very little chance of any human being able to duplicate it.

Some of the Ovarrow looked away from the wallscreen, but Cerot and Esteban couldn't stop looking at the planet below. Connor noticed that Dash was quiet, letting the Ovarrow have this moment to themselves. Connor couldn't remember the exact date of when human beings had first left Earth, but he knew it was well over two hundred years before the *Ark* had left the Sol System. Early astronauts and engineers had pushed the boundaries, pioneering the effort for humanity's next great frontier. They hadn't been brought into it by an alien species. By the time Connor was born, going into space was commonplace. There were space stations engaged in robotic asteroid mining, as well as colonies on various moons throughout the solar system. This was a rare opportunity to witness a species' first time leaving their planet.

Several cargo ships flew within view of them on their way to the lunar base where the CDF shipyards were. The orbital defense platforms were farther away, but they wouldn't be able to see them. Connor hoped the experience would spark a flame within the Ovarrow to push past their limits.

They were able to see the reentry into the atmosphere. The video feed on the wallscreen glowed red on its edges from the heat dispersal. Connor watched as the Ovarrow winced away from it, and he heard Dash try to calm them down.

"I don't know why you put so much stock in the Ovarrow," Samson said.

"They're our link to the past and our only link to the Krake."

"I understand that. We've learned some things, but you're pushing for an alliance. There are only ten thousand of them in that city, and let's say there are two or three times that number in stasis that haven't come out yet. That's not much of an army if we're looking for an alliance."

"I see what you're saying," Connor replied. "Think of it this way: either they might never have awakened because of the faulty tech they used to go into stasis, or they might've awakened in the middle of our war with the Krake, only we didn't know as much as we needed to and the Krake surprised us by coming back here. We know they routinely check, however many worlds they keep track of."

"Yes, but the arch that they were using was under water, so it was inaccessible. I read the report."

"So, what are you saying?"

"I don't know how much help the Ovarrow can be. I mean,

think about it. Their entire strategy for dealing with the Krake was to hide themselves in stasis. Are we going to do the same thing?"

Connor shook his head. "No, we're not going to hide in stasis."

"I didn't think so. So, what are you hoping to get from this other group of Ovarrow?"

"We need to find out more about them—confirm their history. If they didn't go into stasis, that puts this whole situation in a different light. They were survivors of an ice age on a planet where everyone had almost wiped themselves out fighting each other and the Krake."

"Not exactly the kind of person I want guarding my back or fighting at my side. So, the same question applies," Samson said.

"The answer doesn't change. They might know the Krake better than anyone who went into stasis. The records we were able to uncover indicate that the Ovarrow who went into stasis didn't all go at the same time. Ultimately, we need to get them to talk to us. We don't know how many there are. Maybe there are a lot of them—enough to make a difference in a war."

Samson was quiet, and Connor regarded him for a few moments. "What would you do?"

Samson frowned. "About what? There are so many moving parts to this, but I don't know if I'd go looking for the Ovarrow here. If the Krake are the real threat, then I'd want to know about them—where they live, what their capabilities are, what their weapons are, their tactics . . . probably all the things you already said in those Security Council meetings you and Nathan frequent."

Connor twitched his head to the side. "You wouldn't be

wrong about that. The real question is: how long do we have before the Krake come here? And what do we do when they come?"

Samson looked at him for a few moments. "No wonder they don't want to work with you. I understand you're trying to bring awareness, but you know people don't think straight if they're scared all the time."

"Then they'll just have to learn how to cope better. I didn't create this situation, but I'm damn well going to do something about it," Connor said.

"Works for me," Samson replied. "And I'm sure they'll appreciate the hard line from you."

"They appreciate things like facts and data. We need something that's irrefutable. Otherwise . . ." Connor said, pausing for a few moments, ". . . I really am crazy to keep pursuing this."

"They thought you were crazy about a threat coming from Earth, too, but who am I to judge?"

Samson got up and walked away, and Connor shook his head. Samson had lived outside the colony on his own for years, deep in the New Earth frontier, and Connor wasn't sure if Samson was the best judge of his mental status. Samson was good with tangible threats—a combat situation or achieving an objective—but he lacked some of the finesse for intelligence gathering.

There was an open space in the middle of the troop carrier that was commonly used for briefings. Connor had Dash bring their Ovarrow guests to that space so he could watch their reactions to the city and ask them questions.

They'd come up with a way to categorize Ovarrow cities by size, and a capital was the largest. The city they were heading to covered an area of over six thousand square kilometers.

Samson brushed up against Connor's elbow as he leaned toward the holoscreen. "That's gotta be over a hundred kilometers across."

Connor nodded. "Not quite a square but close enough, even with a big river running almost through the middle."

Fragmented spires pierced the overgrowth, but they could see more of the bronze-colored buildings the closer they got to the coastal area.

"We could've used Flint and the 3rd to help recon these ruins," Samson said.

"They're on a training exercise at the lunar base," Connor replied.

"War games on the moon," Samson replied. "I'm sure that's the only reason they're not here," he added sarcastically.

"Gotta keep those skill sets sharp, and if you're implying that I deployed them in the wake of recent events, I can neither confirm nor deny any such actions."

Connor highlighted the northeastern part of the city. "Send word for Layton and the other carrier to begin scouting this area here," he said and then looked at Dash. "Do they recognize anything?"

Dash looked at Cerot and repeated the question.

"None of us have ever been here. There were pockets of fighting that divided the continent," Cerot said.

Connor took control of the city map on the holoscreen and zoomed in closer. "This is the area where we found the arch."

Cerot and the other Ovarrow peered at the map. "It looks like a Mekaal research facility," Cerot said, gesturing to the barely discernable perimeter.

Once the Ovarrow pointed it out, Connor saw it—an Ovarrow military research facility. That made a lot of sense.

"Recon drones aren't showing any ryklar activity and no deterrent signal," Dash said.

Connor nodded, brought up a recon drone feed, and put it on the holoscreen. The drone flew through the dimly lit corridors, racing to its objective. The Ovarrow watched its progress intently. It entered a vast chamber and increased its altitude, giving them a higher vantage point.

"Where'd it go?" Dash asked.

Connor frowned and watched the video feed. Where the Ovarrow arch had once been was nothing but rubbled remains. "Someone destroyed the arch."

"Why would they do that?" Dash asked.

"They didn't want us coming back here," Connor said.

"They probably didn't want us turning it back on," Samson said.

Connor frowned in thought. "The whole city is dead. There isn't any power here. Besides, we took critical components from it, so it wouldn't have worked anyway."

"Yeah, but still," Dash said. "Why go through the trouble of destroying something that already couldn't work?"

Connor peered at the holoscreen, trying to think of a reason but couldn't.

"It's simple," Samson said, his deep voice drawing their attention. "It means 'go away.'"

Connor scratched his eyebrow. "That's not going to work. We're not leaving. Have the pilot find us a place to set down and we can begin searching for them."

# 8

TRIDENT BATTLE GROUP orbited around the New Earth candidate. The NEC had experienced an extinction-level event that was so catastrophic that most of the planetary surface was uninhabitable. Gabriel, the *Vigilant*'s AI, estimated that the cataclysm had occurred within the last thirty to forty standard years.

Sean had sent salvage teams over to the orbital bombardment platform where a derelict ship had been docked. He was heading toward the main hangar bay where a combat shuttle waited to take him over to the wrecked ship. Bill Halsey, the lead engineer aboard the *Vigilant*, insisted that Sean come see the Casimir power core. The man lived for ships and knew them backward and forward, particularly their power cores.

Salvage teams had been exploring every inch of the ship. Sean thought Oriana would've preferred to be on one of the away teams, but she had all but locked herself in her lab with her team. She'd review the information the salvage teams found.

Sean entered the main hangar where an eagle class combat shuttle was ready to be launched. Captain Chad Boseman stood by the loading ramp and gave him a salute as he approached.

"Are we ready to leave?" Sean asked.

"Now that you're here, we are," Boseman replied.

If any of the scientists were lagging behind or running late, they wouldn't be going. Sean kept to a tight schedule that didn't include waiting for anyone who couldn't arrive on time.

The loading ramp closed and the combat shuttle was cleared for launch. As Sean ambled up to his seat, he was greeted by the rest of Boseman's team. He recognized Sergeant Benton, who had a philandering reputation; however, since they were about to fly over to a Krake ship, he was all business-focused, just like the rest of the Spec Ops team.

Sean could always count on Boseman to come up with creative solutions to what others would consider impossible objectives. It had been Boseman's idea to use communications drones to storm the *Yorktown* during the mutiny. When failure wasn't an option, they didn't.

Sean glanced at the Spec Ops platoon and felt a slight pang of regret. He'd led his own Spec Ops platoon for years, and they'd been a small, tight-knit, highly capable group that had been given objectives by their superior officers—mostly Connor and, later on, Nathan. But the more he thought about it, he supposed very little had changed over the years, with the exception of the resources at his disposal. He'd gone from leading a platoon to a company of soldiers, then to a brigade, and now Trident Battle Group. They represented the CDF fleet's offensive line until they could build more ships.

The combat shuttle flew toward the derelict Krake warship. It was a smaller-class vessel than the destroyers they'd encountered in previous combat engagements. The ship had no power, and there were several sections that had been impacted by Krake combat drones. They hadn't found any space gates in the area, which worried Sean. Why had they been given these coordinates if they weren't going to be contacted?

There was a significant hull breach around the middle of the ship where they'd inserted an emergency docking tube. The pilot flew the combat shuttle and docked with the tube. Sean wore a Nexstar combat suit, but he wasn't armed. He didn't expect any trouble aboard the derelict ship. Search teams hadn't found any latent systems on standby, waiting to be triggered by the next hapless visitor.

The Krake were of similar size to the Ovarrow, which made them slightly taller than the average human. The pale interior of the ship held the remnants of organic matter that had been combined with the Krake version of a nanorobotic composite. The structure seemed solid, and the floors of the corridors contained enough metal for their magboots to work.

They headed for the main reactor room. He'd been in a number of main reactor rooms aboard CDF ships and even Vemus ships that had once been part of the NA Alliance military. They were massive constructs for the larger ships, but they all had certain similarities among them. There were containment systems, coolant systems, and emergency shutoffs, but Sean didn't see any of that in the Krake power core.

Captain Halsey came over to Sean, positively bursting with excitement. "Colonel, what do you think?"

"It doesn't look like one of ours. What am I looking at here?"

"We believe this is a Casimir power core. It draws energy

from a vacuum and is much more efficient than even our fusion-based reactors. Zero-point energy creation is the holy grail of power generation."

Sean wished he understood what he was looking at. "So, they can generate more power, which means everything else stems from something like this. I'm surprised the Krake don't use more energy-based weapons, given their superior power core."

Halsey bobbed his head. "Maybe they do, and we just haven't found those systems yet. But I've been over to one of the main engines, and there's evidence of overwearing. We've done some preliminary analyses of the materials they use, and with that kind of power output, these engines won't hold up for extended voyages. We've also had teams that have seen stress fractures at key load points on the hull, which we think is directly related to their powerful engines."

Sean frowned in thought for a moment. "Was this power core retrofitted to this ship?"

"I was thinking that as well. Maybe they had some kind of technical leap and started outfitting their ships with these," Halsey said, gesturing toward the power core. "We'll need more time to figure that out."

Sean nodded. "Understood. Any idea how long the ship has been here?"

Halsey shook his head. "That's outside my area of expertise. I did hear a couple of the science teams mention that the ship has been here as long as the planet's been unlivable."

Sean took another look around at the area.

"We've been scanning everything we can find in here and recording things we don't understand, but in order to really understand how this power core works, we need to bring it back with us. Take it apart," Halsey said.

"You'll have to do the best you can. I don't know if we could take the ship with us."

"I thought you'd say that, sir. But if we could bring this ship back with us and reverse-engineer some of their systems, it might make our weapons more effective against them," Halsey said.

"Do the best you can, and I'll see what kind of options we can come up with. For now, keep trying to figure out how that thing works, but don't turn it on," Sean said.

He expected Halsey knew better, but the man was excited about this find. Sean thought it better to remind him to pay attention and be careful.

"Understood, sir," Halsey said.

Sean left the main reactor area, and Boseman led him toward weapons operations.

"They didn't leave much behind," Boseman said. "I would love to have found some of those attack drones so we could figure out how they work."

"Agreed," Sean said.

They spent the next few hours going over the Krake ship. The bridge of the ship was nothing like the bridge of any CDF ship; it was a multilevel, circular room. Sean guessed the CIC was above normal ship operations.

A comlink request came from the *Vigilant*.

"Colonel," Russo said, "the *Albany* reports a ship detected on sensors."

Sean stopped what he was doing. "How many ships are there?"

"Just the one ship, sir, but it's on an intercept course. Their speed is quite slow. I think they want to be seen," Russo said.

Boseman glanced at him questioningly.

"I think we've worn out our welcome. We need to get everyone off the ship," Sean said.

Boseman nodded and opened a broadcast comlink.

"Colonel," Russo said, "at the current velocity, it'll take them several hours to reach us."

"Understood, Captain. How did they sneak up on us?"

"We're not sure, sir. We still haven't detected a space gate or a gamma burst from a gate being used. The ship is on the smaller side. There might be an arch on the planet, so they could have come from there," Russo said.

"Have they tried to communicate with us?"

"Negative, Colonel."

"I'm heading back to the *Vigilant*. Keep me apprised of any new developments," Sean said.

Using an arch on the planet made sense to Sean, unless the Krake had some sort of stealth technology that hid them from CDF scanners. Sean didn't like to think about that, but it was a possibility. However, since it was a smaller ship, it could've used an arch on the planet. They hadn't had time to thoroughly investigate. He had to get back to the *Vigilant* and hopefully find out what they wanted.

# 9

THEY WERE able to evacuate the derelict ship relatively quickly, even with Halsey lamenting the loss of such a technological sample of superior capabilities. Sean was pleased that the teams had gotten as much information as they had in the short amount of time they were on the ship.

He wasn't taking any chances where the Krake were concerned. They'd only detected one ship, and it had a different profile than the warships they'd encountered. But the safety of the people under his command was paramount to him. He wouldn't risk their lives needlessly.

Sean staggered Trident Battle Group's formation for maximum coverage on the Krake ship as it slowly approached. The *Vigilant* was positioned to be on a direct intercept course.

"No other ships detected, Colonel," Lieutenant Scott said, giving the result of the recent active scans of the area.

"Very well," Sean replied.

"Sir," Captain Russo said, "shouldn't we try to open a communications channel with them?"

"Negative. They knew we were here, and they're coming right for us. I expect them to initiate comms."

Oriana glanced at him. She probably agreed with Russo, but he'd made his decision. The Krake rebels had initiated this first contact when they transmitted these coordinates. Sean knew they hadn't tripped any type of alarm on either the orbital bombardment platform or the derelict ship. There was absolutely no power on any of those systems, and Sean hadn't allowed any of the systems to be brought back online. They had carefully monitored for any outgoing signals and hadn't detected anything.

The Krake ship steadily approached until it fired its braking thrusters and then held its position fifty thousand kilometers from Trident Battle Group.

"Colonel, I have an incoming transmission from the Krake ship," Specialist Sansky said. "They're sending our first-contact protocols back to us."

"Acknowledged. Initiate a comlink to that ship," Sean said.

First-contact protocols included a way for an advanced civilization to be able to communicate with them. He didn't want to use subspace communications because he didn't believe the Krake had that capability. They hadn't detected anything like a subspace comlink in their previous encounter, and he didn't want to wave an advantage like that under their collective noses.

"Comlink is active, sir," Sansky replied.

"Krake ship, I am Colonel Sean Quinn of the Colonial Defense Force."

A video comlink became active on the main holoscreen and

showed a Krake sitting in a command chair. The video comlink vantage was relatively close to the speaker, and Sean could see that the Krake had an elongated, wedge-shaped head with twin cranial lobes. Its azure eyes were framed under a thick brow and cheek bones. The Krake's skin had a bluish hue, and the thick flesh sprouting from its chin appeared like a beard that vibrated when he spoke.

After the Krake finished speaking, a verbal translation could be heard.

"Acknowledgment of transmission. Krake ship designate DH-Crillian. Commander designation Aurang speaking."

Sean leaned forward, and his eyes widened for a moment. "We received these coordinates from a Krake warship that had come to our aid. Are you who we're supposed to meet?"

Trident Battle Group didn't have a translator for the Krake language. They'd been using an Ovarrow translator, since that was believed to be based on the Krake language. Since the Krake had obviously analyzed colonial first-contact protocols, they should be able to understand Sean.

Almost a full minute went by without a response. "Are you receiving me?" Sean asked.

"Delayed response due to translation learning. We are not the Krake who helped you, but we are of the same group," Aurang said.

"What happened to the Krake who helped us?" Sean asked.

"Sacrificed in our war with the overseers."

"Why did they help us?"

"You fought overseer military, though you're not Ovarrow, but you've translated part of the Ovarrow language."

The Krake stopped speaking and seemed to be waiting for Sean to reply.

"We have encountered the Ovarrow. We've also encountered Krake warships. They would not communicate with us and, instead, attacked us. We defended ourselves," Sean replied.

"Are the Ovarrow with you?" Aurang asked.

Sean regarded the Krake for a few moments. "No. Are the Ovarrow with you?"

"There are no Ovarrow on the ship, but they fight the overseers as well. The overseers attacked you because they believed you were a new group of Ovarrow from an unknown beta universe," Aurang said.

The Krake was volunteering information, but Sean's gut instinct was not to trust him. It was interesting that the Krake military practiced a shoot-first methodology. "Why did you help us? What group do you represent?"

"You fought the overseers. You are aware of the Krake and what they do to other Ovarrow worlds."

"We're not the Ovarrow," Sean said.

"No, you're not."

"We are humans, and we prefer not to fight a war with anybody."

"War has already begun. We all fight it. The overseers will find your world. That is what they do."

"Is war the only option? Can't we have peace?" Sean asked.

"There has never been peace. All that matters to the overseers is dominance. They are aware of you and are searching for your world. They will search for your universe, but I can help you stop them," Aurang said.

"Why would you help us?"

"Because of your warships. You are capable. You've used clever tactics to take what you want. I represent a group that resists the overseers because we believe that the individual is as important as the whole. For that, the overseers want us annihilated."

Sean suspected there would be strings attached to whatever the Krake offered them. "What do you want from us?"

"Our operations have been compromised, and it's only a matter of time before the overseers seek retribution. We need your help to stop this from happening."

"And in exchange for our help, you promise to stop the overseers from invading our world?"

"Yes."

"You'll have to forgive me if I don't believe you. If the overseers are as powerful as you say, then how is helping you going to prevent them from invading our home?" Sean asked.

Aurang was quiet for a few moments. "We have an operation in place that is set to take out the overseers. They will be removed from power. New overseers will be appointed, and the Krake will stop. Many things will change."

Sean had seen the Ovarrow ruins on New Earth. All colonists were aware of them. The Krake manipulated the Ovarrow, and Sean felt that what he was hearing was too good to be true.

"We'll need time to consider your request. In order to do that, I need to understand exactly what you need from us."

"You have resources. Our communication network has been compromised and it's not safe for me to contact our fighters. I will transfer the data I have for you to review."

Sean glanced at Specialist Sansky.

"Data uplink has been initiated. Dumping data to secure virtual sandbox for analysis," Sansky said.

"The Krake are not all the same. There can be peace between us," Aurang said.

"We'll need time to consider your request for help," Sean said.

The comlink went dark. Sean sat back in his chair and sighed. He felt as if he'd just gone on a long-distance run and then learned that he still had miles to go.

# 10

An hour had passed since they'd received Aurang's request for help. Sean wanted some time to analyze the data and make sure there wasn't anything hidden that could infiltrate their computer systems.

Sean and Russo left the bridge and headed for the nearby conference room. When they walked inside, Oriana was already there, along with Chad Boseman and Bill Halsey. Major Shelton, who was commanding the *Yorktown,* was online, along with the rest of the commanding officers of the battle group, half of whom were familiar. The other half were too new to know well.

"Thank you all for coming. By now, you've had time to review the data Aurang sent us. I'm going to open up the floor so you can voice your concerns, but before I do that, I want you to know that I don't have any reason to trust Aurang," Sean said.

"He's hiding something, sir," Boseman said.

"I'm sure he's hiding a lot, but he also provided some

detailed information. Gabriel didn't detect any type of data tampering or latent protocols that would infiltrate our systems, so at least the data he provided is clean, but I wouldn't say it's free of risk."

"How was the data verified?" Oriana asked.

"I isolated the data on a secure system and ran it through a number of different analyses, including time acceleration that allowed the Krake data to sit there for the equivalent of ten standard years. No hidden subroutines were detected," Gabriel said.

There was silence for a few moments. Sean hadn't expected any of the junior officers to speak up.

"Sir," Major Shelton said, "they've only given us a list of targets, along with a briefing about what they need to accomplish there. This isn't enough for us to make a 'go' or 'no-go' decision."

Aurang had given them images of multiple Krake facilities, as well as star system information, including defenses and space gate and arch locations.

"Agreed, and the mission requires coordination with Aurang and whatever soldiers he has aboard his ship. Anyone else?" Sean asked.

"Sir," Lieutenant Richard Pitts of the *Babylon* said, "he's making a promise that he can stop the Krake from finding our world if we help them overthrow the current leadership. I understand he wants to protect his intelligence network, or whatever the Krake wants to call it. I think what he's promising you is something he can't deliver. It's intangible. I would call it 'pie in the sky' where they promise us the world and then ultimately can't deliver it."

"Good point, Lieutenant Pitts. How do we know this isn't a

trap? How do we know we aren't being manipulated right now?" Sean said.

"Then we treat the entire operation as if it's a trap, sir," Boseman said.

Sean nodded. "That's what I'm thinking."

"Sir," Pitts said, "if we aren't going to trust the Krake or this Aurang, why would we even consider a military operation with them? Why wouldn't we decline his request and return to New Earth?"

Sean took a moment to look at the other holoscreens. Whether or not they should return home had been one of the crucial points of the entire mutiny. Pitts wasn't his staunchest supporter, but Sean could work with that. "Because of our mission out here. We've been tasked to learn all we can about the Krake and whether or not we can find a way to defeat them. We can't recon our enemy if we don't take any risks, but we can all agree that there's a high degree of risk in this undertaking; however, there's also the potential for a greater reward, meaning that we could learn something crucial about the Krake. We're all out here to protect our home, and I intend to build into our planning a way to send word back to COMCENT in the event that we fail."

There was dead silence for a few moments.

"Colonel, what about the Krake prisoners?" Major Shelton asked.

"We've questioned them before, and they've refused to communicate with us. At this time, I'm not entertaining any option to force cooperation," Sean said.

"Would they be more cooperative if they thought they were being returned to their people?" Shelton asked.

"Possibly, but I want to keep them as a bargaining piece in case we need them," Sean said.

"Sir, are you sure this is the best course of action regarding the prisoners?" Lieutenant Pitts asked.

Sean had called this all-hands meeting to keep the senior officers invested in the mission. "Do you have a suggestion, Lieutenant?"

"Just that it might be dangerous to bring them back home with us."

"I'm positive we can secure two prisoners," Sean replied. "Thank you all for your participation. I will, of course, inform you of your orders, but if you have any concerns in the meantime, raise them with your immediate superiors."

The meeting ended, and Sean returned to the bridge. He brought Chad Boseman with him so he could watch the encounter with Aurang. At the top of the hour, a comlink from the Krake ship was initiated.

*Right on time*, Sean thought.

"Colonel Quinn, you've had time to consider my request for aid. Have you reached a decision?" Aurang asked.

"Not yet. We need to perform our own analysis. If you want our help, you'll need to give us the coordinates of the targets and we'll have a look for ourselves."

"This is unacceptable. My people are in danger from the overseers. We must go at once."

"Then my answer is no. We will not assist you," Sean said.

"The data I provided is current. Why do you need to see these targets in order to make a decision?"

Sean leaned forward. "Because I don't trust you. You haven't given me any reason to trust you."

Sean thought he might've offended the Krake, but that wasn't the case.

"Understood, and this is to be expected. What do you want to know most about the Krake?"

Sean frowned. He hadn't been anticipating that kind of question. "I want to know how much you know about us. Is it possible to negotiate a peaceful end to hostilities?"

"No, I already told you this is impossible. The overseers will never stop searching for you because they need to substantiate how much of a threat you are. In order to achieve that, testing is required."

"That's why we must do our own reconnaissance, and then we can tell you whether or not we can help you. I want to know what communication protocols the Krake use. I want to be able to communicate with other Krake and not be reliant on you to translate for us," Sean said.

"If I provide this, will you help us?"

"No. If you provide this, then I'll consider helping you by doing our own reconnaissance of these targets."

Aurang was quiet while he considered Sean's reply.

"Giving this to us is a show of good faith. If you want to help your people, this is a small token toward building trust between us," Sean said.

"Very well, I will give you a copy of our communications protocols, as well as the translator. I would like to now discuss the use of your space gate," Aurang said.

"Continue," Sean said.

"I cannot bring this ship through the arch and go to the target universe. I will need to use your space gate."

"That is out of the question," Sean said.

There was no way he was going to allow a potential enemy

ship among the battle group to watch how they used their space gate.

"Then how will we communicate?" Aurang asked.

"You can find your own way to the target universe and we'll meet you there. Give us a way to contact you. If we contact you, then you'll know our answer," Sean replied.

"What assurances do I have that you'll even honor your end of the bargain? The lives of my people are at risk if I have to wait for you and you decide not to help," Aurang said.

"You came to us for help. I want to know the coordinates of Krake outposts and the home world, or wherever it is that your overseers reside."

Aurang snarled. "I will not reveal our home world to you."

Finally, an emotional response. That was something, at least. Sean had been wondering how far he could push him before he pushed back. If Aurang had promised to give them that information, then he'd have known this entire thing was a lie.

"But I can provide you with operational data of our current outposts. That data is in the main facility that holds the operational intelligence of our group. I can give you access to it," Aurang said.

Now they were getting somewhere. "I'll be in touch after we do our own reconnaissance," Sean said.

"Sir," Boseman said, and Sean looked at him. "A quick moment, sir. This concerns the Krake."

Sean gestured for Boseman to come over. He looked at Aurang. "Give us a few moments," Sean said and muted the channel.

"Sir, that ship would fit into our main hangar, so we could bring them with us without allowing them to monitor our space gate. We could also confine them to their ship if we needed to. And if they betrayed us, we'd get one more piece of Krake tech to bring home with us," Boseman said.

Sean frowned in thought for a moment. Only the *Vigilant* or the *Yorktown* had enough room in their hangar bays to accommodate the Krake ship. He gave his friend a nod, and Boseman returned to his post.

Sean unmuted the comlink channel. "Aurang, I think we have a way to accommodate your request to come with us."

"Fortuitous! I'm eager to hear it," Aurang said.

Sean told him.

"Your caution is acceptable. We will comply," Aurang said.

"My helmsman will provide you with the coordinates," Sean said and transferred the comlink to Lieutenant Edwards.

Aurang provided the data they requested, including a translation program. Then the Krake ship was guided to the *Vigilant*'s main hangar.

"Helm, set a course for beta coordinates in the outer system," Sean said.

"Sir, I have a subspace comlink from the *Yorktown*," Sansky said.

"Send it to my personal holoscreen," Sean replied. A moment later, Major Shelton appeared on his holoscreen.

"Sir, remind me never to play poker with you," she said and grinned a little. "I know we're expecting a trap, but I find it suspicious that he expected us to up and go right now."

"Maybe the Krake are used to dealing with the Ovarrow. Either way, we'll have enough transit time to test out the Krake translator he gave us," Sean said.

Major Shelton's eyes widened. "You had already planned to ask him for that, hadn't you?"

"It was one of the things. I didn't expect he would share the location of their home world system, but his response was revealing, I think. I don't think he was expecting it."

"No, I think you're right. He wasn't expecting it."

"I'll send a copy of the data to you. If there's anyone else you want to bring in on our analysis of this, let me know. Otherwise, I'm going to keep this between us," Sean said.

"Understood, sir."

The comlink went dark and they got to work.

# 11

TWENTY-FOUR HOURS HAD PASSED and Connor was no closer to finding the Ovarrow. He'd divided the 7th into ten squads and they'd spent the night among the ruins of the Ovarrow capital city. With the use of recon drones, they were covering a lot of ground, but they hadn't found any evidence of the Ovarrow they'd encountered when retrieving critical pieces of the arch. Recon drones spotted a few ryklar scouts out on the fringes of the city, but they only found older ryklar tracks inside. Mostly they saw various flying creatures, some of which might have been considered birds.

The night before, they'd seen a large group of bats take to the skies near sunset, which had startled the soldiers on guard duty. The bats that lived in this region were much larger than the similar species on Earth. Connor didn't know much about them, but Dash, ever curious about New Earth, had enlightened him about them the night before. Bats on Earth were small and harmless, and they liked to eat insects. On New

Earth, they weighed six kilograms and had a wingspan of almost two meters, on average. They had a healthy set of canines, which they used to penetrate the green and yellow fruit they preferred to eat, but they also ate insects, which were quite large in this region. Connor had sampled the fruit before. It was bitter and too full of seeds to be enjoyed, so the bats could keep all that fruit they wanted. And the insects were a nonissue since humans weren't going to eat those either.

The bats had taken up residence in a few of the tall buildings that the colonists thought were monuments. They thought this because rather than being constructed from bronze, metallic-alloyed plates, these were obsidian on the outside. They were dark but shimmered when the sunlight reflected off them. When hundreds of the giant bats took to the skies at sunset, the sounds of their flapping wings ricocheted off the surrounding buildings like thunder. It was no less impressive than watching several wings of Hellcats take off and fly in formation from a CDF base.

As they explored the city, the only reports that came in indicated smaller, rodent-sized creatures scurrying throughout the city. Camping there reminded Connor of exploring other ruins with Lenora when he'd been retired from the CDF. The sleeping arrangements had been better back then, but the 7th was filled with a good group of soldiers.

New Earth was a place that explorers dreamt about. Even after living on this planet for as long as they had, the newness of it hadn't quite worn off. The planet would never be what Earth had been, but most colonists had come to love their new home as much as their old home, and Connor was no exception. Why else would he fight so hard to protect it? New Earth was a world worth protecting. This was his home.

Connor walked over to the command area where Samson was organizing troop deployments for the search grids they were going to hit that day. The group of squad leaders dispersed once they had their assignments and the comlink to the other camps flickered off.

"Layton had several squads explore some of the underground tunnels on the western side of the city, but most had cave-ins blocking them," Samson said.

The cities they'd explored had extensive sewer systems connected to dormant water treatment facilities. Now, they were little more than an underground river system that connected to major waterways.

"Were any of the cave-ins recent?" Connor asked.

"None that they could tell," Samson replied. "If I were fortifying a city against an invader, I'd block off all the underground entries," he said and glanced toward where Dash was speaking with the Ovarrow. "Especially if they were sending in their attack dogs."

Connor nodded. Ryklars could burrow and squeeze through some tight spaces when they wanted to. "It makes sense, but they wouldn't have walled themselves off completely, and we still don't know if they were just guarding the area. They might live somewhere else. I've had satellites scouring the area, but the analysts haven't found anything either."

Samson frowned, his mouth forming a grim line while he peered at the map on the holoscreen. "They could have destroyed the arch and then packed up and left."

"Maybe, but you can't cover up the movement of a big group like that. When the ryklars attacked, there were quite a few of them. I think we need to go back to the arch chamber. It might be our best lead. We know they were there and that there were tunnels in the area."

"Just say the word. I'll have the engineers bring equipment to clear a path if we need it," Samson replied.

"We'll need it," Connor said and was quiet for a few moments while he studied the map.

Samson shifted his feet. "I can hear the wheels turning."

Connor looked at him. "We assumed that they might have been living somewhere in a section of the city itself, but that could be wrong. If they've been hiding their presence for . . ." he said and paused, glancing at the Ovarrow for several seconds, ". . . a few hundred years, then maybe they abandoned living on the surface altogether. Living below ground would prevent them from being detected by the casual observer. When the Krake were cycling through different universes, their goal was to identify a place worth scouting. The Ovarrow were definitely monitoring the arch here."

Samson rubbed the stubble on the bottom of his chin in thought. "Living underground for years is a bit of a stretch."

"I don't think so. If they never went into stasis, they'd have had to survive the ice age somehow," Connor said.

"Wouldn't they have just migrated south to where it's warmer?"

"Maybe, but that would mean bringing a lot of equipment with them, which we've never found evidence of, so I'm not sure that explanation works. They could have migrated, but why come back when the ice age was over?"

"We should ask *them*," Samson said, twisting his head toward the Ovarrow.

Connor shook his head. "They wouldn't know. Maybe the warlord would but not Cerot or the others. They're young."

"So, we need a reason for them either coming back here or staying here. Maybe they were just guarding the arch?"

Connor nodded. "It's the obvious choice. I'm just not sure it's reason enough for them to stay here. They'd have to feed themselves and train future generations not to abandon their posts, but that doesn't tell us why," Connor said.

"Why do we guard anything?" Samson said. He had a point.

"They only destroyed it after they found us scavenging it for parts," Connor said. "What if they intended to use it? Or what if they'd kept it as a fail-safe in case the Krake came back through that arch we found at New Haven?"

Dash walked over and looked at them. "Am I interrupting something?"

"No," Samson said. "Connor's just trying to figure out why we haven't found them yet and why they'd stay here in the first place."

Dash's eyes flicked toward Connor. "Well, given what we've seen, I wouldn't put it past them to figure out a way to survive without giving away their presence to the Krake, or anyone else who might come looking for them."

"At some point, the Krake stopped coming here," Connor said.

Cerot and the other Ovarrow were standing nearby, and Connor considered them for a few moments. Dash looked at him questioningly and Samson merely waited. Connor scratched his eyebrow. "When we brought them out of stasis and moved them to their city, they went to work making it livable. It's what we expected them to do, but the Ovarrow here must be different."

"Should we recall the search teams then?" Samson asked.

Connor shook his head. "No, but send them an update to

look for anything leading underground—hidden entrances inside buildings or anything we could potentially squeeze through."

Samson nodded and opened a broadcast comlink to the rest of the $7^{th}$.

Dash looked at Connor. "That's going to slow them down."

"I'd rather go slower and find something than move quickly and miss something important," Connor replied.

Dash smiled and nodded. "The places Cerot or others have checked don't look like they've been used in a while. Esteban and Felix found a few buildings that hadn't been opened in a long time. With no power, it's hard to get access to these places. It just makes me think that no one has lived here for a long time."

Connor powered off the holoscreen and the map of the city disappeared. "That's what they want us to think. We wouldn't have come here in the first place if it hadn't been for Raylore, but he's not the one in charge anymore."

"I'll stick with Cerot and the others."

"I want them with me, so stay close. Just remember to pay attention. They didn't want us here the first time," Connor said.

"Let's hope they'll be more willing to talk. I mean . . ." Dash said, glancing at Cerot for a moment, ". . . they should be willing to speak with their own kind, wouldn't you think?"

"I'm hoping for that."

"And if they don't?"

"I'm not leaving until I find them," Connor replied.

"Yeah, but if they—"

"It doesn't matter. They were here, so we should be able to find evidence of where they went."

They left the camp and headed for the area where they'd

found the arch. Remnants of a few long spires that ended in jagged edges pierced the skyline, so it wasn't difficult to find. As they made their way closer to their destination, thick overgrowth covered most of the buildings in the area. Connor wondered whether the overgrowth in the area was a natural occurrence or something the Ovarrow had engineered. The broad leaves of eggplant-colored flora grew on thick vines that blocked much of the sunlight and created natural canopies between the buildings. The air was humid and hot, and there was a faint odor of mold that came from the moist ground. The last time Connor had been there, they'd flown over much of the city to reach their destination, so this was new to him.

He kept looking for any signs that there were Ovarrow living there, but the city looked like it had been abandoned many years ago. How had these structures survived all the wars that had been fought across the vast continent? Connor remembered seeing evidence of a bombardment at some of the other cities they'd explored but not this one. They hadn't detected any ryklar deterrent signals, but something had made the creatures abandon the city.

They finally entered a familiar, wide-open area, and Connor led them across the way. Three intertwining triangles adorned the entrance to the building they were headed for. It hadn't changed all that much—still bronze-colored and seemingly reinforced with thick plating. It was an Ovarrow military research center, but there were no latent lockdown systems waiting to ambush them. A ramp led downward. Several soldiers took point and the rest of them followed. Recon drones were already scouting ahead of them.

They headed inside and Connor used his implants to check

the recon drones. They hadn't detected any energy signatures. The place was still dead.

The ramp curved around, leading them deeper into the building, and soon they were underground. There were no plants this far into the facility, and the wide doors they passed through were already open from the last time they'd been there. The first time, they'd had to force the doors open. They continued for twenty minutes until they reached a vast, open area. Their lights penetrated the darkness, but the CDF soldiers also had implants with night vision. Across the way were the remains of the arch that had been there. Connor ordered flares to be shot to the far side of the room so the Ovarrow could see better. As red flares ignited in the distance, large, intact pieces of the arch reflected the light along the ground in glistening pools.

Connor glanced to the side, scanning for the elevated platform to the right of the arch.

"Looks like they took out the command center," Dash said.

Where the elevated platform should have been there was only a heap of twisted metal blackened by scorch marks. Connor looked at Samson and gestured toward the remains of the command center. "It looks like they used some kind of explosive material. Have a team run an analysis on it."

Samson sent a team over while the rest of them made a sweep of the area.

"What are they looking for?" Dash asked.

"The type of accelerant used in the explosive. We might be able to track them with it," Connor replied.

Dash considered this for a few moments and nodded. Then his eyebrows drew up in concern. "Do you think they set traps for us?"

Connor twitched his head to the side once. "Now you're thinking like one of us."

Cerot had been watching the exchange and read the translation on the wrist computer each Ovarrow had been provided. "Mekaal tactics include the use of sabotage. We'll help watch for this."

Connor thanked him. "If you notice anything, let us know and we'll investigate it."

The rooms on the other side of the chamber were structurally intact, but the consoles had been destroyed. Dash had extracted all the data from those consoles the last time they'd been there, so there wasn't a loss. The fact that these Ovarrow were covering their tracks was indication enough as to their intentions. They must have hidden for so long that it had become part of their culture. Getting them to communicate might prove more difficult than it had been with the Ovarrow who'd slept in stasis pods for hundreds of years.

"I'll need your help when we find them," Connor said to Cerot.

"I understand, General."

Connor walked over to the remains of the arch that the CDF had taken components from for their own arch. The Ovarrow had left it intact for hundreds of years, only to destroy it now. Connor couldn't rationalize it. The components they'd taken from it would have prevented it from being used even if the Ovarrow had somehow restored power to it. Why destroy what remained? They might have anticipated that the colonists would return there, so preventing them from using the arch might have been one of the reasons. But that couldn't be the only one. Were they afraid the Krake would discover its existence and use it as a way to come to this universe?

Connor turned toward Samson and Dash. "I don't get it. Why destroy the arch?"

Samson shrugged. "They don't want us to use it."

"I thought of that, too, but that can't be the only reason." Connor looked at Dash. "Were you able to find anything in the data you got from the consoles the last time we were here?"

Dash frowned in thought for a few moments. "Just log entries—old ones—and some of the data was corrupt. We know they used the arch. I showed Cerot and the others some of that data on our way here. They said they were maintenance logs. They could have been testing it."

Connor nodded. "They spent who knows how long trying to reverse-engineer it, so that might make sense," he said and pressed his lips together in thought. "I can understand testing the arch to see if they could make it work. How much of a stretch would it be that they actually used it?"

Samson shook his head. "Not that much. They used it. They must have."

Connor gestured toward the wreckage of the arch. "Paints all this in a new light."

"How so?" Dash asked.

"Think about it. We debated whether we should use the arch, and they probably did the same. So, they could have destroyed this one to prevent us from using it and . . ." He paused for a second. "Or they did it to prevent other Ovarrow from using it—either the ones we've been bringing out of stasis or perhaps among themselves."

Samson exhaled forcefully and shook his head. "And you want to talk to them?"

"We need to."

"I'm going to see about opening a few of those hidden doors

you suspected existed the last time you were here," Samson said and walked away.

Dash waited a few moments and then said, "Why is he upset?"

"Trust me, you'll know if Samson is upset. He just prefers a straight-up fight. We used to work together before . . . before the colony. Anticipating group activities was the whole intelligence-gathering part of the job."

It wasn't difficult to identify the hidden doors. They used a sonic-wave generator to cause subtle vibrations. If an echo was detected, the indication was a passageway beyond. They found five of them. Two of the passageways angled back the way they'd already come. The remaining three appeared to be intact. Recon drones flew down the passageways, scanning for ryklars, and the data they sent back was used to map the area. These tunnels connected with other tunnels.

"There's a city underneath the city. This is going to take a while to explore," Samson said.

Connor studied the holoscreen that was displaying the ever-expanding map of the underground tunnels beneath the city. "A while" was a bit of an understatement. He used his implants to update the data being shown on the holoscreen. Soon, there were paths highlighted in red. "There, that helps a little bit. The highlighted areas are where ryklar tracks were detected."

"It's broken up over here," Dash said. "Oh, I see it now. Those are probably old sewage ways, so there's water there."

"We don't know how old those tracks are, but we don't need to. They're all going in the same general direction to this area here," Connor said. He nodded to himself. "That's our target," he said and looked at Samson. "Captain, let's get everyone ready."

"Yes, sir," Samson said and began bellowing orders.

The Ovarrow had been able to conceal their presence aboveground, but underground was a different story. The tunnels underneath the city showed signs of being recently used. Even the waterways they'd crossed had reinforced bridges. They were on the right track. Some of the tunnels narrowed to barely three meters across, while others were much wider. Connor didn't want to have to fight a battle down there because of the risk of bringing the tunnel down on top of them.

Samson assigned Corporal Alanson to keep track of the recon drones and their updates to the map they were following. Connor, Dash, and the rest of the Ovarrow stayed close to the front. Connor carried an AR-71, which was standard issue for the CDF. The nanorobotic ammunition made it a versatile assault rifle.

They'd been walking up the main tunnel for the last half hour. There were offshoots, and Corporal Alanson spoke. "General, there's movement detected in some of the adjacent tunnels up ahead, sir."

Samson was about to order a scout force ahead, but Connor told him to wait. "Corporal, engage the recall signal for the ryklars," Connor said.

The tunnels lit up in a blaze of light flashing across the visual spectrum of colors. Movement in the adjacent tunnels ceased. Connor had the corporal repeat the sequence, and then they waited. The recon drone flew to one of the entrances of the adjacent tunnel and scanned inside. The ryklars had left. They were definitely on the right track.

With the presence of the ryklars confirmed, Samson had more soldiers brought to the front, armed and ready. His reasoning was that even though they were able to mimic the control signal for the ryklars, they didn't know if the Ovarrow had some way to order the ryklars to attack regardless of which light they were showing them. Connor had to agree with that. The sonic deterrent signals would work down there, but these ryklars had been mutilated by having their auditory systems removed. His mouth formed a grim line at the thought. It must've been extremely painful for those creatures. The ryklars were dangerous, but so was anything else that wanted to live. There were other predators, like berwolves, that were nearly as dangerous as ryklars, but they were nowhere near as smart. Berwolves were the size of Old Earth grizzly bears but with the agility of wolves. The ryklars were something different. They were highly intelligent. Connor had heard the term "sapient intelligence," meaning they had the potential to be almost as intelligent as human beings, but that was a bit of a stretch, even for Connor. He wasn't an expert in evolutionary science, but he'd spoken with experts in that field enough to at least appreciate that yes, there was a strong possibility that if ryklars were allowed to evolve over millions of years, they had the greatest potential of becoming an intelligent species. Right now, their intelligence was considered to equal that of an Old Earth bottlenose dolphin. They had highly complex brains and lived in a small society. It was these traits that had probably drawn the Ovarrow to utilize them the way they had. But at some point, the way the Ovarrow had used the ryklars was just cruel. Connor had never broached the subject with the Ovarrow—at least not yet.

Connor had killed hundreds of ryklars, but there had been

no other choice. He'd seen potential in the ryklars when Siloc had taken him prisoner. Left to their own devices, they weren't entirely wild. That didn't mean he'd voluntarily go unarmed into a pack of them and expect not to be killed, but there was potential there. He remembered ryklars leaving him alive while killing Siloc at the Mekaal secret base. There was nothing that would convince Connor that this was because the ryklars were preoccupied with their desire to kill Siloc. They'd made a decision not to kill Connor. It was what had led him to learn as much as he could about them.

Connor heard Dash speaking in urgent tones with Cerot and the others and made his way over to them. "What's the matter?"

"They're worried about the ryklars."

"Did you explain to them how these ryklars are different?"

"Yes, but I don't know if they completely understand," Dash replied.

The ryklar tracks led to a major adjacent tunnel, and they followed them. The CDF soldiers held their weapons with practiced efficiency. These were all seasoned combat veterans.

By now, they could hear the ryklars, and it seemed that they'd gathered in a vast chamber the tunnel connected to. The entrance to the chamber was a natural cave opening. Connor heard sounds of an underground river echoing off the sides of the cave. There was moisture in the air, but there was a generally cool temperature beneath the ground. They sent the recon drones out of the tunnel and up to take a survey of the area. There were large cisterns across the chamber, and hundreds of the mutilated ryklars were gathered. Walking among them were Ovarrow soldiers, some of whom wore ryklar skins.

Two bridges crossed the wide river. The bridges were easily defendable, but it was nothing the CDF couldn't handle. However, he didn't believe it was a coincidence that the Ovarrow had taken their stand there. He wondered what was beyond this chamber that was worth defending. It could be their homes, or it could be something else.

Cerot and the other Ovarrow erupted into a quick debate. Connor glanced at Dash, who gave a slight shake of his head.

"What are your orders, General?" Samson asked.

"I'm going to try to talk to them. Let's move up to the bridge. Have the men spread out so they can cover us if we need it," Connor said.

"Understood, sir. What about our guests?" Samson said and nodded toward Cerot and the others.

Cerot gestured toward the bridge and then to the other Ovarrow.

"Let them come with us," Connor said.

They walked toward the bridge, and Connor peered at the ryklars gathered on the other side. Their bearded tentacles were gray or almost black, indicating that they were not in a highly agitated state. When ryklars were highly agitated, which occurred through the use of the control signals, their bearded tentacles became bright red. But the fact that the ryklars weren't highly agitated didn't make them any less dangerous. They drew in deep breaths and seemed to be a moment away from charging across that bridge to attack them.

Ryklars had two sets of arms. One set was directly in front of them and was a bit shorter than the heavily muscled ones on the sides. They had thick claws that could rend even the battle steel of their armored vehicles. Leopard-like spots spilled across their gray coats.

It was strange for Connor to see them waiting, and even stranger was the fact that there were definitely Ovarrow soldiers walking among them. They were easy to pick out. Standing at full height, they were head and shoulders taller than the ryklars' stooped forms. They wore dark armor, similar to what Cerot and the others wore. The reconnaissance drone detected power sources from the weapons they carried. The Ovarrow rifle could shoot a particle beam. They required recharging, but they were powerful enough to get the job done. The CDF had superior weaponry, but Connor wanted to communicate with them, not start a fight.

One of the recon drones flew up, taking a position several feet above Connor's head, and a large holoscreen appeared above them.

"Ovarrow, my name is Connor Gates, and I'd like to communicate with your leader."

The Ovarrow translator put up a series of symbols. Connor waited, but there was almost no reaction from the small army across the bridge—not exactly the warmest greeting.

"Is there a warlord among you?" Connor asked.

He noticed several Ovarrow soldiers shifting their feet. Cerot let out a harsh grunt, and Connor gestured for him to come stand next to him. Cerot came over and then spoke in rapid succession, raising his voice so the Ovarrow across the bridge could hear him. The Ovarrow had multiple vocal cords as part of their physiology and could generate sounds beyond anything the colonists could duplicate.

A loud blast of acknowledgment came from an Ovarrow across the bridge. Cerot went quiet and waited. One of the Ovarrow soldiers across the bridge strode purposefully to the entrance. He was tall, like most Ovarrow. He sported lean muscles that could be seen where the armor didn't cover, and many age lines crisscrossed his face. He uttered a short staccato series of sounds.

"What is that?" Connor asked.

"I think that's his name," Dash replied.

Cerot used the translator and a single word appeared. The name was Brashirker. Then came the title "Warlord of the Ovarrow."

Brashirker spoke again and then slammed the butt of his weapon to the ground.

"The abandoners are not welcome here," Brashirker said.

Connor frowned for a moment and then glanced at Cerot. He saw that Dash had made the connection as well. He'd brought Cerot and the others, hoping they'd be able to open the lines of communication; however, Brashirker was sending a clear message that this wasn't the case.

"How accurate is the translation?" Connor asked.

"This is accurate, Connor. It stems from the logic used in their subroutines for their programming. Some tasks are just abandoned. This isn't a mistake. He doesn't want them here," Dash said.

Connor looked across the bridge and tried to think of a way he could salvage the situation before it became untenable. Why didn't anyone want to talk to anyone else?

## 12

CONNOR HEARD Samson provide a status to the other soldiers. Cerot and the other Ovarrow were still staring across the bridge at another member of their own species.

Brashirker made a sharp sound, and two ryklars scrambled to his side and waited.

"What's he doing?" Dash asked.

"Either he's showing off, trying to intimidate us, or he wants protection," Connor said. He took a few steps forward, leaving the others behind, and spoke to Brashirker. "I doubt anyone is welcome here, yet here we are. Your people attacked mine not that long ago. Now you've destroyed the arch. We have a common enemy, and I want to talk to you about that."

Connor sent the recon drone across the bridge and the holoscreen above it expanded to include his entire message. He wanted to be sure Brashirker could read it. He took a few more steps forward and Samson joined him, along with Lieutenant Mason. Both held their weapons loosely, but only a fool would believe they weren't moments from being at full readiness. If Brashirker or anyone else across the bridge attacked, Connor would shoot them.

Brashirker moved forward with the ryklars at his heels. Several other Ovarrow soldiers followed him, but it was only a small group. Connor did the same, and Samson called other soldiers to follow them. He heard Dash asking Cerot to wait behind.

Connor caught his first real look at Brashirker and the other Ovarrow. They looked more like aged veterans than the Ovarrow they'd rescued from stasis pods.

Brashirker began to speak, but the translator couldn't decipher the Ovarrow's spoken language. When it became apparent to him that he was to use the holographic interface and select the symbols to convey his message, he scowled and gestured for one of his soldiers to use it. The Ovarrow soldier gingerly touched a symbol and it appeared on the screen. They weren't strangers to an interface like this. It had been designed to mimic what they'd found on the Ovarrow consoles, so it seemed that the Ovarrow hadn't abandoned their technology.

"You were attacked because you were in forbidden territory. Access to the arch is prohibited," Brashirker said.

"We needed components from the arch to make ours work."

"It is forbidden."

"We've faced the Krake. It's one of the reasons we came back here," Connor said.

He'd expected more of a reaction from the Ovarrow at the mention of the Krake, but that wasn't the case. They were quiet, just waiting and listening. They acted very unlike the Ovarrow who'd come out of stasis.

"You've faced the Krake and you come here? They will

follow you. They always follow you, eventually," Brashirker replied.

"Have you ever fought the Krake?"

"Our ancestors fought and died. You've seen what's left of their war."

"Did you know that we were here on this planet?" Connor asked.

"We were aware of your presence, but you kept your activities far away."

"Did your people go into stasis?" Connor asked.

His question brought an instant reaction from not only Brashirker but the Ovarrow soldiers with him—a murmuring growl that sounded like the Ovarrow were clearing their throats but with more intensity. The ryklars sat back on their haunches and merely waited.

"I meant no offense," Connor said. "I want to know more about you."

"Why?" Brashirker asked.

Connor waited a few moments before answering. "As you said, we have observed the aftermath of your wars. We know that your ancestors fought each other, as well as the Krake. But we don't know about *you*. We know that some of you—the Ovarrow—went into stasis pods. We found many of them, but some of the pods were in a state of disrepair. The Ovarrow who survived suffered from health issues that we've been able to help them with."

"That is a mistake. My ancestors never went into stasis. They didn't have the resources. They were pushed out of the strongholds that had stasis pods. We refused to sacrifice our young to live in a world without the Krake."

Samson leaned closer to Connor. "What does he mean by 'sacrifice their young'? Is the translator broken again?"

Connor shook his head. "No, the stasis tech that the Ovarrow used could only support juveniles and near adults, as well as older Ovarrow. The younger ones wouldn't survive."

"They abandoned their young so they could live?" Samson asked quietly.

"Some of them, maybe. Not all of them," Connor said. His chest tightened, and a sneer lifted his lips. It was hard for him not to judge, but he needed to keep Brashirker talking. There were so many questions he wanted to ask, but he knew this was a delicate situation. The slightest misstep would end the conversation prematurely. "How did you survive?"

"Our ancestors created strongholds of their own upon the bones of the old world. We lived underground. Some moved to the southern reaches, but none of them survived," Brashirker said.

"What happened to them?" Connor asked.

"The Krake found them. We severed all ties," Brashirker said.

Dash had come forward and was standing next to Connor. "He has to be talking about the beginning of the ice age. I wonder how long the Krake were active here."

Connor looked back at Brashirker. "How did you stop the Krake from coming here?"

Brashirker seemed to consider this for a few moments. "Many years had passed and the Krake kept coming here despite the long winter. We disabled the arch here, but there were more across the continent. We sent groups to destroy them. We knew they had succeeded when the Krake stopped coming."

Whoever had gone in search of the arches had sacrificed themselves. They must've known it would be a one-way trip. It was hard for Connor to put together a timeline without making a lot of assumptions, but at least he had a high-level overview of what had happened.

"We thought the Krake had returned when systems from the old world began to come online. If it wasn't the Krake, then it was the abandoners who were finally waking up," Brashirker said.

"It wasn't the Krake; it was us exploring your world. I can understand why your ancestors held resentment of the Ovarrow who went into stasis, but what are *your* reasons? This happened hundreds of years ago."

"We remember."

Connor's eyebrows knitted together in a frown. "I don't understand."

Brashirker took a step forward. His muscles rippled as he clenched his weapon. "Your lack of understanding is what will bring the Krake to this planet. Some of the Ovarrow who went into stasis worshipped the Krake. The Krake are their masters, and they will seek to reestablish contact with the Krake now that they've been brought out of stasis."

"How? We found one arch that was at the bottom of the lake. We've built a prototype. Are there more?"

Brashirker leaned back. "Possibly."

"Then you should work with us so we can prevent anyone else from contacting the Krake."

"It is too late for that. You've crossed paths with the Krake, and they will come back to this world."

"All the more reason to help us. Tell us what you know

about the Krake. I need to find their home universe to stop them from coming here," Connor said.

He expected a similar response to the one he'd received from other Ovarrow—something along the lines of "the Krake can't be stopped," but instead he was answered with silence.

"You will wait. Your machines will not follow us," Brashirker finally answered.

The Ovarrow warlord turned and crossed back to his side of the bridge. The others followed him. Connor recalled the recon drone and withdrew to the other side of the bridge. The Ovarrow soldiers and the ryklars withdrew into several different tunnels, leaving a small token force to stand guard at the tunnel entrances.

Connor looked at Samson. "We're going to make a camp right here. Contact the other teams and let them know our status. They are to proceed as ordered."

Samson walked away to convey Connor's orders.

"I've never seen ryklars look so calm," Dash said.

"Neither have I. What did you think about what he said?" Connor asked.

"It confirms the history we suspected. But we don't have detailed records. We don't know if this is where they live or how many of them there are."

Connor nodded and glanced at Cerot and the others. The Ovarrow were speaking to each other. "Brashirker wouldn't even speak to them."

"He thinks they're Krake sympathizers who went into stasis," Dash replied.

"It's more than that. Whatever happened to them, that dedication or commitment to those beliefs might've formed the foundation of their society. Don't look at me like that; I paid attention. What I don't know is whether I can convince them to help us."

Dash was quiet for a few moments while he considered what Connor had said. "So, you want to find the Krake's home universe and stop them there? That's the first time I've ever heard this."

"That's where we need to get to. If the Krake find us first, it'll be a lot worse for us."

"It took months to convince the Ovarrow that we were trying to help them when they came out of stasis. I think you took them by surprise. Maybe they just need some time," Dash said.

Connor's eyebrows raised. "I'm sure they didn't plan on us showing up here."

"I mean beyond that. I don't think they expected you to say the things you did. Considering that they might've been aware of our presence, they've never interacted with us. Darius often told me not to underestimate the small steps. They can add up," Dash said.

"Let's hope so," Connor said, and meant it.

# 13

CONNOR HAD SENT a few teams out to patrol the surrounding area. They were camped in the main cavern and they could see the Ovarrow soldiers across the way, but he had no intention of letting his guard down. He wasn't going to give them the opportunity to sneak around his team. Dash seemed surprised by this because he still had a certain amount of naiveté about the world. He was a very capable young man, but he was still young enough to retain some of youth's innocence.

"This has to be rough on them," Samson said and gestured toward Cerot and the other Ovarrow. "They came all this way on the hope that they were going to meet more of their own kind, only to find out that their own kind wants nothing to do with them. It's like the Ovarrow have no concept of hospitality."

Connor barked a laugh and shook his head. "Did you forget the last time Diaz and I went to your camp?"

Samson shrugged, his features impassive. "That's how I welcome everyone."

"What happened?" Dash asked.

"Let's just say that Samson has a gift for making people feel *un*welcome. His camp had a lot of traps, and Diaz got caught up in one of them," Connor said and drank some water.

Dash's gaze darted to Samson and then back at Connor. "So, that's why Diaz . . ."

Connor nodded. "Yes, that's about right."

"He's only mad," Samson said, "because he wasn't paying attention."

An image of Diaz strung up by his feet, dangling above the ground and shouting curses appeared in Connor's mind. He exhaled softly and glanced over at Cerot. He was speaking with Esteban, Joe, Felix, Luca, and Wesley. They'd followed the conversation with Brashirker, probably better than Connor had. They understood what—

He stopped that train of thought and looked at Cerot. Dash had been watching and activated the Ovarrow translator.

"Were you able to understand what Brashirker said?" Connor asked Cerot. He knew it was an obvious question, but he couldn't afford to take too many chances on an assumption.

"I could understand him. Vitory and Senleon are aware of the Krake worshippers," Cerot said.

Connor regarded the Ovarrow for a few seconds. Cerot was the warlord's second-in-command, known as the warlord's First. Connor had no way of knowing if any of the Ovarrow he'd brought with him were Krake insurgents. Connor looked at the others. It was so hard to get an idea of what they were thinking. Cerot seemed to sense that Connor wanted more of an explanation.

"General Gates, the only thing I can tell you is that we are aware of the issue and are working to deal with it."

"Cerot, you know there was Ovarrow involvement in the bridges that collapsed in your city. You have a group that seeks to undermine the authority of your leaders. We're aware of this too, and we understand that none of this has been easy for you."

"I appreciate your understanding. Your partner saved my life. This is a debt I would like to repay, which is why I chose to come with you."

"Did you know there were Ovarrow who weren't allowed into bunkers with stasis pods?" Connor asked.

Cerot was quiet for a few long moments. Connor waited him out. "We knew. I knew about it. We didn't expect anyone to survive. The effort was to preserve our species. We knew we couldn't save everyone."

Connor considered this for a few moments, thinking about the video message recorded by his son while the Vemus were storming the bridge of the *Indianapolis*. Those brave souls on Earth had given the colonists a chance to survive the Vemus. They'd sacrificed themselves, but he did wonder whether there were pockets of humans who had somehow survived the Vemus back on Earth.

"I'm not here to judge you, Cerot, or the rest of the Ovarrow. What I'd like to do is understand. You've been given a second chance. But it may take them some time to accept the fact that you're here," Connor said, gesturing across the cavern where the descendants of the Ovarrow who hadn't gone into stasis stood guard.

"I don't think they will ever accept us," Cerot replied.

"They might not, but don't give up so easily," Connor answered.

The soldiers who were standing watch opened a comlink

to report that Brashirker and the Ovarrow soldiers had returned and were waiting at the edge of the bridge. This time they didn't bring the ryklars with them. Connor and a group of soldiers walked to the middle of the bridge and waited. Brashirker met them halfway. Cerot and the other Ovarrow stayed behind so as not to stress the situation any further.

Brashirker had been gone for almost twenty hours. He couldn't have gone far to have returned so quickly. Dash activated a communications drone and sent it over to Brashirker with the Ovarrow interface engaged.

"Our ancestors have used the arch in the past. They sought, as you do, to find the Krake home world by exploring different universes. They were not successful. Eventually, they abandoned those efforts and instead disabled all the arches on this planet to prevent the Krake from coming here. They weren't able to find them all," Brashirker said.

"We've also explored other universes, both from here on this planet"—Connor gestured above him—"and from beyond." He knew the Ovarrow weren't a spacefaring race, and he wasn't sure how acquainted they were with the Krake's capabilities. "Do you have any records of when your people explored other universes that you could share with us?"

Brashirker was silent for a few moments and then looked at Connor. "We only have the historical record that our ancestors did do these things. But the specific things that you are asking for have been destroyed. Even if they hadn't, I wouldn't share them with you."

"Why not?"

"You believe you know the extent of what the Krake are capable of. You don't. They are too powerful. Our people will make preparations to find another location. We would advise you to do the same."

Connor clenched his teeth for a moment. "Hiding and hoping that the Krake won't find us isn't a long-term strategy. You were lucky the first time. There's no guarantee that will happen again."

Brashirker met his gaze. "It is the *only* strategy."

"I urge you to reconsider. We have powerful weapons. We can help each other," Connor said.

Brashirker made a show of looking at the CDF soldiers gathered on the opposite end of the bridge. "We've observed your machines, and we know their capabilities are beyond what we have. You don't take any steps to hide your presence here. This is a foolish mistake. You believe that you are powerful, but you've never fought a war with the Krake. This isn't a fight that you will face on a single battlefield. If you persist in antagonizing the Krake, this war will be fought among you, and it'll be fought among your allies," Brashirker said and gestured toward the small group of Ovarrow that waited among the CDF soldiers. "The Krake will study you—your reactions, your behaviors, your vulnerabilities. And when they're done studying you, they will crush you."

The cold words appeared completely dispassionate on the Ovarrow translator, but the look on Brashirker's face was one of absolute certainty. He believed that the best choice was to hide.

"We won't hide from the Krake. Since you're so convinced that they're coming here, aren't you concerned they'll find you? Don't you want to take steps to protect your people?" Connor asked.

"When the Krake come here, they will be preoccupied with

you. They won't care about us. We'll be around to observe the aftermath," Brashirker said.

Connor inhaled explosively and then tried to clamp down on his rising temper. He'd never met a group that was so determined to hide from a problem. Some people throughout history might've endured a tyrant until such time that they could rise and overthrow him, but these were the ancestors. And they wouldn't even consider fighting the Krake.

"This is a mistake. Your ancestors made those decisions because they were probably the best decisions they could make at the time. This is different. *You* should be different."

"We *are* different, but we study our history. We learned from their mistakes. We won't repeat them. I have spoken with other leaders, and none of them will consider helping you," Brashirker said.

Connor clenched his teeth. Thoughts raced like wildfire in his mind. Brashirker had said they didn't have the records from when they used the arch. If that was true, then what history did they study? What if Brashirker was lying? Or what if someone else was lying to Brashirker?

"I have given you an answer to your question," Brashirker said.

"Well, your answer sucks," Connor said. Chances were that the Ovarrow translator didn't have a symbol that would translate his colorful metaphor of the situation, and he didn't care. Connor took a few steps toward Brashirker. "You came here with your display of force using the ryklars. You were posturing so we would know what your strength was. You haven't been to the other worlds. You think you can hide from this and you're wrong. You don't believe me because you have your precious history. But I've *seen* other worlds where the

Krake have been. I've seen worlds they've destroyed. They'll come here and do the same. Then you can record your precious history of how you just hid in a cave underground while the world burned around you because that's the best your people could do. Well, that's not who we are. So hide. Stay here and hide underground like a rodent and dream of the past because you won't have a future as long as you stay here."

Connor stood for a few moments and waited for Brashirker to finish reading the message. He intended to look this bastard in the eye so Brashirker would know just what Connor thought of him. He was a coward—a coward dressed in wolf's clothing.

Connor spun on his heel and walked off the bridge. "Captain, we're leaving."

"Understood, General," Samson replied.

# 14

CONNOR SLIPPED into a cold fury as they followed the network of tunnels to return above ground. He called off all the search efforts. Samson saw to the details of organizing the withdrawal as Connor walked ahead at a brisk pace. Even Dash didn't ask him any questions.

At first, he just needed to calm down, and then he kept going over his exchange with Brashirker. Cerot and the other Ovarrow had been given a transcript of the exchange with Brashirker, but he hadn't offered to leave Brashirker a way to contact them. He supposed someone like Darius Cohen, a lead diplomat, would've handled things differently, but he was just so furious. There were so many people who questioned his objective of gaining any kind of intelligence about the Krake from the Ovarrow. It had been one of the main drivers for the effort to assist the Ovarrow in coming out of stasis, and now they'd found a completely different group of Ovarrow who'd never gone into stasis—Ovarrow who'd survived for the past two hundred years through an ice age and a superior enemy force hunting for them. But he couldn't understand how a group like that wouldn't want to defend their homes.

He heard the high-pitched whine of troop carrier engines as they flew overhead to the designated egress points. They were leaving, and he wasn't leaving anything behind except a whole lot of regret. As far as he was concerned, there was nothing left there for him or any other colonist.

He walked up the loading ramp of the troop carrier and headed for the command area so he could be alone. The soldiers aboard hushed their conversations as he stormed by. They knew things hadn't gone well, and by now the news of his failure had probably spread. He was going to have to write a report and submit it to Governor Wolf's office. Although, if he was following a strict protocol, he'd have to send it to Nathan first, who would then send it to Governor Wolf's office. The price of his previous actions had come with a demotion.

He glared at the bulkhead of the troop carrier for a few moments. He just wanted to unleash his rage, to slam his armored fists against it and obliterate it while howling in fury. The Ovarrow had been a thorn in his side ever since he'd woken one up out of a stasis pod. He lowered his chin and clenched his teeth. Why wouldn't they listen? These Ovarrow had survived for two hundred years through an ice age. They'd come up with a way to control the ryklars for protection and had made them immune to the ryklar control signals. These feats were not inconsequential, but if they weren't willing to take the next step and fight the Krake when the time came for it, what good were they? They would become fodder for the Krake or maybe even seek an alliance with them against the colony.

Lars Mallory had posited that the Ovarrow couldn't be trusted, and he'd gotten all the intelligence he could by torturing them. He'd used their fear against them. When Connor first learned about it, he'd thought it was wrong and that Lars had been severely misguided to do those things. They were better than that. But the more he thought about it, he wondered if perhaps he'd been the one who was wrong. The lives of the colony were at stake. Should *he* have been the one to lead those efforts? Would he be in a different position now if he'd done what Lars had done? Would he have the knowledge he sought from the Ovarrow if he'd been more ruthless? Connor squeezed his eyes shut, shook his head, and a soft growl escaped his lips. He could've done it. He could've ordered it and explained it in such a way as to perhaps convince someone like Governor Wolf that it was necessary. Maybe she would've even believed him.

He inhaled deeply and sighed, thinking about his home. He thought about Lenora, who was home right then with Lauren. He thought of his baby girl, staring up at him with the intensity of someone trying desperately to make sense of the world around them as quickly as possible. One day, when she became a woman, she'd judge the man he was. Could he ever explain the actions he was considering to her? Would she hate him if those horrible actions might be the only way she could live? Could he live with himself?

Connor drew in a deep breath and sighed again. He wanted to hold his daughter right then and there, feel her soft cheek up against his face and breathe in her scent. She had an easy smile, and her eyes were a deep blue like her mother's. And when she looked at him, he melted . . . The thought of her calmed him like splashing soothing, warm water on his face, and the tension evaporated. No, he wouldn't torture the Ovarrow to get the information he needed. He wouldn't become that.

Dash cleared his throat from nearby. Connor hadn't even heard him approach.

"Excuse me, Connor. I'm sorry to interrupt, but Cerot has a request I thought you'd want to hear."

Connor rubbed his brow, releasing the tension, and sat down. He leaned back in his chair and looked up at the ceiling for a few moments, then looked at Dash. "What does he want?"

"They'd like to see one of our cities. They've only seen images of them on a holoscreen. I think it might be good for them to see it, and we do have a unique opportunity since they're already here with us."

Connor frowned in thought. For a few moments, he thought about the bureaucratic red tape he'd be required to go through to facilitate Cerot's request. Then he decided he didn't care.

"We'll bring them to Sanctuary. Are you okay with babysitting them for a little while longer? I'll assign protective details to accompany you because they'll need escorts," Connor said.

Dash's eyebrows raised in surprise. "I'm fine with staying with them. I'll even show them around. Cerot, in particular, is keen to keep the lines of communications open between us."

"I appreciate that. I am . . . I can't think about this right now," Connor said and shook his head. "I don't know what time we'll reach Sanctuary, but show them around and we'll meet up after. I just need a few moments to myself."

Dash took a step back, raising his hands in front of his chest. "I understand. I'll take care of it and send you an itinerary of where we'll go. I just wanted your approval. I'll leave you alone now."

For the duration of the trip back to Sanctuary, Connor was alone. Samson hadn't come back to check on him, which probably meant that Dash had warned him to stay away unless it was absolutely necessary.

Connor drafted a few orders for the officers in the $7^{th}$ to file their reports with his office within the next twenty-four hours. Then he began writing his own reports. Disclosing exactly what had happened was easy; Connor had nothing to hide. It was the parts where he included his views on what they should do next that his ideas came to a halt. He allowed his thoughts to scurry down a few proverbial rabbit holes in the hope that one of them might swing the pendulum to a way forward that he could commit to.

An alert appeared in the upper right corner of his holoscreen, informing him that they were making their final approach to the CDF base at Sanctuary. He wanted to go home and see his family, but he couldn't. It wouldn't have been fair. He'd be home, but he'd be distracted by the work that needed to be done. He didn't want to disappoint Lenora like that. She deserved better. Both his wife and daughter deserved to have his full attention when he came home.

He turned in his weapon and walked down the loading ramp. New Earth's rings were visible in the night sky, even amid the lights of the CDF base and city beyond. He hardly remembered the walk across the base to reach his office, but he soon found himself standing inside. A few holoscreens powered on when the identification from his implants authenticated his clearance. Long lists of messages from text to vid-mail came to prominence on the centermost holoscreen, and Connor gestured for the comlink system to go on standby. He didn't want to check any of his messages. Instead, he went into the bathroom in his office and took a shower. Jets of hot water pelted down on tight muscles. He rolled his shoulders and stretched his neck from side to side, staying in the shower for a long while. Then he heard someone call out to him from inside his office.

"Just a minute," Connor said and rubbed the water from his eyes.

He shut the shower off and heard someone access the door controls. Muttering a curse, he hastily grabbed a towel. "Hey, I said—"

Whatever he was about to say died on his lips as Lenora stepped boldly into the bathroom. Her long auburn hair was braided, making her delicate cheekbones more pronounced. She was a tall woman, nearly two meters, with tanned skin that sported a few freckles and soft lips the color of frozen raspberries.

"So, you don't want some company?" she asked with a wry smile.

Connor smiled back. "Your company? Always."

Lenora gave him a quick hug and a kiss. "I'm glad I'm not one of those jealous wives because I'd be wondering who else has interrupted one of your showers before."

Connor shrugged. "Anyone else would be wasting their time."

Lenora grinned. "Good answer, love," she said and locked the door.

A short while later, they both took another shower. She told him that Lauren was visiting Ashley.

Ashley Quinn was a close friend. She was one of the first people Connor had met coming out of stasis on the *Ark* all those years ago. There may have been a few incidents involving several shock-batons, something that had become a bit of a joke between them over the years, but Ashley loved to dote on his daughter.

They went into his office where a couple of trays of food were waiting, along with a pot of coffee.

Connor glanced at Lenora.

“I thought you'd be hungry, and if you weren't, I was certain we'd work up an appetite,” Lenora said and sat down at the small meeting table in his office. She eyed him for a few moments. “All right, you might as well tell me what happened.”

Connor sat down at the table and poured them both a cup of coffee. “You mean Dash didn't fill you in?”

“Does it matter? I want to hear it from you.”

Connor told her what happened while they shared a couple of sandwiches. The food was actually quite good, and Lenora told him she'd gotten it at the Salty Soldier on her way here.

“Diaz says hello, by the way,” Lenora said and finished her coffee. “So, there's another group of Ovarrow who never went into stasis. It's amazing if you stop and think about it, given what we know about the planet.”

“I thought so, and I would've thought they'd be more willing to share information with us.”

Lenora pursed her full lips in thought for a moment. “Actually, it sounds like they shared quite a bit with you.”

Connor shrugged. “They used the arch to try to find the Krake home world, or at least their ancestors did, but that doesn't help us.”

Lenora regarded him for a few moments. “I haven't seen you like this since the Vemus War. Don't give me that look, Connor. You know what I mean. I know you know better than this. It's disappointing, and I agree with you. The Ovarrow should be falling over themselves to help us since they have a better idea of what we're facing than we do."

"You won't get any arguments from me, but the fact of the matter is that we have one group that simply won't help us, and the other group—the ones we brought out of stasis—is incapable of helping us."

"Don't you think that's a little harsh?"

"Not really, no."

Lenora gave him a level look and then nodded. "All right, what was the outcome you were hoping for?"

"Honestly, I was hoping for a lot more cooperation from them. And by 'them' I mean both of them—both groups of Ovarrow," he said and held up his hand. "I know they're worried and all that, but still, we're not the bad guys here. I really wanted to get more information from them. It's like we're going to be fighting a war with hardly any knowledge of our enemy. Back on earth, we had thousands of years of history to draw from. And despite all the efforts here to uncover the Ovarrow's history," Connor said and smiled at Lenora, "we don't know nearly as much as we need to. Everything is new, and we don't have a lot of resources to spare. And this might shape up to be a very long war. Most small wars in history were meat grinders. The conflict comes down to logistics and numbers. How many of our soldiers will it take to achieve an objective, and how much will it cost the enemy to achieve theirs? I don't want to start thinking in those terms but . . ." He let the thought go unfinished.

"It may come down to that," Lenora said, finishing for him.

Connor rubbed his fingers on the tabletop for a moment. "Honestly, Lenora, I dealt with generals in the NA Alliance, and I don't know hardly any of them who were as concerned with the lives of their soldiers as I am. And they didn't have to deal with this."

"Then I'm glad you're here and not them. Maybe we don't need any of the military leaders from your past."

"They might be able to offer something that I just can't," Connor admitted.

Lenora shook her head and steeled her gaze. "I don't believe that for a second. And neither do you, not really. Maybe you believed it at one time but not anymore, Connor. I don't care how angry you are at the Ovarrow. You're the best chance this colony has to survive. And everyone knows it, even if they won't admit it."

She reached across the table, gripping his hand for a moment.

"I appreciate the support, but I think you're just a little biased when it comes to me."

"That's funny," she said in a bit of a light tone. "I was sure you'd say I was one of your staunchest critics."

Connor grinned a little. "Brashirker doesn't understand what the CDF is capable of. Hell, even Senleon and the rest of the Ovarrow we brought out of stasis don't know what we're capable of."

"They're doing what they've always been taught to do," Lenora said.

"The Ovarrow are defeated in their hearts hundreds of years later. What can I do to show them that it can be done?"

"It might come down to that. Inspire them."

"I don't know anything about inspiring anyone. Well, if the Ovarrow aren't going to help us, we'll have to do it alone," Connor said.

"What's so bad about that?"

"It carries a heck of a lot more risk, for one. And two, I'm not sure if the Security Council will approve of scouting missions through the arch. They want credible intel for us to act on, and I can't really blame them, even though it's frustrating," Connor said.

They were both quiet for a few moments, and then Lenora spoke. "So, don't ask for approval."

"Weren't you always telling me that I should try to function within the system we have here in the colony?"

"And aren't you the person who takes action when the situation calls for it for the good of the colony?" Lenora replied.

"I'm still paying the price for the last time."

"Oh, poor me," she replied. "Stop. Nathan supports you."

"He does, and we agree that the Krake are a threat worth investigating. So that's what I'm going to do," he said and looked at Lenora for a moment. "I'm not going to just send teams of soldiers through the arch. I intend to lead them. I need to see this for myself."

Connor watched as Lenora inhaled deeply. She didn't want him to go, but she wouldn't tell him that. She didn't need to remind him of what he'd lose if he didn't come back home. That was the bedrock of their relationship, and it had taken years to build.

"Be careful," Lenora said.

"I will. You know I will," Connor replied.

Lenora looked to be on the verge of saying something else, but a comlink chimed from the wallscreen next to them. It was from Nathan.

Connor acknowledged the comlink and Nathan Hayes appeared. He smiled a greeting at Lenora and then looked at Connor. "I heard things didn't go well with the Ovarrow."

"No reason why anything should be easy where the Ovarrow are concerned, but I'm still finalizing my thoughts on it," Connor said.

"Understood. But that's not why I am contacting you. Do you remember a few years ago when we sent out probes to explore neighboring star systems?" Nathan asked.

"Of course," Connor answered. "They were sent to star systems that might have habitable planets, but we're still a few years away from hearing back from them."

"That's correct, but we heard back from one a little bit quicker than we thought we would. You see, once the scientists working on the subspace communicator got a stable working prototype, they got the idea that they could send our exploration probes instructions to build a subspace communicator of their own. Theoretically, they're well within subspace communication range. However, to make a long story short, they sent out instructions for the probes to build one, and at least one of them has gotten back to us. They found a habitable planet that's just a few light-years away from us," Nathan said.

"That's amazing," Lenora said. "Did the probe send back any scan data?"

Nathan nodded. "Some. This news is getting a lot of attention, particularly with the Security Council. I'm giving you a heads-up because we're going to have an all-hands in just a few hours."

"That quickly? Why would they do that?" Lenora asked.

"Because," Connor said dryly, "they're considering whether we should leave New Earth."

Lenora frowned and glanced at Nathan for a moment. "That's a bit premature, don't you think?"

"I agree," Nathan replied. "But as farfetched as the option is, it's still an option we need to consider."

"Is it really an option though? We have double the colonists now, and our resources are spread throughout the star system," Connor said.

"There are also the Ovarrow to consider," Lenora added, and Connor threw her a look that said he agreed.

Connor looked at Nathan. "She's right. We need to consider the Ovarrow. We brought them out of stasis. The Krake are aware of our presence and are looking for us. When they do find this planet, are we going to leave the Ovarrow at the mercy of the Krake?"

"Are you proposing to take them with us if we leave? Would they even come with us?" Nathan asked.

"I think we're getting ahead of ourselves here," Connor replied. "We'll need to work the problem through because there's a lot more to it than the three of us can think of at the moment."

Nathan nodded. "All right. I just wanted to warn you what was coming. When can you be at Sierra?"

"I'd rather stay here and attend the meeting remotely," Connor said, telling Nathan about their visit with the Ovarrow.

After some more back and forth, Nathan agreed that it was best for Connor to stay in Sanctuary. The comlink closed and both he and Lenora stood up.

"I didn't see this coming," Lenora said.

"Me either. I didn't think we'd find a habitable world so close, but there has been some discussion about whether leaving New Earth is a viable option. This discovery is going to force us to reexamine the viability of that choice."

"Do you think we should leave?" Lenora asked.

"No," Connor replied.

Lenora sighed. "I almost thought you were going to say something about weighing all our options. I don't want to leave either, but . . . well, you know."

"This is our home," Connor said. "And besides, what's to stop the Krake from following us to a neighboring star system? If we stay here, at least we can put our energy into fortifying our position. If we decide to run to another world, we'll have to not only build up our defenses, but also build new homes at the same time."

Lenora grinned, and Connor looked at her questioningly. "Your answer is purely rational, but not everything is so cut and dry. You'll see."

Connor frowned. The decision of whether they were to leave New Earth or not seemed obvious to him, but for as long as he'd known Lenora, she'd demonstrated time and time again that she was a shrewd judge of colonial politics. Her keen insight into these matters might've come from all her experience as an archaeologist, piecing together ancient civilizations, or she just had the uncanny capability of seeing right to the heart of the matter. Either way, if he were to bet on the outcome, he'd bet on Lenora's insights. She was usually right about these things, and he'd learned long ago to trust her judgment.

# 15

THE ALL-HANDS MEETING was pushed back to the next day, and Connor was able to go home and spend some time with his daughter. As usual, coming home was always easy, but leaving was getting increasingly harder to do. The last time Connor had left a child of his at home was over two hundred and thirty years ago. His son had been three years old, and Connor was shipping off for a six-month assignment. That six-month assignment turned into a multiyear operation, which had broken his marriage and ultimately ended with Connor being smuggled aboard an interstellar colony ship bound for New Earth. He was a different man now. Lauren would know who her father was because he'd be there to raise her.

The personal holoscreen on his desk cycled through pictures of his family and his friends. For years, his work areas had been devoid of personal effects, but now he liked having visual reminders of the people in his life. They helped him keep things in perspective and remember what was important.

The meeting with the Security Council had begun a short while earlier, and he'd noticed that only half the participants were in Sierra to attend the meeting. It wasn't practical to have in-person meetings as often as the Security Council met. However, at least once a month, they did gather in person, and it had been agreed on by the majority that the meeting would be hosted at any one of the four colonial cities. In a few months' time, the meeting was scheduled to be at Sanctuary. Policies like this had been put forth by Dana Wolf as a way to convey to the rest of the colony that Sierra wasn't the seat of power for the entire colony. It was a unifying effort, and Connor approved.

Bob Mullins was chairing the meeting. Bob was of average height with dark, oily hair, mud-colored eyes, and a few days' worth of beard growth on his face. He had an athletic build, and his voice had a calm, soothing quality to it except when he addressed Connor. They didn't get along. In fact, Connor was of the opinion that Bob kept the stubbled growth of a beard simply because he thought it made him look more appealing to the women in the room. Diaz had often joked that there were many faces of Bob Mullins as he sought to ingratiate himself and get people to trust him. That mask was usually dropped when they were discussing anything related to CDF efforts, which was why Connor didn't like him. He didn't have to like him in order to work with him, but things would be so much easier if Mullins would simply go away.

"We pushed the schedule for this meeting back so everyone would have a chance to review the briefing about the space probe data we've received," Bob Mullins said. "We've found a viable planet that makes an ideal colonization candidate. The planet is well within the Goldilocks zone, with a chemical composition that will meet our needs. It's estimated that the gravitational field is above Earth normal but nothing we couldn't adapt to. The preliminary data provided by the probe exceeds our standard criteria for colonization candidates. It's a prime world."

A man sitting next to Governor Wolf indicated that he wanted to speak. "Dr. Trautmann, you have something to add?" Mullins asked.

Lionel Trautmann was Dana Wolf's newest scientific advisor who held specializations in multiple disciplines.

"The data from the probe is promising," Trautmann began, "but the probe is still in the system's Oort Cloud and hasn't made it to interior planets to do an adequate scan of the system."

"That is correct, but we have access to the information already gathered a lot sooner than we thought we would," Mullins said and glanced at Nathan. "Given the potential threats to the colony, there are quite a few people on this council who feel it's worth discussing whether or not we should establish a colony on that planet."

Connor reached toward the speaker button, which would indicate that he wished to contribute, and let his hand hover over it for a moment. His fingertips must've grazed it because the request was sent, and as Mullins turned toward him, his gaze narrowed.

"General Gates," Mullins said.

Connor wasn't about to admit that he'd hit the button by mistake, so he decided to go along with his initial thought. "The briefing doesn't just imply the establishment of a new colony. It implies that we need to make a decision on whether to move the entire colony to this planet."

By default, once Connor was through speaking, the floor was turned back over to Mullins.

"That is something we'll be discussing. I'd like to highlight the fact that this is just a discussion. We're not requiring decisions to be made," Mullins said.

Connor had lost count of how many items had been "just a discussion," and then, more often than not, were the precursor for an approved project. He stabbed the speaker button again, and Mullins glowered a little.

"The question is not whether or not we can colonize this other planet. We can, but the question is whether or not we should work toward that goal," Connor said.

"General Gates," Mullins said, "I will not let you domineer this discussion and rush a conclusion to these talking points. You make valid points but—"

"He has hardly begun making his point," Dr. Trautmann said, interrupting.

"Bob," Governor Wolf said. "I, for one, would like to hear what Connor has to say, and so do a lot of other people in the room. We facilitate discussions, but in order to do that, we need to listen to what people say."

The tips of Mullins's ears became red, and he nodded. "My apologies, Governor," he said and turned toward Connor. "General Gates, please proceed."

"Thank you," Connor said, directing his gaze at Governor Wolf. "I don't want to beat around the bush here. We're worried about the Krake and the threat they are to this world. That's the driver for whether or not we colonize another world in the immediate future, but I'd urge everyone here to be cautious when considering this option. We live in an established colony. We can build ships.

Actually, we can build anything we could possibly need. This is a resource-rich star system. The preliminary probe data indicates that the star system in question has resources for us to use as well, but we don't know how much. However, even though it might be a safe assumption that we could colonize that world, that's not dealing with the main issue—the Krake. Let's be honest. If we leave this world, it's because we're running from the Krake."

"Excuse me, General Gates," Mullins said. "Just so I understand. You're putting forth that there are circumstances that would necessitate relocating to another world?"

"Absolutely, but only as a last resort," Connor said. "If we were to move this entire colony to a new world, it would take us years to do it right, even working at breakneck speeds, and at the end of the day, what happens if the Krake follow us?"

"The reports concerning the Krake indicate that they largely operate not only within this star system but in many different universes," Mullins replied.

"That knowledge is based on a few different scouting expeditions, one of which is overdue, as you're all aware. Our own scientists and many senior officers are divided on the capabilities the Krake have. Some of their technology seems superior to our own but not everything. It's not quite an equal playing field, but if the Krake wanted, they could follow us wherever we went."

The reactions from the people in the meeting were mostly supportive, but not all of them.

"We can't make any guarantees here," Mullins replied, "but right now, we have an option open to us, and it's something we can't afford to ignore—that is, until we know more about the Krake, but there's also a significant risk in doing that. If we keep antagonizing the Krake, we'll give them a reason to come find us."

"The Ovarrow believe that the Krake will come here, especially now. There's no use arguing about whether or not we can put the genie back in the bottle."

Mullins shook his head. "That's just my point. Continuing to antagonize the Krake will bring them here faster."

Several speaker requests came in from the other attendees.

"Gentlemen," Governor Wolf said, "there are a lot of strong opinions here, and I don't want this meeting to descend into a theoretical debate. There are multiple issues coming to a head, and I have no choice but to address them here. Most of us would agree that we can't afford to put all our eggs in one basket, meaning that each decision we make carries with it a certain degree of risk. As Connor has highlighted, if we committed to moving the entire colony to this new star system, we'd have to start from scratch, and how much time would we really buy ourselves by doing that? Especially where the Krake are concerned. In fact, it might make it even more difficult to find a way to protect ourselves from the Krake, as General Gates has also suggested.

"However, I don't see any issue in drawing up plans on *how* we'd relocate the entire colony. We're not committing to doing anything, but colonizing this other planet is an option, and a serious one at that. It wouldn't be prudent for this council to ignore either of these options at the expense of the other. I think there are ways we can accommodate both. One"—she gestured with her index finger—"just off the top of my head is based on a discussion with Dr. Trautmann—before the discovery of this new planet, I might add—that we send a smaller colony and let them establish the planet's viability. It doesn't cost as much in resources and is certainly within our reach. There are a lot of options open since we have the capacity for subspace communication. Distance is still a factor, but a smaller colony of five thousand is something that's definitely within our reach. And an effort like that wouldn't detract from any military efforts. It could, and I stress *could*, be an avenue we might explore further."

Clinton Edwards, the Mayor of Delphi, hit his speaker button. "How would we pick the people who would go?"

"That's something we'd need to consider," Mullins replied.

"We're not going to hash out all the details here," Governor Wolf said.

"What about the Ovarrow?" Connor asked. This drew a few questioning looks in his direction. "I know we're tiptoeing around the subject, but if we do decide that leaving here is our best option, what about the Ovarrow? Do we abandon them? Do we offer to bring them with us?"

Trautmann was nodding enthusiastically. "This is an excellent question. We hadn't considered this, and it's something we should discuss."

"Yes," Mullins said in a mild tone. "There are always the Ovarrow to consider. Thank you for that, General Gates."

Connor caught the double-edged meaning of Mullins's last statement, and he wondered if anyone else did as well. It was because of Connor that they'd found the Ovarrow in the first place, and Mullins had never been an avid supporter of bringing them out of stasis. Connor was still surprised that they hadn't found any evidence to link Mullins with the rogue group activities that had been led by Meredith Cain. Either he'd covered his involvement even better than Meredith Cain, or he hadn't been involved.

"Governor Wolf," Nathan said, "this might be a good time to bring up the request for authorizing additional scouting missions to worlds potentially occupied by the Krake."

Connor noticed the hint of recognition in Dana Wolf's gaze. She'd been expecting the question.

"Indeed," Governor Wolf replied. "I see no compelling reason not to authorize more scouting missions."

"Excuse me, Governor Wolf," Mullins said quickly. "I think we should put restrictions on future CDF scouting missions."

Governor Wolf leaned back in her chair. "What kind of restrictions?"

"I agree we should go look for the Krake, but I don't think we should exhaust our resources doing so. And I don't think there should be an open policy for the CDF to conduct the scouting missions without getting any results. The purpose of these missions is to acquire intelligence about the Krake and find out what they know about us. However, every time there's been a mission to an alternate universe, it has cost a very high price in terms of lives, and it's also been a significant risk to this colony. I propose that we don't give the CDF free rein on how many operations they can conduct to scout these alternate universes. Each mission should have a clear objective and be approved by the Security Council."

Connor clenched his teeth. "Would you like a report every time we leave a room too?"

Mullins smirked. "I think you of all people should be acquainted with the concept of accountability. This ensures accountability."

Connor's response was on the tip of his tongue, but at the last second, he glanced at Nathan, who gave him a slight shake of his head. It wouldn't be the first time Connor's mouth had gotten him into trouble, so he shifted his gaze to Governor Wolf.

"The Colonial Defense Force was established based on accountability," Connor said. "We already have defined objectives of scouting alternate universes to look for the Krake."

"Yes," Mullins said, "but there's the lack of an approval step. Not all missions are the same."

"That's correct," Nathan replied. "Not all missions carry with them the same degree of risk."

Connor wanted to invite Mullins on the next mission. That way, he could leave him on an alternate world. *Accountability* . . . These were the same people who'd let someone like Meredith Cain infiltrate and manipulate the upper echelons of their government.

"I think what would help here . . ." Governor Wolf began. "A briefing should be sent out to the Security Council about specific scouting missions. That way, everyone is kept in the loop. Individual scouting missions don't require Security Council approval, but a briefing should still be sent to my office."

For a few moments, Connor thought they'd cancel all the scouting missions so they could hammer out an approval mechanism for him to operate under. Sending out a briefing about scouting missions would give Mullins part of what he asked for, but Connor knew when someone was angling to increase their influence. Mullins shouldn't have any influence on CDF affairs. He was just a governmental advisor, yet he had a satisfied expression that indicated he'd gotten exactly what he wanted.

The meeting went on for another hour as they discussed more

of the specifics about the colonization of the new planet. Connor didn't pay much more attention to it. He kept thinking about the implications of what Mullins had done, and he wondered if Nathan had caught on to it. Sending out a briefing to the Security Council also gave them a window of opportunity to voice concerns, which could propel Governor Wolf to act accordingly—and not just Governor Wolf but future governors as well. Governor Wolf had another two years to serve on her term, but Mullins was playing the long game. Connor would have to keep an eye on him.

The meeting ended, and Connor received a comlink request on his private line. Only a select few people had access to that, so he answered it immediately.

"Noah, how's—how are you?" He'd almost asked how the recovery was going, but Noah was sensitive about it.

"I'm fine," Noah replied. "In fact, each day I wake up and I'm not in a coma, I call it a good day." He said it jokingly, but there was a slight edge of bitterness as well. Connor could relate. He'd been quarantined and then strictly observed at the end of the Vemus War because of his exposure.

"Excellent. What can I do for you?"

"This is more about what I can do for you," Noah replied.

"I'm going to stop you right there because Kara will kill me if I don't. No, you're not cleared to assist in the scouting missions," Connor said.

Kara had almost breathed fire when she'd learned that Connor had brought Noah along on the op to capture Lars Mallory.

"You need me for this kind of work."

"You're right; I do, but not until the doctors clear you. You spent almost a year in a coma, Noah. I'm not telling you anything you don't already know. It's just going to take some time."

Noah looked away for a moment. "I know it hasn't been that long. Honestly, the reason I contacted you is that I've been looking at the documented differences between the arch and the space gates."

"All right, I'm listening."

"The Ovarrow were attempting to reverse-engineer the arch, which is how we stumbled upon subspace communication, but I think it goes further than that," Noah said.

"Well, they *did* teleport several buildings to another planet, and we haven't been able to duplicate that. I think they were doing multiple things with technology they didn't fully understand," Connor replied.

"That's just it; the Krake never used it for that, but I'm at the point where I need some resources to conduct my own experiments."

"What are you trying to do?"

"I'm trying to overcome the five-minute window where we lose the subspace communication signal. Sometimes it's less, but it's never more, so there's got to be something we're not doing right," Noah replied.

"Have you consulted with the scientific teams already working on this?"

"I have, but there are some things I'd like to try. There are fundamental differences between the arch and the space gates, and I'm still wrapping my head around that," Noah said and paused for a moment. "Who have you been bringing with you on the scouting missions?"

"Dash," Connor answered.

Noah grimaced and looked away again.

"Noah, I promise I'll keep you in the loop. If we find anything I think you could help with, I'm not going to keep it from you. Now, can I ask how you're feeling?"

"I'm surprised you're not just looking at my medical records."

Connor shrugged. "You know I won't do that now that you're awake."

Noah sighed. "I still get painful headaches. Sometimes vertigo. The doctor believes it's temporary," Noah replied.

"Well, take it one step at a time and listen to the doctor. Send your request to my office, and I'll either make sure you have what you need or give you clearance to a place that does have it."

Noah thanked him and closed the comlink. Connor sat, staring at the empty space where the video comlink had been active. Noah had almost died. Connor could really use his help with scouting for the Krake but wouldn't involve him until he was back to normal. If Noah was never normal again, Connor would just have to find another way to solve the technical problems he faced regarding Krake technology. What he wouldn't do again is bring his friend into dangerous situations. Noah had sacrificed enough.

# 16

Sean walked down the corridor, heading to where the Krake prisoners were being held. They'd initially captured six Krake, and three of them had committed suicide. The remaining three had attempted to end their lives, but Sean had stopped them. Using the Ovarrow translator, they'd told him they were already dead and nothing would change. Sean had found the entire exchange with them appalling. He didn't like being in the room with them, but it was necessary.

"Are the civilian mutineers being held nearby?" Boseman asked.

"Yes, they are, but I don't know how much longer I'm going to keep them here."

"Why is that? Are you getting soft in your old age?"

Chad Boseman was in the Spec Ops platoon assigned to the *Vigilant*. They had served together for years and were friends.

"Maybe." Sean said. "It's tight quarters, and I need them to work. We can't afford any freeloaders. As long as they behave themselves, I won't keep them down here, but they'll have to answer for their actions when we get home."

"Morale is a fragile thing. Who's to say that if we let them out they wouldn't cause trouble," Boseman said.

"They're scared. That's why they did what they did. And Lester used that to convince them to help him."

"That man is a disgrace. We tried to take him alive, but he already knew he was going to die."

Sean clenched his teeth a little and his mouth became a grim line. "It was either going to be you or me. The moment he put us in that situation . . ." His voice trailed off, and Boseman gave him a firm nod.

They walked to the end of the corridor toward the Krake holding cells. The doors to the cells were translucent and the Krake prisoners could see each other. Sean wanted them to know that the others were still alive. He'd thought it would entice them to cooperate. They hadn't.

There were two CDF soldiers stationed nearby, and they saluted Sean as he went by. Sean walked to the center holding cell within full view of the others. They were under constant watch, and there was nothing in the room they could use to take their own lives. They'd had to be restrained after multiple suicide attempts.

*Are all Krake as fanatical as these salvagers are?* he wondered.

Sean opened the door and walked inside. Boseman followed, and the soldier outside closed the door. The prisoners had been captured from a Krake salvage ship they'd ambushed.

Sean activated a holoscreen and brought up an image of Aurang. The Krake prisoner stared at the image for a few moments.

"We've met other Krake who are willing to communicate with us. Can you understand me?" Sean asked.

The Krake prisoner winced and its eyes darted to Boseman and then to Sean.

"I'd call that a yes," Boseman said.

"Say something," Sean said.

The prisoner seemed to draw himself up to his full height. "Betrayers," he said and charged toward Sean.

Boseman stuck out the stun baton, releasing a high-powered jolt into the Krake's side and bringing the prisoner to his knees.

"If you'd just cooperate with me, I'd let you go. The same with the others. They can hear us," Sean said, gesturing toward the other holding cells where the Krake prisoners were listening. "Aurang wants us to help him against the overseers."

The Krake prisoner winced and scrambled back. "There is no outcome other than death. There is only death."

The prisoner came to his feet and charged them again. The other prisoners began banging their heads against the wall, each of them chanting that there was only death.

"Colonel," Boseman said.

Sean saw that the Krake prisoner was lying on the ground, not moving, and there was a dark ring around the side of his head. Boseman was staring at the stun baton in disbelief.

"When he charged me, he grabbed my hand and put the stun baton to his head. He held it there. I tried to pull it away, but they're strong."

Krake blood was pooling dark gray under his head. The prisoner was dead. Sean spun and hastened to the other holding cells. The two soldiers rushed inside to restrain the others.

Sean and Boseman helped get them strapped to the beds.

"You don't have to die. Stop doing this. Stop struggling," Sean said and gritted his teeth.

The prisoner struggled even more, trying to break free of his restraints. A few moments later, a medic arrived and sedated the Krake. Both the remaining prisoners were strapped to their beds, unconscious.

"They're crazy," Boseman said. "They're determined to kill themselves."

Sean looked at the unconscious Krake prisoners and shook his head. Most people had an innate drive to stay alive. It was hardwired into their DNA. Even the Ovarrow were the same. They'd fight to survive, just like most creatures of New Earth.

"It's like they've been brainwashed," Sean said.

Boseman's eyes widened for a moment. "You think this is conditioning?"

"It's not rational, unless their entire society rigidly adheres to these types of conventions. Aurang isn't like that, so there must be some kinds of established protocols for the salvagers to follow, which means we're not the first ones to capture a Krake ship," Sean said.

"They're crazy. It might be better for them if we let them die," Boseman said.

Sean was tempted to agree with this friend. The Krake prisoners were a danger to themselves and to others. He couldn't afford to set them free because of what they'd seen on the ship. "I'm not going to kill them."

"Understood, sir."

They left the area. At least they had confirmation that the Krake translator worked. Sean had strongly suspected that it would, but there was nothing like a true test. On a secure system, Sean had authorized the use of the Krake translator to interpret the data they'd taken from previous Krake places they'd been. They'd been able to cross-check the translation with the Ovarrow translator they'd used in the past. Gabriel had confirmed that the Krake translator was superior to what they were using. Sean had been concerned that there could be a subroutine hidden within the translator that would infiltrate the *Vigilant*'s computer systems, which was why he'd only authorized its use on secure systems that were isolated from everything else.

"There's something I need to ask you about," Boseman said. "A Dr. Evans requested assistance from someone under my command. Do you know anything about this?"

"Oriana is working on a lot of things, but I'm not sure why she'd need someone from your team."

"I'm not concerned about the request. I just thought it was odd. We're ready to lend a hand whenever we can, but I was surprised by who she asked for," Boseman said and paused. Sean's eyebrows raised. "Benton."

Sean frowned. Benton had a reputation for pushing the limits of acceptable behavior aboard ship. When they'd first had civilians mixed with enlisted personnel, there had been more than a few complaints about him.

"I don't know. I can check with her if you want," Sean offered.

"Negative. I already did, and she needed Benton's help. I even offered to send her someone else."

Sean shrugged a little. "You don't need to worry about Oriana. She can take care of herself."

Oriana had never been shy, but she'd gotten used to living aboard ship among the CDF. After the mutiny, she'd become more serious. They all had, but Oriana and her science team had been held captive by Brody and the other mutineers. Sean had been teaching her self-defense, including how to disarm an opponent. He rarely had occasion to utilize his training and welcomed the opportunity to revitalize his skills.

They'd had little time together after the mutiny. Each of them preferred to be as active as possible, which included downtime. Sean required very little sleep because of his military-grade implants. Oriana wanted her implants upgraded with the same capabilities, but there hadn't been enough time.

Others began to notice their workouts and asked to join them, which gave them a chance to practice against all kinds of opponents. Boseman was among the best hand-to-hand combat specialists on the ship and wasn't shy about humbling Sean when they practiced together.

They headed to the meeting room near the bridge. Dean Stonehill was already inside, along with Jane Russo, his XO. Major Shelton and Captain Martinez were on the holoscreen. Oriana should have been there, so she must have been running late for some reason.

Sean sat down at the table. "We're scheduled to meet with Aurang in a little while, but we needed to speak first."

They were in the alternate universe and had been studying their targets as best they could for the past twenty-four hours. No alarms had been raised and no Krake scout forces had been sent out, so it was safe to assume that their presence had gone unnoticed. But Sean didn't like assumptions. If this was a trap, Aurang could've arranged for the Krake defenses to simply ignore their presence for the time being.

"Gabriel, send a message to Lieutenant Pitts that I'd like him at this meeting now," Sean said.

"Message has been sent, sir," Gabriel replied.

His request drew more than a few puzzled frowns. "It's nice to know that I can still surprise all of you."

A few moments later, Lieutenant Pitts appeared on an additional holoscreen.

"Thank you for joining, Lieutenant. To bring everyone up to speed, I called this meeting with all of you because of your ability to think outside the box," Sean said.

Sean noticed that Pitts frowned for a moment and seemed to be glancing at the array of holoscreens from his ready room aboard the *Babylon*.

"So far, the Krake haven't detected our presence here. I've been able to confirm that the Krake translator does, in fact, work. Boseman and I," Sean said and twitched his head toward Boseman, "successfully communicated with our prisoners. We did get a response, but there isn't much to share on that front. Behavioral analysis indicates that these particular Krake might've been brainwashed."

"Colonel Quinn," Pitts said, and Sean gestured for him to speak. "Behavioral analysis applies to humans. While the response you received from the Krake could be conditioned, it might be premature to assign a prognosis based on limited testing."

"It's a theory, and it's supported by our senior medical doctor on board," Sean said. "We haven't detected any Krake ships at the NEC. The planet has a single moon, but there is a sizable asteroid belt relatively close to the planet. Analysis indicates that it was a dwarf-sized planet. The Krake could have an attack force hidden there."

"The lack of Krake ships in the area," Major Shelton said,

"confirms what Aurang told us about how the Krake conduct operations across multiple universes."

Sean nodded. "It makes sense if you think about it. They have a ready force to deal with alerts that come in. This saves a considerable amount of resources with maintaining a fleet across multiple universes, but I don't want to get blindsided."

The door to the conference room opened and Oriana hastened to an open seat.

"There's an operational lunar base," Sean continued, "as well as an orbital defense platform. In order for this mission to work, we'll need to disable the space gate, but the timing must be in tandem with the ground force that will infiltrate a Krake military research and development complex on the surface. We'll need to hit all of these targets almost at the same time in order to prevent the Krake from mustering a response. But the attack must occur after the regular status check-in from the Krake complex. After that, disabling the space gate is key to preventing Krake warships from responding if they're able to raise an alert."

"It's the ground force operation that I am most concerned about, sir," Major Shelton said. "We're supposed to trust that Aurang will be able to infiltrate the R&D systems right before the Krake send their scheduled update to their version of COMCENT, which will then have updated orders so the fifth column will be freed or at least taken off the watch list. And in return for our help, he plans to give us operational data, particularly around the multiverses they have a presence in."

"I don't trust them either," Sean said. "That's why I'm going to equip Captain Boseman and his team with another tool for exfiltrating data from Krake systems. We refined it based on the new Krake translator interface combined with proven techniques used to remove data from Ovarrow computer systems found on New Earth."

Sean gave them a few moments to consider. "This is where I need you to raise questions if you have them."

"Ovarrow computer systems," Lieutenant Pitts said, "are a rudimentary version of Krake computer systems. How do we know that when Captain Boseman attempts to steal the data, he won't trip any of the alarms?"

"We won't know," Sean said pointedly. "There's no way around this. This mission carries a significant risk factor."

"Colonel Quinn, if I may," Boseman said, and Sean nodded. "My team is going to be thrown into the fire, but this is what we do. We'll learn something worthwhile about the Krake and their systems. There are redundancies in place that will get whatever it is that we learn out of there even if my team doesn't make it."

"Worst-case scenario, but we'll have combat shuttles on standby to extract the Spec Ops team," Sean said.

"Sir," Lieutenant Pitts said, "it just seems that you expect Aurang to betray us. So why go through with this?"

"You want to know if the risk is worth the reward. We don't have the luxury of making decisions in hindsight. We've learned a lot about the Krake these many months we've been away from home, but it's not enough. We've gathered some credible intel, but we need more if we're to begin an offensive against them. That's the purpose of our mission. Aurang could be misinformed, and we'll have to be able to adapt to that. So far, everything he's provided has been proven accurate."

"Understood, sir," Pitts replied.

"This is the first system that has a significant Krake presence, and this is what we came to find. It'll be the most complex mission we've executed to date. Let's go over the particulars of the mission," Sean said.

They discussed the plan that Sean and Vanessa had put together, even though most of the people who were at the meeting had contributed to it. Sean had decided to bring Lieutenant Pitts along because he'd been the most vocal about the state of morale after the mutiny. He asked good questions during their review of the mission, which reaffirmed Sean's decision to bring him into the meeting.

"Colonel Quinn, I have one more question," Lieutenant Pitts said.

"Go ahead."

"According to Aurang, the next window to begin this mission is in twelve hours."

"That's when Aurang wanted us to go, but we're not going to comply with that request. You see, there's a delicate balance here. If we go in twelve hours and there's an ambush waiting for us, they'll be expecting us. If we delay several cycles, they won't know when or if our mission will begin," Sean replied.

Lieutenant Pitts's eyes widened and he actually smiled. "Understood, sir, and thank you," he said.

Something in that moment changed in Lieutenant Pitts. Sean spotted it, and he supposed Vanessa had seen it too. She wouldn't be his XO for the Trident Battle Group if she couldn't identify that moment when a soldier became a believer in the mission. There was the chain of command, but there was also trust to be built.

"Aurang will be here in a few minutes. Major Shelton, I want you to brief the commanding officers of the battle group," Sean said.

The holoscreens flickered off as the comlinks to the other ships were severed.

"Colonel, I'm sorry I was running a bit late," Oriana said.

"Understood. What did you think of the way they wanted us to disable the space gate?" Sean asked.

"It should work, and we know that if there's a misalignment with the space gate cubes, you can't establish a stable gateway. I also wanted to run something else by you," Oriana began to say but stopped when the door to the conference room opened.

Captain Russo walked in with Aurang and the soldiers who were escorting him.

The chairs in the conference room couldn't accommodate Krake physiology. Their long limbs made using the chair too awkward, so Sean and the others stood up.

"Colonel," Aurang said, "you've had adequate time to consider my request for aid, and you've done your reconnaissance. What is your answer?"

"I've conferred with my senior staff and we agree this mission is possible. So far, everything aligns with the information you've given us," Sean said.

"Excellent. So, we can begin in the next cycle," Aurang said.

"That won't be possible," Sean said and began to hold up his hand so he could further explain but then realized the gesture would be lost on the Krake, who didn't understand human mannerisms. "Our teams need to train for the mission. We'll need at least twenty-four hours before they'll be ready to go."

It was a lie and everyone but Aurang knew it. Sean had no intention of telling the Krake when they would begin the mission.

"I'm very disappointed. Tell me, if I requested to leave your ship, would you let me?"

"You wouldn't make that kind of request," Sean said.

"You haven't answered my question," Aurang replied.

Sean regarded the Krake for a few moments. "If you were to make that request, I'd assume that everything else you told us was a lie. You came to us because you have nowhere else to go. That's what you told us. The overseers are about to annihilate your entire network of operations. You want to protect your people, and so do I. That means not rushing into anything. Do we understand each other?"

It was difficult trying to gauge the Krake's response. There seemed to be an exactness in how they responded to anything that was almost devoid of emotion.

"Colonel, I have teams in place that require what I have on my ship."

"And if we don't show up during this next cycle, what will they do?"

Aurang regarded Sean for a few moments. "They will wait, but time is running out for them. We have contingency plans in the event that we cannot—" Aurang stopped speaking.

"We need to go over the plan so everyone knows what's expected of them," Sean said.

Aurang glanced at the others in the room for a moment. "I will answer your questions."

# 17

"I JUST HEARD THE NEWS," Samson said.

Connor had left the main administration building at the CDF base in Sanctuary only moments earlier. "Good. Have the 7th assemble so we can be underway ASAP."

"Oh, we'll be ready, but I have a couple of concerns," Samson said, matching his pace with Connor's.

Connor checked the status of the message he'd sent to Dash, and it had been received. One less thing to worry about. He looked at Samson. "We were bound to succeed, sooner or later."

Since they hadn't gotten any help from the Ovarrow, Connor was determined to get the intel he needed from the Krake by finding one of their worlds. They needed to find out more about them, but more importantly, they needed to find out what the enemy knew about the colonists. Connor had converted a CDF storage facility located over a hundred kilometers from Sanctuary into a working compound for the purpose of utilizing an archway to find a Krake world. The concept was simple. They were using the data they'd gotten from the Krake forward operating base, starting with the coordinates taken from that facility. However, the task had proven to be a lot more complicated than that.

"Since we're only bringing one platoon for the scouting mission, we shouldn't bring the Ovarrow with us," Samson said.

"Why is that?" Connor asked. He didn't want to make any assumptions.

"They're an unknown quantity. They've had some combat training, but it'll be dangerous for them. We're already bringing one civilian with us, and honestly, it's one too many," Samson said.

"Dash has a skill set that we don't have in the CDF. He's a specialist, and that's why he's coming with us. Having some of the Ovarrow will help speed the process along," Connor replied.

"Yeah, but do we need to bring all six of them? Why can't we just bring Cerot?" Samson said.

"Because Cerot is the warlord's First. He's second-in-command of their military. He'll insist that he bring some kind of protection, and he would be right to do so."

"I understand that, but this is our operation. He doesn't have to come."

"It's essential that he comes with us. We need somebody who can speak the language. And right now, Cerot and the others have agreed to help us," Connor said, silencing Samson with a gesture. "Now hold on a minute. I agree we don't need to bring all six of them. We'll probably bring only three—Cerot and whoever he chooses to bring with him. They're professional soldiers, albeit they're not us. They did fine when we went to the city."

Samson tried to think of an argument but couldn't. Things could rapidly spiral out of control, and they'd be cut off from New Earth. They'd spent the last few days strategizing on how to deal with that, which included a bunch of secondary protocols in the event that unforeseen circumstances occurred. Samson was aware of it. He was minimizing the potential impact of things outside his control, which included the Ovarrow. He was doing his job, and Connor couldn't be frustrated with that.

"To be honest, I didn't expect they'd find anything so soon," Connor said.

They made their way to the airfield where the troop carrier transports waited for them. Connor had sent the preliminary alert to Nathan to make him aware of the situation. Connor was going on-site to do a more thorough analysis and determination of whether sending a scout force to the world they'd found was required. He was due to return to the CDF compound anyway.

Dash and the Ovarrow arrived, and Connor gestured to one of the containers aboard the troop carrier as where they'd stow the Ovarrow's armor and weapons.

"Come on," Connor said. "I'll brief you on the way."

They walked up the loading ramp, and this time the Ovarrow were a lot more familiar with the troop carrier. They went to the section that was dedicated to them, and Cerot and Dash followed Connor to the front. It was always hard to gauge what the Ovarrow were thinking, but Connor speculated that Cerot looked a little excited to be on the troop carrier again. He was keenly interested in any of the vehicles the colonists used, be they for military or civilian applications. He'd even brought up the possibility of convincing the high commissioner to request a few of the rovers for their use. The Ovarrow equipment they'd found stored was several hundred years old, and anything left unused for that long wouldn't be in prime operating condition. However, there were some bunkers that'd been hermetically sealed, so they hadn't deteriorated over time. But they'd also sat unused, and there was a lengthy process to make those vehicles operational again. The Ovarrow were primarily restricted to ground transportation, but Connor wondered how long it would be before they were able to restore more of their vehicles. They were capable of creating machines for atmospheric flight.

"Are we heading to the base at New Haven?" Dash asked.

Connor shook his head. "No, there's a compound closer to Sanctuary. We have an arch there."

Dash's expression was one of appreciation. "That was fast."

"Once we had the first one working, we built a second and then a third. We didn't want to be reliant on finding a Krake version. And I don't know how many arches they had on the planet. Anyway, it's quite a setup, and you'll get to see it," Connor said. He activated a holoscreen. "We opened the arch and sent a reconnaissance drone through. It has a look around and then comes back. This video is from a world where we believe there's a Krake city."

The others watched the holoscreen. The video had been taken from the vantage point of the drone as it ascended. In the distance, there was a distinct outline that was purely artificial. It wasn't a natural occurrence, and the recon drone attempted to zoom in on the structures in the distance. They looked to have been artificially created. It was a large series of buildings that could be the beginning of a small city. Then the video feed cut off.

"This is the first world we've seen that has any kind of structure on it," Connor said.

"How do we know this is of Krake origin?" Dash asked.

"We can't be one hundred percent sure," Connor said. "It could be an Ovarrow settlement or something else entirely. The universe coordinates were taken from the Krake forward operating base. It wasn't one they visited, so we suspected it was something they came from. That's why we think this location is associated with the Krake and not the Ovarrow. It's our best lead so far, and we're going to have another look. There's a good chance we'll be sending a scout force through."

Cerot informed them that he was going to give an update to his soldiers. Once he was gone, Connor motioned for Dash to come closer.

"I need your opinion on Cerot and the others. You've spent the past few days with them. What's your impression? Are they ready for this?" Connor asked.

Dash glanced at the other end of the troop carrier where the Ovarrow had gathered. The CDF soldiers nearby watched them. "I think it was a good idea to allow them to come to Sanctuary. That gave them more of an insight into us. Even though we still have communication barriers, I just get a sense that there's more of an understanding. There are a couple of them who . . ." Dash said and paused for a few seconds. "They're very quiet, so I don't really have an impression of them. It's Esteban and Wesley. Joe, Felix, and Luca seem more open-minded about learning new things. There's a big difference with Cerot because he seems young, but at the same time, he's . . . you can tell he's been through a lot."

Connor thanked him, and the troop carrier pilot announced that they'd be reaching their destination in a few minutes.

"Dash, I know you've agreed to come with us, and I appreciate that, but I wanted to give you the option of staying behind," Connor said, and Dash immediately protested. "No one would think less of you if you did. Exploring New Earth is one thing, but having been through this a few times, I can tell you it's quite different and very dangerous."

"I understand, Connor, and you don't have to worry about me. I'll keep my head down and do as I'm told—you know, leave the soldiering to the professionals."

Connor gave him a long look, considering. "That's just it. You're much more capable than the average citizen, but you're not a soldier. You'll be armed, and you might be called upon to do more than you ever have before."

Dash gave him a determined look. "I won't let you down."

Connor had trained a lot of soldiers throughout his career. There were some who excelled in a training environment, only to freeze up during a hostile situation. Even though Dash had never been through a CDF boot camp, much less any of the additional years of training that ranger companies went through, he'd been in some tough situations. Connor could have brought in another specialist or a soldier who knew the Ovarrow translator interface and had a basic rudimentary knowledge of it, but nothing could take the place of the years of study Dash had done at the Colonial Research Institute and in the field on New Earth. Dash knew the Ovarrow to a degree that very few had attained.

Connor had also seen it with Lenora. This was an important mission, and he needed answers as quickly as possible because lives might depend on it. And even though Dash thought he knew what it was going to be like, Connor actually had a better idea. The platoons that made up the 7th Ranger Company were all seasoned soldiers, but it was Carl Flint's men who'd actually been to another world and engaged the Krake. Connor had absolute faith in Samson, but he wouldn't have minded Flint being with them. The trouble with finding truly capable soldiers was that they tended to be put in charge, and sometimes that spread the forces pretty thin.

The troop carriers headed to the LZ inside the walls of the compound. There were habitat units on the other side where the permanent residents stayed, but the bulk of the compound was in one large warehouse capable of holding several squadrons of combat shuttles or dozens of the troop carriers they'd flown in on.

As they went inside the warehouse, Connor caught his first glimpse of the arch. It was on an elevated platform that was capable of either maintaining the arch at ground level or raising it thirty meters straight up. That had been a last-minute addition when they discovered that some of the universes they opened a gateway to had different elevations on the other side. The gateway could still be opened whether it was aboveground or beneath it. They wouldn't be able to go through if it was beneath the ground, but the goal was to explore what was on the other side. Massive power cables coiled on the ground near the platforms that raised the arch. Connor knew that a great deal of effort had gone into maintaining the alignment so they had a stable gateway. The arch itself was six meters tall and fifteen meters across at the base.

While everyone else waited below, Connor, Samson, Dash, and Cerot walked up to the command center, which maintained its elevation to be level with the arch. They used the staircase outside the command center to reach it, and even though the steps were wide enough for the average human foot, the Ovarrow's feet were both longer and wider than the average human's. But Cerot didn't hesitate to go up the stairs. Dash told Connor it was only the second time the Ovarrow had ever used stairs. In their cities, they typically built long ramps to ascend to upper levels.

Connor entered the command area and Major Kent Henderson greeted him. By his side was the familiar face of Dr. Volker, whom Connor had had transferred from the CDF base by New Haven for the purpose of this project.

"General Gates," Henderson said, "welcome to Independence Compound. We've just completed our second scouting run and have some additional intel for you."

"Show us what you have," Connor replied.

Henderson brought up several holoscreens and gestured to a particular area. These were more detailed images of the structures Connor had initially seen. Even though it was still quite distant, they were able to see large groups of figures moving in the distance. They couldn't tell whether they were Ovarrow or Krake, and he also couldn't discount the possibility that they were something else altogether. Scientists believed it was highly unlikely that they would find another completely different species. This made perfect sense to Connor because the Krake had obviously been using the multiverse for quite some time, and nothing indicated that they'd found anything but a variance of themselves in these different universes.

"General Gates," Volker said, "these images are very exciting. I was alarmed by the number of mixed results we had in the beginning."

"What were you expecting?" Connor asked.

Dr. Volker scratched his dark beard. "I was expecting more worlds like ours, but what we've been seeing is a lot of variation that goes well beyond different climates. Some of them have a completely different composition and are entirely lifeless. But not this one. There's a civilization here, but with the type of reconnaissance we're allowed to do, we're limited to a peek on the other side."

Connor nodded. "We don't want to draw attention to ourselves."

"I completely understand. I was just hoping to provide more information that you could base a decision on," Volker replied.

"I have to agree with him," Major Henderson said. "You brought a team with you, so will you be launching an operation to go through the arch?"

Connor glanced at Cerot. "Do you recognize those buildings?" he asked and gestured toward one of the images on the holoscreen.

The Ovarrow peered at the image and then opened the translator interface. "They appear to be of Krake design, at least partially."

Connor glanced at Dash.

"I see what he means," Dash said, gesturing toward a different part of the image where the buildings appeared to be rounded at the top. "These are more in line with the architecture we've found here, so they must be Ovarrow, at least at one time. But these other buildings don't match anything we've seen so far. Maybe they built something temporary," he said and asked Cerot a question.

"I've never seen these types of materials before. Therefore, they are Krake," Cerot answered.

"General, I don't think that's enough to go on," Major Henderson said.

"That's the problem," Connor replied. "We're making our best guess. I think this warrants us taking a closer look."

"We have armored rovers, but we don't have any stealth ships here," Major Henderson said.

Connor glanced at Samson for a moment, and they shared a look. "No, we need to minimize our footprint. We'll be going across in combat suits. They can keep up with any rover, and they give us more flexibility with the terrain we can cover."

Dash cleared his throat. "Excuse me, General Gates, but what about the Ovarrow? Their powered armor isn't as capable as the combat suits are."

Dash was right, and there was no way they could adapt the combat suits for Ovarrow use. He looked at Major Henderson.

"All the equipment here is designed for us," Henderson said.

"If they want to risk it," Samson said, "they could hitch a ride on the combat suit heavies if we had to move quickly."

"I'm not sure they'll like that," Dash said. "Isn't there something else they can use to keep up?"

Connor frowned for a moment and shook his head. "I'm afraid not. Everything is designed for us, and we want to reduce our presence so we're not bringing any vehicles."

"I'll go get the $7^{th}$ ready, sir," Samson said and left.

Dash explained the situation to Cerot. Connor knew the Ovarrow were used to walking long distances, but if they got into a situation where they really had to move, they wouldn't be able to keep up with the soldiers in combat suits.

"What about a couple of MPSs?" Dash asked. "They're designed to be worn by—well, by anyone, and despite certain physical anomalies between humans and the Ovarrow, they're bipedal. The suit doesn't have to actually provide protection, but it could enable them to move faster than they otherwise could."

Connor shook his head. "They don't know how to use them, and there's no interface for them to utilize the features. MPSs are reliant on the standard implant interface. They wouldn't be able to turn them off and on. The MPS isn't going to help."

He tried to think of something they could bring that could help the Ovarrow, but there wasn't really anything that would fit the parameters. Most importantly, they couldn't leave anything behind. Samson was right. The Ovarrow would have to hitch a ride.

Cerot looked at Connor. "Stealth is most important for scouting missions. The Mekaal will not be a burden."

"I'm glad you understand. We're taking a small force through the archway. Therefore, I can only allow three of you to come with us. The others will have to stay behind," Connor said.

Cerot read the translation and turned to look at the arch for a few moments. Then he looked at Connor and gave him a single nod. Cerot had picked up on a few human gestures, and he'd seen Cerot and some of the other Ovarrow mimic human mannerisms when interacting with the colonists.

Connor left the command center and headed back down, Dash and Cerot following. A CDF soldier met him at the bottom of the stairs and saluted.

"General Gates, sir, I'm to escort you to your combat suit," Corporal Julia Bradley said.

"Lead the way, Corporal Bradley."

Bradley turned smartly on her heel and set a brisk pace,

leading them over to the staging area. Cerot went to speak to the other Ovarrow.

Connor was already wearing an MPS that had been specifically designed for him. The suit redistributed its mass so it wouldn't weigh him down all that much, and he kept it on when he climbed into the Nexstar combat suit.

Dash gave the Nexstar an appreciative look. It added several inches onto Connor's already impressive height. "We need a civilian version of this."

"You have the MPS series 7, which is quite capable," Connor said.

Dash slipped into his MPS and it immediately adjusted to his body type. "Yeah, but the combat suit has all the extra bells and whistles. It has things like thrusters."

"I know, but don't underestimate the MPS. It can allow you to do most of the things I do from in here. But not everything. It's only a matter of time before we see more MPSs being used instead of these combat suits," Connor said.

He used implants to bring the combat suit's systems online. It went through a quick diagnostic check on startup and then showed green across the board on his internal heads-up display. The Nexstar was constructed of composite material that was quite strong without weighing the wearer down with needless bulk, which affected power consumption. The suits could operate out in the field for almost a full week before needing to recharge. All but three of the 1$^{st}$ Platoon in the 7$^{th}$ Ranger Company wore similar combat suits. Those three exceptions wore combat suit heavies. These carried heavy weapons capable of massive amounts of destruction, and they could also carry immensely heavy loads.

Corporal Bradley came back to them and handed Dash a

hornet class SMG. "Mr. DeWitt, I'm told you're a capable marksman, but you're not qualified for the standard AR-71 assault rifle. This is the next best thing." She proceeded to go over the capabilities of the hornet and its operation. Connor agreed that it was the best suited for a nonmilitary person to use if they had to go into a dangerous situation. It had the option of becoming fully automatic. And even though a single dart wouldn't punch through the armor of a Nexstar combat suit, the next hundred fired inside a few seconds would chew right through it without any problem.

"I think I got it," Dash said. "I mean, I got it," he tacked on quickly.

Connor walked over to where Samson stood, and the men and women of the 1st Platoon gathered. Connor glanced at the arch behind them for a moment and then turned back to his soldiers. Dash stood with Cerot, Esteban, and Felix. The Ovarrow had put on their armor and carried their long rifles with them.

The soldiers quieted down, and Samson gave him a nod.

"In a few minutes, we'll be the first of many scout forces that will be sent through the arch. Our objective is clear. We're to scout out Krake installations for the purpose of gaining intel on our enemy. We need to know more about them so we can develop a strategy on how to beat them. This is where the groundwork gets laid—right here by all of you," Connor said, allowing his gaze to sweep across the men and women who stood before him. "We need to know what they know about us. To help speed up our intelligence gathering, we're bringing a few specialists with us," he said and gestured toward Dash and the Ovarrow. "You're here because you're among the elite. You've proven that you can adapt, and you're part of the most capable Spec Ops companies in the history of the Colonial Defense Force. Most of you have seen what the Krake are capable of. We're going in first because we do what no one else can, but remember the mission objective. We are a scout force. When it comes time for us to fight the Krake," Connor said, pausing for a moment, "we'll be able to do it more effectively because of missions like this."

Samson leaned over so only Connor could hear. "Are you planning to go on all the scouting missions?"

"I can't let you have all the fun. We'll see. You never know what we'll find," Connor said.

Samson let out a soft chuckle.

A large holoscreen came on next to the arch, and then a countdown appeared. The timer reached zero, and there was a brief shimmer in the space at the absolute center of the arch that spread to the edges. The arch was elevated about seven meters into the air, and a large loading ramp was moved into place. Two squads went up the ramp and through the arch gateway. A few moments later, they received an "all clear" message.

Connor heard Lieutenant Layton order Corporal Bradley to pick two soldiers and stay with Dash and the Ovarrow. They were behind Connor and Samson. When Corporal Bradley took up a position by Dash, Connor heard him mutter a comment about "babysitting duty." Bradley's no-nonsense look cracked into a lopsided smile for a moment, and then she was back to business.

Connor walked up the ramp and approached the edge of the gateway. For some reason, when they went through the gateway, they all leaned forward a little bit as if they expected to meet some kind of resistance. But going through the gateway didn't entail any resistance whatsoever; it was as simple as stepping through a doorway, except that when they stepped through, the ground under their feet changed to whatever was on the other side, and their view was one of emerging from the warehouse and stepping onto the plains of another universe. The gateway remained active for a few moments after the last person was through, and then it disappeared. There wasn't any flash of light; it was as if the window or doorway back to New Earth had simply ceased to exist.

They were on a schedule now. Back in the warehouse, Major Henderson would open the gateway at twelve-hour intervals. They had to adhere to the clock back on New Earth, but they also had to account for the fact that time might flow differently here. The days could be longer. They could immediately measure that the gravitational pull was three percent less than on New Earth. Initial scouting missions involving just reconnaissance probes had broken the theory that every gateway led to a world that was only slightly different from the one they called home. That wasn't the case at all, and they had to be prepared for those differences that may not be readily apparent.

Before they'd gone through the gateway, Major Henderson informed Connor that they'd moved the arch forward one hundred meters in order to allow them to emerge under cover. There were medium-sized trees about eight meters tall, with ground-sweeping branches of muted yellow and gray leaves and stout trunks with some exposed roots of dense black bark that transitioned to white in the broad, rounded crowns at the tops. The ground was covered with discarded leaves, and the air was crisp and dry.

Connor ordered stealth recon drones to be sent out. They

were about a meter in length, with an elongated bulge in the middle. Reflective plates were used by a cloaking mechanism that projected the imagery of the surrounding area. The drones flew low for about half a kilometer, going in opposite directions, and then flew higher in the sky, noting significant movement toward the northwest of their position. Between the data sent back from the drones and their own observations, they were able to compile a map of the immediate area.

Connor looked at Samson. "Let's stick to the high ground on this ridge. That'll give us a better view of our approach."

They set off at a quick pace, allowing Connor to monitor the drone feeds, which were on an open channel for the officers. There was no one nearby, and they were able to move a bit quicker than he would've expected. The drones were closing in on the small city, and he was able to make out more of the details.

"They look like Ovarrow soldiers," Samson said.

There were several hundred Ovarrow soldiers with multiple types of weapons and armored ground transportation bringing them toward the city.

Connor programmed one of the drones to speed ahead, while the others monitored it to give a better view. If the first drone was detected, they'd at least have the others in reserve.

As the drone flew overhead, Connor got more of a bird's-eye view. There was now a significant group of Ovarrow soldiers marching directly for the city.

"They have thousands of soldiers there," Connor said. "Looks like a full division, and they're storming that city."

"We just happened to pick the day that a battle is going to be fought," Samson said and shook his head in dismay.

The drone had reached the city, and Connor noted

blackened craters from some kind of bombardment. "This isn't the first day of battle. There's been a lot of fighting here."

Bright flashes from particle-beam weapons came from the Ovarrow soldiers and their ground assault vehicles. Krake soldiers returned fire from the broken shells of the outer buildings. The Krake's dark gray armor had streaks of black and glowed yellow along the arms. Parts of the armor looked like they were organic, as if the armor had been grown rather than manufactured. Connor could see muscle-like tissue, even from the distance the drone flew overhead.

As the CDF soldiers made their way closer to the city, the Ovarrow began pushing toward the city that the Krake were trying to reinforce. The Ovarrow ground assault vehicles concentrated their fire, punching a hole through the Krake defense, and Ovarrow soldiers surged forward. Connor could appreciate the tactics used, but he much preferred surgical strikes rather than waging all-out war. He kept looking up in the sky, wondering why the Krake hadn't used any type of orbital bombardment, which would end this fight rather quickly. There had to be more going on here than what they were seeing.

They got within two kilometers of the city and circled around the outskirts so they could keep watching the battle. There were several bright flashes of light and thunderous sounds. Another bright flash of green lit up the sky, and a steaming swath laid waste to hundreds of Ovarrow soldiers from some kind of Krake heavy turret. Several more rose from the ruins of the city wall. There was a buildup of power as the weapon primed and then unleashed its god-awful fury onto the battlefield. The Ovarrow army scattered out of the way. Connor's enhanced vision saw that the weapon had been fired from within the city and cut through the buildings as much as it had the soldiers, as if the Krake didn't care about actually protecting the city. This was more about killing than protecting.

As the Ovarrow began to withdraw, they heard the high-pitched whine of several ships breaking the sound barrier from above. Krake combat shuttles raced down toward the battlefield and unleashed their weaponry on the retreating forces. Waves of Ovarrow soldiers came to a halt and then ran back toward the city, only to be shot at by the vicious cannon.

Samson looked at Connor. "This isn't a battle; it's a slaughter."

Connor watched as the Ovarrow soldiers tried to fire their weapons at the Krake, but they had no effect on the armored shuttles. Eventually, an estimate from the recon drones appeared on Connor's heads-up display, showing that less than fifty percent of the Ovarrow soldiers remained. He looked at Cerot and the others, who watched the carnage with grim fascination, and Connor realized that they were just as bewildered as the rest of them.

The Krake combat shuttles wheeled away and flew off, heading west. Connor sent a reconnaissance drone after them. There was a Krake military compound on the outskirts of the city that had a similar structure to what they'd found in the forward operating bases but on a much larger scale. The weapons ceased firing and the Ovarrow seemed to limp away.

"I think they're heading toward our egress point, General," Samson said.

Connor looked at the path the Ovarrow soldiers were retreating on. The area the CDF team had used for their transition into this universe had a lot of tree cover.

Dash came over to his side. "What just happened? They

killed so many of them, and then they just stopped. What was the point?" Dash asked.

The second drone was making another pass over the Krake soldiers, and Connor saw that they were walking among the dead Ovarrow, killing any of the survivors. There were different groups of Krake doing the killing, and they utilized different weapons for their task.

Connor glanced at Cerot as he and the other Ovarrow watched the grisly scene, grimly acknowledging something they'd already witnessed many times before. There was no mistaking it. When a soldier had seen battle, they didn't react the same way as someone who'd never fought in one. Connor was beginning to feel that he might have been too hard on Cerot, Vitory, and the other Ovarrow.

"General, you need to see this," Samson said. He brought up the image taken from the drone video feed and made a passing motion to Connor.

Connor looked at it and saw thousands of habitation units that were cordoned off behind walls. It looked like some sort of encampment, but there were guard towers all around. Connor's mouth dropped open a little. It was a prison camp that held thousands of Ovarrow soldiers. Then he looked back at the battlefield.

"They aren't soldiers," Connor said. Dash looked at him, his mouth agape. "These are prisoners. They're being forced to fight." He looked at Cerot. He couldn't quite connect the thoughts in his mind, but he knew the brutal truth.

"This is a weapons test," Samson said. "And they are the targets."

Samson was right.

Cerot began tapping symbols urgently. "We have to help them."

Connor peered at the battlefield using his internal heads-up display. It showed different features that weren't within direct view but that his cyber-warfare suite in his combat suit knew were just beyond view based on the drone data.

"We can't help them. That's not why we're here," Connor said.

"There has to be something we can do," Dash said. "If this is a weapons test and the Krake are arming the Ovarrow, why would the Ovarrow go into that city in the first place? Why not just run away?"

Connor brought up the drone footage, looking for something he'd missed, and found a deep crater roughly in the middle of the city. There was an arch at the bottom. There were glowing lights on the outside of the arch and a slight shimmer on the inside—an active gateway. Connor looked back at the retreating Ovarrow soldiers, and it only took his brain seconds to put it together.

"You promised to help the Ovarrow," Cerot said.

Connor looked at him. "I promised to help you and your people. To prevent something like this," he said, gesturing toward the battlefield, "from happening to you on New Earth."

"They *are* us. We are the same. There are more prisoners," Cerot said.

Cerot wasn't able to see the drone video feeds, but he'd made the logical leap that there must be a place where the prisoners were kept.

A high-pitched siren sounded from the city, and the Ovarrow soldiers stopped their retreat immediately. They turned around almost as one, and Connor watched as they checked their weapons. Then, they began to march back toward the city. The siren was almost ear-piercing, and it went on for a few minutes. Several of the soldiers attempted to run the other way, only to be shot by the nearest Ovarrow soldier, who then resumed his march back toward the city. There was no retreat, and apparently there was no surrendering either.

"What do you want to do, General?" Samson asked.

Dash had left the Ovarrow communicator on, and the words were translated for Cerot and the others. They watched Connor warily.

"We have ten more hours before the gateway from New Earth is activated. We need to do more reconnaissance. There's a Krake military installation. I think we can circle around and have a closer look," Connor said.

Samson considered this for a few moments. "We can make it back in time if there was—if we wanted to leave at the next check-in."

"You're right, but we need to send a status report back. I don't want to leave a comms drone, so let's send a small team and then they can catch up with us," Connor said.

Lieutenant Layton, who'd been listening, ordered three soldiers to wait, and when it got closer to the time for the check-in, they'd send a comms drone directly to where the gateway from New Earth would appear.

Connor looked at Cerot. "I can't make any promises. We need to assess the situation further."

"Understood, General," Cerot replied.

They took their time circling well away from the city. Connor and Samson expected that there would be defenses in place that might even be capable of detecting them. They moved slowly and steadily, carefully navigating the battlefield and keeping as close to cover as they could. The drones continued to survey, providing valuable data on the layout of the area.

As they were circling around the city, there were two more attempted sieges by Ovarrow soldiers. Even Connor was beginning to wonder how many prisoners the Krake had there. He was impressed that they didn't run away; they threw themselves at the objective, and there was no mistaking that they were trying to reach that arch. He didn't know where the gateway went, and he wasn't about to risk sending one of the drones that close.

---

FIVE HOURS HAD PASSED since they'd observed the first grisly battle. The ground began to shake under their feet, followed by several large explosions east of their position. Connor spun around, as did Samson. Lieutenant Layton attempted to open the comlink to the soldiers they'd left behind. After a few moments, they got a reply. After a short conversation, Lieutenant Layton looked at Connor. "They're fine, but it looks like the Krake have added an orbital bombardment to their weapons testing. The area we came in through is now a massive crater a half a kilometer across and several hundred feet deep. We're not going home that way."

Connor muttered a curse. "We have contingencies for this. Tell them to leave a comms drone and schedule it to go active at the time the check-in is scheduled. Briefly update, explaining what happened. We're surveying the area to come up with another egress point, but we don't have one right now."

Lieutenant Layton relayed the orders.

Connor had been in more than a few hot spots throughout his career, but this was different. They were on someone else's battlefield, and they didn't know all the rules. More than a few soldiers glanced above them, wondering if the next orbital strike was going to be on them.

"We need to move closer to the city and head toward the Krake military compound," Connor said.

"Move closer? But won't they detect us?" Dash asked. His voice was high, but he was keeping it under control. Corporal Bradley said something to Dash, and he quickly glanced away from Connor. "I'm sorry."

"It's all right. Calm down. We're moving closer because there's less chance of the orbital strike occurring in the city. Otherwise, there'd be no city left," Connor said.

Dash nodded and pressed his lips together, determined to keep his mouth shut.

Connor looked at Samson and Lieutenant Layton. "Let's move."

# 18

As Connor and the rest of the 7th made their way closer to the city, the reconnaissance drone flying overhead showed no sign of Krake forces being aware of their movements. The battle being fought a few kilometers away had gained in intensity, and the bombardment hadn't stopped. The Krake must've changed their tactics because they were attacking with smaller ordnance. They didn't restrict their activity to one particular area. Instead, they seemed to be blanketing the entire area, with an occasional shot that came closer to Connor and the others. As they got closer to the city, they found makeshift barriers and shallow tunnel networks from previous attempts to infiltrate the city. Also, the closer they got to the city, the ground cover lessened, leaving the area open, which would make them easy targets if the Krake were watching. There were several louder explosions that Connor equated with bunker busters, which penetrated deep into the ground.

They slipped into a pattern of evaluating the next fifty

meters, then moving forward and repeating. Bright flashes made the thick cloud cover above them blaze with a blinding light. Something pierced an area over the battlefield, and then a new blossom of light appeared in rapid succession on the ground.

"Take cover!" Samson shouted as a bright flash of light appeared directly above their heads.

Connor grabbed Cerot's arm and pulled him down, shielding him. The sound of the explosion was deafening, but the combat suit dampened the sound. The ground shook, and Connor squeezed his eyes shut for a few moments, waiting for it to be over. There was nothing he could do. Cerot covered his ears, and when the roar of sound was finally over, Connor glanced around. He saw Dash a short distance from him. Corporal Bradley helped Cerot to his feet. Other CDF soldiers had protected Esteban and Felix, but the Ovarrow were disoriented and it took them a little while to regain their feet.

Connor looked up and saw that there were more bright flashes as the bombardment continued along the surrounding areas of the city. Had they been spotted? He couldn't be sure. The only time *he* would order an orbital strike that blanketed a specific area was when he couldn't find the enemy, but this was different. The Krake knew exactly where their Ovarrow prisoner army was attacking from, which meant this tactic was just as much a mental attack as it was physical.

Connor looked at Samson, who was surveying the area. "Containment strategy," he said.

"That's a bit over the top," Samson replied. "We need to find cover. We're too exposed."

The recon drone video feeds showed a large crater fifty meters from their position. Any closer and the force of the explosion would have taken lives. Those types of orbital strikes were meant to take out heavily armored units, and while the Nexstar combat suits had plenty of armor, they couldn't withstand the kinetic force of an orbital bombardment. They had to move.

The rest of the 7th sounded off, and everyone was accounted for. A short distance away, the force of the bombardment had caused the ground to cave in, exposing an underground tunnel. There was water at the bottom that must have been from an underground river system. An artificial path led inside. They couldn't see inside because of the angle of the drone cameras.

Several soldiers shouted an alarm, and Connor glanced over at them. The sky was lighting up again. This area was about to get pounded.

"Move into the tunnel!" Connor shouted.

His orders were repeated, and the 7th ran for the exposed tunnel. Once inside, they kept on going. The tunnel angled down, and they could hear the bombardment above them getting closer and closer until it sounded as if it were right on top of them. The ground shook violently, and they kept moving as fast as they could. Then the bombardment stopped. The Ovarrow coughed, clearing their throats of the dust in the air.

Connor brought up the recon drone video feed, and it showed that the area they'd been in was now a smoking ruin. Samson had one of their soldiers go back and confirm that the way back was blocked off. They weren't going to get out that way.

"Any idea what this place is?" Samson asked.

Connor glanced over the edge of the landing they were walking on and could hear the sounds of water not far away.

The tunnel they were in had a rocky bottom, but it had been built by someone.

"It's gotta be a sewer system," Dash said. "I've seen something similar in the Ovarrow capital cities. We should be able to take this all the way inside. The walls are reinforced, but I don't think we want to stay here very long."

Samson raised his eyebrows and glanced at Connor.

"He's right," Connor said. "The Ovarrow built their cities by major waterways."

Samson looked at Dash. "So, anything else we should know? How bad is this place going to smell?"

"I have no idea," Dash replied. "The running water provides a natural filtration system, so hopefully it won't be too bad. The ones I saw had been abandoned for hundreds of years."

They made their way deeper into the sewer system along drainage pipes that were emptying into the area from the ceiling above. The bombardment had faded to a dull thud but was a constant reminder of the battle being fought above them.

The waterway became deeper the closer they got to the city, and the sounds of a waterfall were almost constant. They found doorways that had been blown open, so they knew they weren't the first to have come down there. They carefully scanned the area, looking for sensors that could detect their presence, but there weren't any. Given the way the Krake were conducting their war games, Connor didn't believe for a second that this was an oversight. They must have some other way to secure this entry into the city.

The drainage pipes that connected to the main waterway were about a meter and a half across, and Connor didn't relish the thought of trying to climb through one of those to reach the surface. They were dark and curved away from view. Anything could be living in there.

The soldiers ahead of him came to a stop, and Connor peered into the distance. The walkway they were on split as they reached a major filtration system where dark shadows scurried amidst the water. They looked like the glistening bodies of wet otters a meter long, and they were clamoring to climb out of the waterway. Some of them came from multiple drainage pipes, as if a clog of them had been shoved out. Dozens of dead otter-like creatures floated by. Their bloated bodies were still, their snouts frozen in agony.

Connor wanted to know what the otters were running from, but typically in nature, if rodents were running from something, it meant there was danger nearby. They reached the area where the walkway split and saw that the otters kept trying to climb up the waterfall, each using the one ahead of it to climb above. It was a savage display of determination to live. Teeth and claws were tearing into one another. Hundreds of screeches and growls pierced the sounds of the waterfalls. Beyond the water treatment center was a giant pumping station. All the waterways were filled with the scrambling otters.

Connor looked at Cerot. "What are they doing?"

"It looks like an infestation. Small numbers are used for maintaining the sewage system, clearing away debris and blockages," Cerot replied.

Across the pumping station, there were several levels above that looked clear of the rodents. Suddenly, a loud roar overwhelmed all other sounds and sent the otters into a frenzy. The soldiers at the rear began firing their weapons. The otters were storming the walkway they were on. Something large bumped into Connor's leg, and the otter flailed as Connor kicked it off over the side and into the water below.

They raced ahead, and the combat suit heavies brought up the rear, decimating the oversized otters attempting to race toward them. The heavy gauss cannons chewed away the walkway, and the otters began spilling down into the water below. But still, they came. Enough of the dead piled up to form a grisly bridge.

Several more loud roars came from the watery depths below, and the otters tried to flee in waves. There was something big down there.

Samson gestured toward the upper levels. "We can get up there," he said.

The Nexstar combat suits had grappling hooks, as well as suit jets. Connor looked over at Dash, and Corporal Bradley was already telling him to climb onto her back. Connor gestured for Cerot to grab hold of his combat suit, while Esteban and Felix grabbed onto the nearest soldiers with combat suits. Combat heavies provided covering fire while they raced to the edge of the walkway and engaged their combat suit jets. One by one, the CDF soldiers launched into the air, using the suit jets to give them a massive boost, and then fired their grappling hooks to the other side. The hooks bit into the walkways above, and the automatic retractors pulled them quickly upward.

Connor felt Cerot give a double tap, indicating he was ready. Connor raced to the edge and engaged his suit jets just as a large shadow burst from the watery depths. As he launched in the air, a gargantuan mouth with savage teeth opened, chasing him. He fired his suit jets at maximum, but the teeth were closing the distance toward him. Cerot shifted, and Connor felt his ascent slow as the suit jets tried to keep him level. They slammed against the far wall, and Connor instinctively reached out to grab hold of anything to avoid falling into the mouth of death. At the same time, the creature slammed into an area beneath them. Connor's armored fingers found purchase, and they stopped slipping. He spun around and paused, making sure Cerot still had a hold. Cerot fired his weapon at the dark beast below, and other soldiers joined him.

Connor couldn't get a good look at the creature. The way above was blocked, and he scrambled to the side. He jabbed his fingers into the rocky wall, and small bits of rock fell. The combat suit assisted his movements, and Connor was able to move faster, almost scrambling around the outcropping as the giant beast below made ready for another lunge. He saw movement above him and realized it was Dash hanging off the back of Bradley's combat suit. There were bright flashes as the CDF soldiers unleashed the fury of their weapons at the monsters below.

Connor reached for a ledge and managed to pull himself up a little bit before it started to break away. He scrambled over to another handhold and dangled, his feet unable to find purchase. He heard Cerot growling as he tried to hang on for dear life.

"General Gates," Corporal Bradley shouted, "we're dropping you a line. Take it and we'll haul you up."

Connor glanced over to the side and saw a synthetic line with a stubby end drop next to him. He reached with one hand to grab hold of it and the magnetic end attached to his suit. He let go of the wall and was quickly pulled up. Once he reached the top, they helped Cerot off Connor's back, and then Connor pulled himself up the rest of the way over the edge. There was a small group of them. Connor took a few moments to catch his breath.

"Is everyone all right?" Connor asked.

Dash nodded, and Bradley said she was all right. Private Marsters was peering over the edge of their shallow outcropping.

"There's no one else down there," Marsters said.

They had been separated from the main group. Connor opened the comlink to Samson. "What's your status?"

Most of the 7th had made it across, but they were still rescuing a few stragglers.

"What's your position? I'll send a team to get you," Samson said.

"Negative. We're down from your position, and I see a way for us to get out. We'll meet up topside," Connor said.

Samson began to protest, but several more roars rocked the cavern, rising above the pitch of the waterfall.

"You have your orders, Captain. Gates out."

Connor closed the comlink and went to the edge of the outcropping, looking up. There appeared to be a maintenance shaft not far above their position. If they could make it up there, they might be able to get away.

"General, those things aren't dead," Marsters said, looking over the edge they'd just climbed up from.

Connor went over to Marsters, and the others joined him. Down below, three of the large monsters were scaling the walls.

"Corporal, there's a maintenance shaft above us. Take Dash and go there. We'll be right behind you," Connor said. Dash hesitated for a moment, but Connor told him to go ahead. "We're going to stall them."

Connor went to the edge and Cerot stood next to him.

Connor looked at Marsters. "Change your ammunition type to incendiary and check your fire so the weapon doesn't overheat."

The AR-71 utilized a nanorobotic ammunition source that was capable of becoming various types of armaments. The monsters' hides had to be thick, and the best thing to penetrate that besides firepower was firepower that was extremely hot. They leaned over the edge and fired their weapons. Incendiary darts glowed red as they streaked down into the faces of the monsters. Cerot shot a particle beam from his Ovarrow weapon, and one of the monsters screeched in pain. Connor aimed for its clawed hands as it tried to lurch upward. As the monster got closer, he saw that its face was speckled with dark liquid. They were shooting the thing up, but it wouldn't stop. Its eyes were almost black, and like a shark that had caught the smell of blood, it was beyond anything even resembling reason.

They backed away from the edge as the creature closed in on them. Connor glanced behind them and saw that there was synthetic rope hanging. He ordered Marsters to get up the rope. Cerot kept firing his weapon, keeping his focus as a giant clawed hand reached over the edge. The Ovarrow weapon wasn't strong enough to do much more than surface damage. Connor told Cerot to get back and launched a grenade.

The grenade blew chunks of the creature's flesh away and it wailed in pain. Connor gestured for Cerot to climb onto his back. Connor secured his weapon and ran for the edge just as a rescue line reappeared. As he grabbed hold of it, his momentum carried him away from the edge. He used his suit jets to angle him away from the enraged creature. Engaging the main thrusters below his feet, he surged upward with Cerot. Corporal Bradley retracted the line and brought them up out of the reach of the creatures.

They went into the maintenance shaft and ran. He wasn't sure how big that monster was, but the maintenance shaft wasn't exactly a tight squeeze. If it was determined enough, it could probably follow them.

The shaft angled upward, and they kept running. Cerot moved to climb off his back, but Connor told him to stay put. As they turned up the speed, he heard the loud roars of the creature entering the shaft. The thing wasn't going to give up. They had to get out of there.

They reached the surface and emerged into a shell of a building from which they could see the gray skies overhead. They were in the city, so at least they wouldn't have to worry about a bombardment. They walked to the edge of the building, and Connor looked down an empty street. Cerot climbed off and walked. Dash did the same. The MPS had kept him safe. Bradley and Marsters were on either side of him.

As Connor took a few steps out into the street, a small ship flew overhead. It was extremely quiet and came to a complete stop right above them. They tried to run back into the building, but the ship quickly sank down and thick, dark cords sped toward them, impossibly fast. The cords wrapped around their waists and yanked all five of them up into the air. Connor tried to force his way free, but he couldn't. The thick cord had one of his arms pinned, and he couldn't even draw his weapon. He heard the others shouting as they sped toward a larger ship. They were going so fast that Connor thought they were going to collide with the hull, but at the last second, a door opened and they were pulled inside.

# 19

CONNOR'S TEETH rattled as he was pulled through the darkness. He slammed into the walls and flailed, trying to break free. He thought he heard someone else screaming, but his senses were jumbled with each bone-jarring slam into the walls of the tunnel. Then he was free-falling for a few moments until he hit solid ground. Between the combat suit and the MPS he wore, he was protected from the impact, but he was still disoriented.

Connor pushed himself to his feet, and the glowing lights of his suit pierced the darkness. Dash called out for him, and Connor answered but couldn't see him. He sounded as if he was speaking through a wall. Looking around, he saw that he was in a dark cell. A large shape detached itself from the wall, and Connor raised his weapon, but when the helmet's night vision adjusted he saw Cerot and lowered his weapon.

Cerot held up one hand as his other hand clutched the broken shaft of his weapon. He took a step and clutched at his side. Pieces of his armor had broken off.

"We're in some kind of a cell. Can anyone see a way out?" Connor asked.

"Same here, sir. They dumped us in a box," Bradley replied.

"We still have our weapons. Can't we just use them to get out of here?" Dash asked.

Connor was thinking the same thing, but he frowned. "I'm cut off from the others. I've got no comlink signal or anything that would reach to the reconnaissance drones. Bradley, Marsters, are you experiencing the same thing?"

"I'm cut off too, sir," Bradley confirmed, and Marsters did the same.

Connor glanced up and saw that there was light coming in from the outside. "There's a window above me. I'm going to climb up and see if I can get a look outside."

"There are no windows in here," Dash replied.

Cerot tried to get up and Connor told him to stay where he was. He walked over to the wall. It was smooth but looked as if it was made of some kind of metallic alloy. Engaging the magnetic sensors on the palms of his hands, his knees, and the tips of his feet, he climbed up the wall to the window, which wasn't a far climb and required minimal effort on his part since the suit did most of the work. He reached the top and peered out the small, round window. It was open to the outside, but there was a faint bluish force field that separated them from the outside. Connor couldn't reach it. It must've been some kind of gas that was keeping the atmosphere sealed in the ship.

The ship banked to the side, and Connor caught a glimpse of the ground below. They were being taken away from the city toward the Krake military compound. He'd wanted to infiltrate the compound, but he hadn't wanted to be a prisoner when it happened.

"What do you see?" Dash asked.

Connor climbed back down. "They're taking us to the compound."

"General," Bradley said, "I'm not detecting any other life signs. We're the only ones in here."

Connor frowned and saw that Bradley had deployed a personal recon drone, which was smaller and was able to leave the area they were in.

"We might've triggered some kind of automated escaped-prisoner retrieval protocol once we got inside the city," Connor said.

"What about the others? Won't they be captured as well?" Dash asked.

"There's no way for us to know, but they're not on this ship, so we'll just take this one step at a time," Connor said.

They checked their supplies. Marsters and Dash had dropped their weapons, so Connor and Bradley were the only ones still armed, which wasn't optimal. Connor opened the panel on the side of his combat suit and activated a personal recon drone. Flying toward the window, it approached the force field slowly. The recon drone was able to fly through the force field and get outside it, at which time Connor lost his connection to it. The video feeds cut off, and he cursed. He climbed up to see if it was just hovering along outside the force field, but it wasn't.

He dropped to the floor and helped Cerot with his wounds. They were trapped. He couldn't risk using explosives because of the close quarters they were in.

"How can we get out of here?" Dash asked.

Connor slammed his fist against the bulkhead wall. It was

solid, and hardly a blemish showed from the force he'd used. "We're not getting out of here," he said.

"There has to be a way. We can't be trapped in here," Dash said.

Connor heard Bradley trying to calm Dash down, but his voice was rising in fear.

"Dash," Connor said in a firm voice, "no one is giving up. Any second now, the ship is going to land. Even if I could blow a hole in the bulkhead, we'd have to jump out. We might survive, but Cerot definitely wouldn't. We'll make our escape attempt when the ship lands. I doubt they intend to keep us in here. I need you to calm down and listen to Corporal Bradley. She'll keep you safe."

"All right, all right," Dash said. "And for the record, telling somebody to calm down doesn't make them calm down."

"Understood," Connor said. "Did anyone get a look at the ship as we were getting pulled up into it? I couldn't get a good look."

"Negative, General. It happened too fast," Bradley said.

Marsters echoed the same.

Connor peered at the ground and saw that it was smooth, with no seams, even along the wall. How were the Krake going to get them out of there? He began putting together a plan in his mind but had to do a lot more guessing than he would've liked. There were no two ways about it. They'd been captured.

"We need to keep our heads. We're going to get out of this," Connor said. Now all he needed to do was come up with a way for them to do just that. He thought about his personal recon drone and shook his head. He should've uploaded a message and set a secondary protocol to search for Samson and let him know they were alive. Once it was cut off from Connor's suit, it would just fly around uselessly until it acquired a signal. If it never reacquired a signal, it would just go into standby and be otherwise useless.

"Is your recon drone still active?" Connor asked.

"Yes, sir, it's still flying through the air ducts," Bradley answered.

Connor nodded. "Good. Let me know if it finds anything."

The only thing they could do now was wait. He hoped Samson and the others hadn't been caught in this trap. He wondered how many of the $7^{th}$ had made it out of the sewers.

# 20

SEAN LEFT the galley just after he finished his meal and was contacted by Gabriel, the *Vigilant*'s AI.

"Colonel, I've noted some power fluctuations near Dr. Evans's lab. There has been a temporary loss of artificial gravity in the area," Gabriel said.

The artificial gravity on the ship was on its own separate system, just like life support. There were redundancies in place to prevent it from failing.

"Is anyone injured?" Sean asked, quickening his pace.

Oriana's work area wasn't far from the galley.

"None reported, sir."

"Thanks for letting me know, Gabriel. I'll head over there right now," Sean said.

An alert flashed on his internal heads-up display as he hastened down the corridor. It was a reminder to return to the bridge for his update with Vanessa. Sean reminded himself for the umpteenth time to thank Colonel Cross for connecting him with Major Shelton. Vanessa had become a real asset.

Sean turned down the corridor to Oriana's lab and saw her standing outside, speaking to a group of people. As he approached, they began to disperse. The door to the lab was open, and Sean leaned over so he could see inside. The place was a mess of overturned equipment and tools.

"What have you done to my ship?" Sean asked.

Oriana smiled. Her long hair was tied up, with a few strands cascading down her neck. "We'll get it cleaned up."

Sean glanced inside the lab again and saw two heavy emitters. Status windows appeared above the control console that showed a growing list of errors. Eugena Yuan was working on the consoles.

"They both redlined," Eugena said, "but I have the calculation that will prevent that. It shouldn't happen again," she said and made a passing motion, sending the data to Oriana's PDA.

Oriana opened her wrist computer and glanced at it. "This looks good. Get this to Halsey when you can," she said and looked at Sean. "I'll explain along the way."

They headed down the corridor and Sean glanced back at the lab. "Are they going to be able to clean all that up?"

"Of course. You should've seen it the first time that happened."

"First time?" Sean said and frowned.

"You asked me to come," she said and paused. "I know it looks bad, but it's actually—well, that's the result of a successful test."

If that was a success, Sean thought, he'd hate to see what failure looked like.

"Whatever you were doing affected one of the core ship systems."

"I can explain that," Oriana said.

For the next ten minutes on their way to the bridge, Oriana explained what she'd been working on. Sean felt like he had a permanent frown on his face while he tried to follow along. He thought he understood what she'd done, or at least he understood the concept.

"But as I said, the power draw will be enormous," Oriana said.

"And you consulted with Halsey on this?" Sean asked.

"Yes, of course. He even helped me get access to some of the equipment I needed, but it's not finished. I just ran out of time . . . You don't look convinced."

Sean bobbed his head to the side, his brows knitting together in thought. "I'm *not* convinced, but I don't think you wasted your time. I don't mean to take anything away from what you've accomplished."

Oriana nodded and didn't say anything. She wasn't angry or anything like that. She knew that there was still a lot more work to be done, but the source of her frustration was the lack of time, which was the source of frustration for all of them.

They walked onto the bridge and headed to the command center. Captain Russo stood up from the commander's chair and went to sit at the auxiliary workstation next to his. Sean sat down and brought up his personal holoscreen, asking Specialist Sansky to open a subspace comlink to the *Yorktown*.

Major Vanessa Shelton appeared on his screen. Sean thought he saw a hint of annoyance in her gaze. He'd decided to keep the *Yorktown* as far away from the hot zone as possible. He'd also transferred the space gate to the *Yorktown*.

"Colonel Quinn, the Talon-V squadrons have been underway for the past twenty-four hours. They reported minimal course correction and should have more than enough resources to rendezvous with Charlie team," Shelton said.

He had divided the battle group into multiple teams to achieve their mission. He'd kept the particulars of their plan from Aurang and had just given him a timeframe of when they would begin. Dividing his forces was necessary for mission success. It would enable him to hit the Krake from multiple angles of approach to their targets.

The soldiers aboard the Talon-Vs had spent the last twenty-four hours coasting through space—twenty-four hours in the same cramped space inside the same flight suits—and they had another twelve hours to go, at the very least, not to mention the time it would take after they delivered the payload to the space gate. They had one of the most crucial steps of the entire operation, and they had to send a small enough force to have the least chance of being detected by the enemy.

"Understood, Major," Sean said. "I know it's not easy staying out of the fight."

"I understand the reasoning, sir. It's the endgame that I don't particularly care for," Shelton replied.

In the event that the mission experienced complete failure, the *Yorktown* and the *Acheron* would egress through their own space gate. He couldn't leave the *Yorktown* completely defenseless, so he'd assigned the *Acheron* to stay with the *Yorktown* under the command of Lieutenant Sutton.

"I don't either, but we need to make sure we can account for anything and everything," Sean said with a lopsided smile.

"Maintenance checks on our space gate don't fill me with

confidence, sir. We've been patching this together as we've gone, and some things are starting to wear out," Shelton said.

What had started out as a prototype mobile space gate had become a cobbled-together piece that contained components stolen from a Krake space gate to keep it operational. "It just needs to work one time for as long as we need it to."

"I have maintenance crews working on it now, and they'll remain working on it until the end of this mission. No matter what, that gate will be operational for you when the time comes," Shelton said.

Sean had considered moving Vanessa to one of the destroyers, but he needed her right where she was, and they both knew it.

"Aurang and our Spec Ops team have already left and are even now speeding ahead. They should reach their target three hours ahead of us," Sean said.

"The Krake are even more paranoid about their security than we initially thought. Who puts the authenticator for a secure facility on the planet on a monitoring station that orbits around the planet?"

"Don't forget the lunar base," Sean said.

Aurang had informed them that there was a mining facility on the lunar base because of the rich deposits of minerals they'd found there. "We have a good plan," Sean continued. "The Talon-Vs will disable the space gate while we disable the communication capabilities from the other Krake targets. It should keep them off balance while Aurang and our Spec Ops team reach their target."

Sean didn't trust Aurang or that part of the plan, which was why he had a few combat shuttles designated to run rescue operations should the need arise.

"I wish we had more time," Shelton began to say and then stopped. "I know I've said it before, sir. All the parts are moving. I just wish there was more I could do. The entire crew of the *Yorktown* feels the same way. You'll be in our thoughts and prayers, sir."

"Thank you for that," Sean said. "Good luck, Major."

"You as well, Colonel."

The subspace comlink went dark and Sean sat back in his chair. He glanced at Oriana for a moment, who was busy working at her console.

"Gabriel," Sean said quietly, "I need to run a few calculations by you." He didn't know why, but most people assumed—and by that he meant scientists and other specialists—that he couldn't do the same level of math they could. If anything, his parents had made sure that Sean had a good education, and the fact that he'd tested so highly in multiple fields had served him well on more than one occasion. Sean was a military man, but he could easily have been one of the specialists like Oriana.

"Okay, Gabriel. Let's begin."

# 21

CHAD BOSEMAN HAD BEEN on more high-risk missions in the past eighteen months than in his entire military career. The reports they filed carried the acronym LPS, which stood for "low probability of success." Among the Spec Ops team there was a different ranking system for these types of missions, and that carried the acronym CD—certainty of death. The CD for this mission wasn't quite at the highest rank. He'd read the mission reports from when General Gates had stormed the Vemus Alpha ship and saved the entire colony. If a mission like that rated the number ten in terms of life expectancy, then this one was a solid eight in his professional opinion.

The entire Spec Ops platoon was in their Nexstar combat suits aboard a rundown Krake transport ship, which could've been a shuttle at one time but looked more like it had been converted for salvage runs. The ship's components hadn't quite vibrated when they'd done their initial burn to speed away from the *Vigilant*, but it had been a close thing. They were all on their own life support despite Aurang's assurances that the atmosphere in the ship would meet their requirements. None of them wanted to breathe the air on a Krake ship.

Aurang was the only one who communicated with them, even though there were five other Krake fifth column fighters aboard.

"I'm surprised they don't call themselves freedom fighters," Corporal Brentworth said.

They'd been aboard the ship for over twelve hours, which was long enough to become more comfortable even though they were on an enemy ship.

"So, we're helping freedom fighters," Brentworth continued.

"Are you kidding me?" Bowren said.

Bowren was in a combat suit heavy configuration and took up a lot more room than the rest of them. The man liked big guns, and it suited him.

"No, I'm not. What's wrong with calling them freedom fighters?" Brentworth asked. Then he looked at Chad.

"You need to study some history," Chad replied. "You know how many groups called themselves 'freedom fighters' who were actually little more than terrorists?" The faceplates on the combat suit were transparent because the armored cross section wasn't engaged, so he could see Brentworth's frown.

"They told us they were rebelling against those overseers," Brentworth replied.

"Yeah, and we can't trust everything they say," Bowren said.

Benton, who'd been unusually quiet, burped loudly. They were all on a shared comlink, but Benton had a habit of leaving his on, much to everyone's chagrin.

"Watch out now," Bowren said and grinned. "Sarge is going to lose it."

Benton grinned, which had started out as a groan. "Not likely."

Chad looked at Benton. "Are you sick? For real, did you catch a stomach virus or something?"

"Negative, Captain, just my insides are a bit scrambled."

Chad regarded him for a moment. Benton *had* been unusually quiet. He opened a private comlink to Benton. "What's going on?"

Benton sighed. "It's been a while since I've been in zero-G, sir."

Chad frowned. "You're telling me you're nauseous because of the zero-G we experienced for a few minutes before we did our burn?"

"No, sir. You know I can take that. It's . . . I just got a little bit of payback, that's all." He was quiet for a second. "Remember that request we got . . . well, *I* got?"

"You're telling me that Dr. Evans did this to you?"

"Not exactly. It was Eugena."

Chad remembered Eugena. Anyone who saw her wouldn't likely forget her anytime soon. She was definitely easy on the eyes. He snickered. "What did they do to you?"

"Well, they asked for my help. They said they needed a volunteer out on the flight deck—someone who could keep a clear head. So, I met them out there. They had me out on the second level. I know you told me to stay away from them, but the galley is a free area, sir. I was respectful," Benton said. "So, Eugena was standing there with a cup of coffee, and she held it out to me. When I went to grab it, she stepped back. Beneath me was the artificial gravity emitter. They reversed the field and had me dangling in the air."

Chad laughed and the others joined in. He'd opened the channel back up so everyone could hear the story.

"*Ha ha*, very funny. Yeah, I know," Benton said.

"How long did they leave you out there?" Chad asked.

"It wasn't so much the length of time but the transference to other emitter fields. They moved me in every direction possible —up, down, sideways, upside down. You name it; they did it. But I told them to. I told them I could take it, and I did," Benton said.

Chad nodded in understanding. There were certain personality traits that were almost a prerequisite for joining Spec Ops. They all rose to the challenge to prove themselves in almost everything that came across their paths.

"Was it worth it?" Brentworth asked.

Benton tilted his head to the side and swallowed a burp. "I got her to agree to meet me for a drink when we get back home. What do you think? I told you she liked me," he said and chuckled a little. "I'd do it all again."

Chad shook his head. Benton wasn't kidding. Not giving up was another character trait they looked for in recruits.

Two of the Krake fifth column soldiers ran past them toward the rear of the ship and the Spec Ops team engaged their helmet protection. They had entered the planet's atmosphere, and if everything had gone according to plan, they were over eight hundred kilometers from the south pole. Their target was in the frigid south, where the Krake ran clandestine operations on this Ovarrow world. They'd entered the atmosphere and were flying low to blend in with the frozen landscape.

"Sounds like our plan just took a turn," Bowren said.

Chad stood up and went toward the cockpit. Several violent

shudders moved through the ship, and Chad had to brace himself.

"Are we under attack?" Chad asked.

They were heading toward a massive storm system, and since they were this far to the south, there were likely blizzard conditions on the ground.

Aurang was flying the ship. "No attack. The ship is breaking. We'll need to secure other options for escape."

Chad glanced at a smaller holoscreen in front of Aurang's copilot. It was showing some kind of video feed. The copilot glanced at him and quickly turned off the screen, but for a second he'd seen an arch. They weren't supposed to be anywhere near an arch on this mission.

"You should secure yourself. This landing won't be soft," Aurang said.

"I thought the arch was on the other side of the compound," Chad said.

"It is, but we also know that this is where we need to secure transport for our escape," Aurang said.

There was a loud bang from the rear of the ship, and they began to lose altitude. Chad looked at the holoscreen and saw that they were heading directly for a building near their target, but now they were veering off course. This was supposed to be a quiet operation.

Chad turned around and went back to his men. "Get ready. This is going to be a bumpy ride."

The storm was getting worse. Ice shards pelted the Krake ship. Then, large chunks of ice slammed into the side of the ship. They just had to hold on a little bit longer until they reached their destination. The storm, despite doing its utmost to bring the ship down, was a blessing because it covered their approach. They couldn't have asked for better cover than what they had.

Something large slammed into the ship, causing one side to suddenly drop downward. There was a loud tearing sound, and gusts of wind sucked out of the hole in the rear of the craft. Chad watched as the two Krake soldiers held on. The ship banked to the side and sank even farther. Then they crashed.

The Krake ship slid on its side for a few moments before the nose wedged itself into the ground, but they had too much momentum and the ship flipped into the air, snapping off the front of the vessel. But when they finally came to a stop, they were still secure in their seats.

Chad checked the combat suit statuses for his team, and they were all green. They'd survived the crash. The two Krake soldiers in the rear of the ship untangled themselves and headed outside. Aurang left the cockpit, followed by two more soldiers, and all of them left the ship. The blizzard was in full swing, blowing so hard that it was difficult to see. The combat suit systems adjusted the display, clearing the way in front of them as best they could. Chad saw that they weren't far from their destination. There was a small city laid out like a spider, with domed living spaces at the ends of long tunnels. There were no roads in. They were isolated.

Chad glanced behind him, and so did Brentworth. "Is it working?" he asked quietly.

Brentworth was carrying a modified field kit that contained a subspace communication device. It was big and bulky, and if it didn't work, it wasn't worth carrying.

"It's green across the board, Captain," Brentworth said, sounding relieved.

They went to one of the buildings on the outskirts. Aurang was able to open the door and they all went inside.

"Captain, I'll need a few moments to confirm the precise location for the uplink," Aurang said.

He was flanked by his two companions while the remaining two watched them.

"Is he serious?" Benton said. "We had a target, and they need to confirm the location?"

Chad didn't reply. Instead, he glanced over to the side where Vladek had circled around so he could have a good view of the console.

Aurang finished what he was doing and turned back toward Chad and the others. "There's been a complication. The area we need to get to has several maintenance crews nearby, along with soldiers. It's probably because of the storm, but there are a lot of defenses active."

"Did they detect us?" Chad asked.

"No, there's only a general warning about the poor weather. I'm going to need you to draw the soldiers away so we can get in to access the communications network. We don't have much time."

Chad was aware of the time constraints. There was a scheduled uplink that was to be engaged from the planet and relayed through the space gate. They had to have their dummy data uploaded by that time, because after that, the space gate would become inoperable, courtesy of the Talon-V squadrons en route to do just that.

"We can draw them off and then meet up with you," Chad said.

Aurang was quiet for a moment. Maybe he'd expected Chad

to protest splitting up their forces. “Very well. We'll meet up at this location here.”

This was the communication hub for the entire star system. Everything was routed through this location, but the authentication was handled through the monitoring station in orbit, which was then relayed to the space gate. Once all those things lined up, they'd proceed with an update to the Krake version of COMCENT. It was also the time they'd receive official updates from whatever command structure the Krake had.

“Captain, I cannot overstate the importance of this. You must get those soldiers out of there in order for us to access this area. Here are the schematics of this place,” Aurang said. “Are you able to perform this task?”

“We'll get the job done. You just deliver on your promise to us.”

“I haven't forgotten, Captain,” Aurang said. Then he and the other Krake soldiers left them.

Outside, the Spec Ops team gathered.

“So now we're a diversionary force,” Benton said.

“That's what *they* think,” Chad said and gestured toward Vladek. “We're heading to the main complex, and once we distract those soldiers, I need you to access this specific console. There should be a linkup there.”

The console was farther from the one Aurang was using, but it was their closest option. Krake communication protocols for high-level access were unique for secure systems. They hadn't had time to duplicate it, so they had to use what was already in place if they wanted to access the same uplink systems.

“I see it,” Vladek replied. “I monitored how Aurang accessed the system, and I should be able to do the same.”

"Remember, we need the most recent updates sent and received. We don't have time for a broad search, so we need to narrow it down to core system targets," Chad said.

"Yes, sir."

They made their way toward their target. They were moving around the outside but there weren't many windows in the complex, and Chad guessed the Krake weren't concerned with looking outside.

"Bowren, let's open some walls up. Target that building over there. It's some kind of processing center. Should be important enough for them to go and investigate," Chad said.

Bowren grinned hungrily. "My specialty, sir."

"Don't wait around for any company. Meet up with us after," Chad said.

They moved into position and then heard an explosion over the howling winds. Chad watched as Bowren sent more explosive charges inside the building, and a few seconds later those explosives detonated, causing massive destruction.

"They had to have heard that," Benton said.

Vladek got the door open and the Spec Ops team went inside. Aurang had expected them to remain outside and circle around to the rendezvous point, but Chad wasn't taking any chances. They had their own objective inside. He just hoped the schematics Aurang had given him were accurate. Otherwise, all the soldiers they'd lured away would come looking for them.

"Sir, I see Krake soldiers heading to the area. We're heading back to you," Bowren said.

They went down the corridor, and near the end was a cross section. Several Krake soldiers ran past, but the last few stopped. One of them gestured toward the Spec Ops team.

Before they could raise an alarm, the CDF soldiers fired their weapons and stopped them.

They ran past the dead Krake, heading away from where the others had gone. They had a target to reach. They headed farther into the building's interior, navigating through open doors and taking out Krake along the way.

There were multiple access rooms that linked to the core comms system, and the Spec Ops team wondered if Aurang would be able to detect when they accessed the system and whether he'd try to stop them. They entered the room and took out the Krake inside.

There was a phalanx of consoles, but Vladek went to a smaller one off to the side. "I'm in, sir. I'll need some time to gather what we need."

Access to this system and the data on it would give them valuable insight into how the Krake operated across the multiverse. Hopefully, it also contained references to the Krake home system where the overseers resided. If they could learn that location, they might be able to end this war before it actually began.

"Sir, I can see what Aurang is doing. They've successfully uploaded their updates and . . ." Vladek said, pausing for a moment, ". . . authentication is complete. Scheduled uplink is about to initiate."

Chad had wanted to add a search for a reference to their home universe, but Sean had denied the request. The risk was too great because the Krake might be able to bring up Vladek's session and trace everything he'd done. They didn't need to point the Krake at New Earth by leaving a search history, despite assurances from Aurang that they could cover their tracks.

"Data transferred and received," Vladek said. A few moments later, he stepped away from the console. "We got it, sir."

"Good work. Let's head to the waypoint," Chad said.

He checked the operations schedule on his internal heads-up display. They were right on schedule. Now they just had to find a way off the planet.

# 22

The *Vigilant* was approaching the equatorial line of the NEC. The *Dutchman* and the *Babylon* were both several thousand kilometers away on different approach vectors in the northern and southern hemispheres of the planet. The *Vigilant*'s target was the main monitoring station in low orbit on the other side of the planet, while the secondary and tertiary targets of the CDF destroyers were the Krake communication satellites that were always pointed at the space gate. According to Aurang, at least one of those satellites had a direct line to the gate, which was located on the other side of the moon.

The best approach for reaching their targets undetected was to use a gravitational assist from the actual NEC. Sean had ordered their approach vector at a specific velocity so they could also orbit the planet for several revolutions without overly taxing their inertia dampeners.

Sean sat in the commander's chair, monitoring their approach, while the crew on the bridge went about their tasks, completely focused. The best scanners in the universe couldn't penetrate through a planet. Line of sight was still a major factor in space warfare. The Ovarrow who lived on this planet were not a spacefaring race, and according to Aurang, they hadn't grown beyond an industrial age. The Krake wouldn't tell them very much, other than that this planet was a simulation where a multitude of tests were being conducted. If the Krake were running simulations on an entire planet of Ovarrow, the number of tests could be impossibly large.

So far, everything Aurang had told them about the defenses had been truthful.

"Colonel, gamma burst activity has been detected, which matches the activity of a space gate," Lieutenant Scott said.

"That will be the scheduled check-in Aurang told us about," Sean said.

He checked their velocity and time to intercept the target. If they arrived too soon, the Krake would be aware of their presence and call for reinforcements. The key to this entire operation was to strike at precise times across all the teams in order to cripple the Krake's ability to respond. Talon-V squadrons were on their final approaches to the space gate, while Charlie team was performing its own orbital assist to cripple the Krake lunar base. Sean was quite familiar with the combat tactic of hitting the enemy where they believed they were safe, and the lack of Krake ships in this system seemed to indicate that the Krake hadn't anticipated an attack here.

"Forward mag cannons locked on target," Lieutenant Scott said.

"Ops, what's the status of the space gate?" Sean asked.

"Still generating gamma waves, sir," Lieutenant Burrows replied.

Once they fired their weapons, there was no going back. They were close enough that the velocity of the slug from the mag cannon would hit the monitoring station before their target had a chance to react. If they used midrange missiles, there was a chance the Krake would detect the attack.

The forward mag cannons were built into the superstructure of the *Vigilant*. Sean had already given his authorization to fire, and Gabriel was programmed with the exact time to do so. At the same time, the *Dutchman*'s and the *Babylon*'s single forward cannons would fire their armament as well.

"Shots away," Lieutenant Scott confirmed.

Sean looked at Burrows and she shook her head. The space gate was still active. This was going to be close. Sean watched as the seconds ticked by.

"Gamma burst has ceased," Burrows said.

"Target has been hit. No alerts on any of the known Krake communication channels," Lieutenant Scott said.

"The *Dutchman* and the *Babylon* each report successfully destroying their targets," Specialist Sansky said.

"Acknowledged. Good job, people," Sean said. "Helm, adjust our heading to coordinates bravo."

"Adjusting course to coordinates bravo, sir," Edwards said.

Maneuvering thrusters became active, and the *Vigilant*'s heading began to change. They were soon flying over the southern polar region of the planet.

"Sir, I'm detecting Krake attack drones. They're hard astern of us," Lieutenant Scott said.

The plot on the main holoscreen began to populate with marks for the attack drones.

"Where are they coming from?" Sean said.

"Sir, they're coming from the planet. No Krake warships have been detected," Lieutenant Scott said.

"Ready HADES Vs. I need a firing solution on the attack drones. Ops, alert the other ships. Tell them to find alternate orbital paths," Sean said.

His orders were confirmed.

"Aurang betrayed us," Russo said.

"Maybe. Either he didn't know or he didn't tell us," Sean replied. "Comms, open subspace comlinks to the other teams. Warn them that the Krake have other defenses in place."

HADES V missiles fired from the *Vigilant*, staggering their approaches to the oncoming swarm of attack drones. The lead missiles detonated, blinding the attack drones and temporarily disabling them, and then the second wave gouged their numbers. But more attack drones kept appearing on the scope. The *Vigilant* was too far away to take out the facility. They needed to get out of there.

Sean did a quick calculation based on the number of HADES V missiles they had and the rate the Krake were replenishing their attack drones. This was a numbers game, and the numbers weren't in favor of the *Vigilant*.

"Colonel, I have a subspace comms from Captain Boseman," Sansky said.

"Put him through to me," Sean replied. He could hear the distinct sound of weapons being fired in the background.

"Colonel, Krake forces are arriving through an arch here in the southern complex. Aurang crashed our ship and we are unable to leave," Boseman said.

"Is Aurang with you?"

"Negative, sir. We're unable to reach the rendezvous point. We need extraction."

"Acknowledged. Deploying combat shuttles to your position. Send them your beacon," Sean said.

Sean studied the main holoscreen. Krake attack drones were flying toward them, and the HADES V missile defense screen could only buy them so much time. But he wasn't going to leave those men behind. He had fifteen minutes to come up with a way to rescue the Spec Ops team on the ground and get them to their own space gate.

# 23

THE FIREFIGHT HAD BEEN brief but intense, and Chad ordered his men to keep moving. There were two combat shuttles on the way, and he had sent them a waypoint for extraction. The video feed from the reconnaissance drone he had hovering near the arch showed Krake soldiers coming through. Reinforcements had arrived. Chad had lost four men so far, and he'd had their combat suits self-destruct what remained of them. They couldn't leave any trace behind.

"That bastard." Benton scowled. "Looks like Aurang and his people found a way off this rock."

Aurang had avoided the Krake soldiers and made his way to one of the landing zones where he'd secured a ship. The Krake shuttlecraft looked to be powering up.

"Captain, Krake comms chatter contains references to a report that has information about Trident Battle Group," Vladek said.

"Son of a—" Chad started to say and stopped. He gritted his

teeth and shook his head. They had monitored Aurang closely, but somehow the Krake rebel had deceived them. He was playing both sides of this.

"Captain, should we warn the *Vigilant*?" Vladek asked.

Chad's first instinct was to do just that. "Negative. The trap has been sprung. Brentworth, I need you to prepare the data we've gathered for a subspace comlink burst. Vladek, help him."

They were outside, sticking close to the buildings and using them for cover. The Nexstar combat suits assisted their movements with relatively low energy expenditure from the wearers. One way or another, they would get the data where it needed to go, even if they couldn't make it off this planet.

They had to move quickly, and the storm provided some cover, but the Krake had an idea of their position. Within minutes, they were on the outskirts of the small city.

A comlink registered to his combat suit.

"Captain Boseman, this is Lieutenant Franco. I'll be at the waypoint position in under a minute. We're flying low and fast, so be ready," she said.

"We'll be here," Chad replied. The comlink closed, and he knew they wouldn't hear the combat shuttles approaching in this storm.

Suddenly, a bright flash from behind them lit up the sky. Then, a blue beam of light fired from the center of the city out toward them. It cut a swath right through the blizzard, illuminating the area above them. The beam then swept the area above them, and Chad watched helplessly as the two CDF combat shuttles exploded. As the Spec Ops platoon dove for cover, the remains of the shuttles descended over the snow-covered ground. After the beam of light stopped, Chad stood up. He scanned the area and saw a flaming wreck with the two combat shuttles raining down all around them.

"Did anyone see where that came from?" Chad asked.

"Looked like it came from the central building in city," Benton said.

Chad clenched his teeth and peered through the blizzard, trying to get a look at whatever the Krake had just fired at them. If they went back into the city, they'd have to face the Krake soldiers. They needed to find another way out.

"Brentworth, I need a subspace comlink to the *Vigilant*, now," Chad said. A few moments later, he had the link. "Colonel, both shuttles are down. The Krake have a defense weapon, and it targeted them. We didn't know it was there. Uploading a data burst of the data we extracted from the Krake's systems. Can you confirm receipt?"

"Yeah, we got it," Sean said.

Benton gestured toward the city and told him that the Krake soldiers were heading in their direction.

"Captain, can you find another ship?"

"Negative, Colonel. All ships are on the other side of the city with too many of the enemy. There's no landing zone nearby. The approach is bad, and the extraction zone is too hot," Chad said. He ordered his men to take cover and get ready to fight.

"I'm sending another shuttle down to you," Sean said.

"It's too hot. We can't reach that weapon to take it out, and Krake soldiers are closing in on us. That data is why we came here. Take it and go," Chad said.

"That's not how this works. Hold your position. That's an order, Captain. Acknowledge."

Chad gritted his teeth. "Holding position. Copy that, sir."

# 24

"OPS, get another combat shuttle ready. I'm not abandoning those men," Sean said.

"Sir, did Captain Boseman say what kind of weapon the Krake were using?" Russo asked.

Sean glanced at his XO. "It's some kind of energy weapon. He did say it was a bright blue beam, which is probably like the Colossus cannon we use for city defenses back on New Earth. It's perfect for atmospheric defense. Probably wouldn't do anything to us up here, though. They didn't have the exact coordinates for it."

"We can't make a precision shot with the information we have, but we can create a firing solution for a bombardment run. It might give our shuttle and the Spec Ops team enough cover for an extraction," Russo said.

Sean frowned. That was a hell of a lot of guesswork, given the conditions down there. They could see the storm system. "We'll risk hitting our own men."

Russo glanced at the main holoscreen and then looked back at Sean. "Colonel, I can do this. Let me give those men one last shot."

Jane Russo had been his tactical officer for years and he knew her capabilities. If she said she could do it, then she could do it.

"Very well," Sean said.

Russo turned her attention to her personal holoscreen and got to work.

"Helm, adjust speed to allow time for a bombardment run," Sean said.

"Colonel, slowing our velocity will allow the Krake attack drones to reach the ship. A successful evacuation of the ground forces to this ship is impossible," Gabriel said.

"Acknowledged," Sean replied. "Comms, open a comlink to the *Dutchman*."

A few moments later, Captain Oliver Martinez appeared on his personal holoscreen. "Captain, listen up. I don't have a lot of time. I have a shuttle en route to extract our Spec Ops team on the ground. It's a hot zone. We're about to blanket the area with heavy fire, but we're unable to secure the evac. Can you give our guys a window and scoop them up?"

"Receiving new mission objective, sir," Martinez said and looked away from his screen for a few moments. "I have the course. We'll pick our guys up but, sir—" he said and stopped.

"After you retrieve the Spec Ops team, head directly to the *Yorktown*. Our gate will be up for your return to New Earth," Sean said.

"Colonel, have the *Babylon* run the evac up. Let us take some of the tactical burden from the *Vigilant*," Martinez said.

"Negative, Captain. I need you on this. There are dozens of

ways this could go, and I need an experienced captain to get our guys out of there. *Vigilant* out," Sean said and severed the comlink. He looked at Russo, who was still putting together a firing solution.

He opened a comlink to the *Babylon,* and Lieutenant Richard Pitts's face appeared on his personal holoscreen. "Lieutenant Pitts, you have just about enough time to use a gravitational assist to break out of the orbit and return to the *Yorktown*."

"Understood, sir." Pitts looked off-screen for a moment. "We can assist you."

Sean looked away from the holoscreen and closed his eyes for a moment. *Dammit, Ward*, Sean thought. Captain Ryan Ward had been the *Babylon*'s captain until he'd turned mutineer.

"Colonel, I know I'm not Captain Ward, but the *Babylon* is ready to assist you. Let me add our combat capabilities to your defense plans. We can increase the odds," Pitts said.

Pitts had been one of Sean's critics about how he'd handled the mutiny; now he was willing to lay down his life to make sure their mission succeeded. Sean looked at the young man. "Stand by, Lieutenant." He then looked at his XO.

"Firing solution ready, sir," Russo said.

"Execute, XO's discretion," Sean said and turned back to his holoscreen. "Lieutenant Pitts, maintain course and heading. We're coming to you."

---

BOSEMAN FINISHED READING the message and called the others over, then opened the comlink to the rest of the platoon.

"There's another shuttle coming, but our egress point is half a klick away in an open area."

"Captain," Benton said, "Krake soldiers are already on their way here. They have our position."

"A shuttle can't get close enough to take out that Krake weapon," Vladek said.

"The *Vigilant* is going to bombard the area, and we need to get clear. In this weather, there's no way for them to make precision shots. They'll do their best to avoid us, but we have to move. Sergeant Benton, send a recon drone ahead. Maybe there's someplace we can get cover."

Boseman saw the recon drone zip away. He lost visual but could track its movement through his internal heads-up display.

---

"KRAKE ATTACK DRONES within point defense range, Colonel," Lieutenant Scott said.

"Acknowledged," Sean said.

They had altered their course so that the bow of the ship was pointed directly down toward the planet, and the forward mag cannons sent a volley in rapid succession to the target area. The helmsman altered course and increased their velocity. Sean didn't want the *Vigilant* to break from the planet's orbit. He had to maintain the angle to utilize the gravitational assist so he could line up with the *Yorktown*. This would require them to orbit the planet one more time.

---

Above the howling winds, they heard loud pops, and streaks of red blazed down from above, heading to the city.

"Move!" Boseman shouted.

The Spec Ops platoon ran from cover and headed to the waypoint as the small Krake city felt the wrath of the *Vigilant*'s weapons. Muted explosions sounded like deep impact wells in high snowdrifts. Krake soldiers fired on them as they ran. Bowren turned and returned fire from his heavy gauss cannon, causing the Krake soldiers to dive for cover, but there were more than a few who got caught in the spray.

There was an orange glow in the blizzard, and black smoke billowed in the howling winds above the city. The attack had been quick and catastrophic. A few of the Krake soldiers pursued them, but most were returning to the city.

Boseman tasked a recon drone to go behind them and make sure the Krake weren't going to follow them. Less than a minute later, the Krake soldiers had turned around and were once again heading right for them. Someone over there knew what it meant to command. Boseman would've chewed out any soldier who'd dared to let the enemy get away from a city they'd just destroyed.

"They're coming. Where's the shuttle?" Vladek said.

Boseman kept thinking he heard the high-pitched whine of a combat shuttle, but it was just the wind. They ran as best they could, but the snow was getting deeper, and he hoped they didn't accidentally fall through to a major cavern beneath them. They didn't have time to rescue anyone if that happened. As the Spec Ops team ran, the bombardment finished and Boseman glanced off to the side, seeing deep crevices begin to form. The ground lurched beneath his feet, and he felt as if he was sliding on a board of ice and snow that was thousands of square feet.

A flash of light appeared ahead of them and a comlink connected to his suit. It was the combat shuttle. The shuttle spun around and the loading ramp lowered. The pilot couldn't land the shuttle, so it hovered in the air.

"Get on the shuttle, quickly," Boseman said.

He climbed onto the ramp and turned around. The Krake soldiers who were pursuing them fired their weapons. He and several soldiers stayed at the bottom of the ramp and returned fire while the rest of the platoon raced to get on.

"Bowren, if you don't get your ass up there, we're going to leave you here," Boseman said.

Bowren turned and leaped toward the loading ramp. Bright flashes of light came from Krake weapons as they fired on him. The combat suit heavy was pelted, and Bowren went down by the sheer force of it.

Boseman raced up the loading ramp and grabbed a metallic tether cable. In seconds, he had vaulted down to Bowren and quickly wrapped the tether cable around him. CDF soldiers returned fire from the loading ramp. The engines engaged and the combat shuttle rose into the air. They were retracted to the loading ramp and helped onboard. Bowren's suit had taken damage, but he was all right. They'd made it.

Boseman walked toward the cockpit and looked at the two shuttle pilots. "Thanks for pulling our asses out of the fire. Where's the *Vigilant*?"

"Several thousand kilometers away from here, Captain. Go strap yourself in. We're meeting up with the *Dutchman,* and then we're getting the hell out of here," the pilot said.

Boseman turned around and headed back to find a seat, ordering his men to strap themselves in. Even though they were off the ground, it sounded like things were just as hot up here as they had been below. They weren't out of this yet.

---

SEAN DIDN'T KNOW why the Krake attack drones hadn't increased their velocity to catch up with him. Perhaps it was because there was something interfering with their navigation system or some other limitation they hadn't accounted for. He could only deal with the situation as it was, which meant that if there were any Krake attack drones left when he finally broke free of the planet's gravitational pull, they'd be able to catch up to his ship before he could reach the *Yorktown*.

"Colonel, I'm detecting a gamma burst from the Krake space gate," Lieutenant Scott said.

"Are you sure? The space gate was disabled. The Talon-V squadrons reported successfully taking out the alignment controls so the gateway couldn't form," Sean said.

"These readings are accurate. Charlie team has already picked up the Talon-Vs and they're heading back to the *Yorktown*," Lieutenant Scott said.

Sean frowned for a moment. It would take them too much time to change their course and stop whatever was happening with the space gate.

"Colonel," Specialist Sansky said, "I have a . . . It's Aurang, sir."

Sean clenched his teeth. "On my screen."

A moment later, Aurang's face appeared on his screen. "There's been a change in our plans. I congratulate you on a successful mission execution. We wouldn't have achieved our mission objective without you."

"You double-crossed us! You left my team on the planet, and you've activated the space gate that we thought had been sabotaged."

"We have fulfilled our end of the bargain. I confirmed with Captain Boseman that they had the data they sought. I'm aware of their operations. Therefore, our temporary alliance is concluded. It has been quite enlightening."

"Aurang, I'm going to hunt you down. I'll have my own update sent to your overseers," Sean said.

"Only if you manage to survive," Aurang said and severed the comlink.

Sean cursed and snarled. He looked at Lieutenant Scott.

"Krake warships are coming through the space gate, sir."

He'd covered all his bases, but once again, his plans were coming up short. There were a few moments of heavy silence on the bridge at the stark realization that they weren't going to get away this time. Sean inhaled explosively and then sighed. "Comms, open a subspace communication link to the *Yorktown*."

A few moments later, Major Shelton appeared on his personal holoscreen and he gave her a tactical update of the situation. "I'm sending a data burst to you now. This is the data we've collected from the Krake."

"Confirm receipt of the data," Major Shelton said.

"You're to open a gateway back to our universe. I want all ships to go through as soon as they reach you," Sean said.

He saw the conflicting emotions on her face, but she didn't make the protest she wanted to. She understood the tactical implications of their current position. This time, Sean had played the odds and was going to lose.

"It'll be close, but the *Dutchman* should be able to reach you."

"Colonel," Major Shelton began.

"Hold the gate open for as long as you can, but no heroics. Is that understood, Major?"

Vanessa met his gaze. "Understood, Colonel. Godspeed, sir."

The comlink severed.

Sean leaned back in his chair and tried to think of something he could do to get them out of this. He glanced at the main holoscreen and saw that the intercept course he'd laid in to meet up with the *Babylon* was only minutes away. The *Dutchman* had reported the successful pickup of the remaining Spec Ops team. This mission had cost them.

Sean stood up and walked over to the tactical workstation, and Captain Russo joined him. He looked back up at the command area and saw Oriana staring intently at her console.

"How many HADES Vs do we have left?" he asked.

Lieutenant Scott brought it up on his screen. "Not that many, sir."

"Get them into the tubes. We can at least stall those attack drones and then make our best speed to the *Yorktown*," Sean said.

"That will get us away from the planet, but what about the Krake warships that just entered the system?" Captain Russo asked.

"It's a race. I don't know if we can win it, but I'm certainly going to try. We can have the *Babylon* fly in tight formation with us, and that might buy us a little bit of time," Sean said.

Russo looked away from him and he knew she was trying to come up with an alternative that had a higher probability of success.

Sean returned to the commander's chair. He looked around the bridge, feeling like a failure. He'd let all these people down by thinking he could achieve this mission and return home.

They completed the last leg of their orbital assist and broke away from the planet's gravitational pull. The *Vigilant* launched all its remaining HADES V missiles and the *Babylon* did the same. The two ships sped away from the planet. Active scans showed that Krake warships were trying to intercept them, but despite being faster than the CDF ships, they wouldn't be able to. They'd have to chase them, but they'd be well within the attack drones' range before they reached the *Yorktown*.

Sean looked at Oriana, and she finally looked back at him. "We have to try it," he said.

"It's not ready."

"It's our only option. The attack drones will eventually get past our point defense systems. If that happens, we won't even be able to try."

Oriana looked away for a moment. "The power requirements for sustained output will deplete the reactor cores on our ship. The *Babylon* can't even do it."

"If the *Babylon* is ahead of us, they won't have to do it."

Oriana was quiet for a moment. "I understand that, but if it doesn't work at all, then . . ."

Sean knew what she was about to say. With all the ship's power devoted to what they were about to try, they wouldn't be able to bring the point defense systems back up in time. It was all or nothing.

"Colonel, I'm not following this conversation. Can you tell me what's going on?" Russo asked.

"There might be a way to increase our defenses against the

Krake attack drones, but it's never been tried and it's unconventional."

Russo's gaze flicked toward Oriana and then back at Sean. "What is it?"

"It's gravity," Oriana said. "It's the only thing I could think of that might affect the Krake attack drones. When they're active, they can generate heat equivalent to that of a G-type main sequence star. So, I realized the only thing that could withstand that kind of heat is gravity. Gravity is what keeps a star together."

Russo frowned and looked at Sean. "You want to generate an artificial gravity field that's capable of stopping the attack drones from reaching the ship?"

"Something like that, but the power requirements are enormous, and there's a bit of a debate on whether it will just stop the attack drones or cause them to be unable to reach us—almost like they're on a slippery surface," Sean said and looked at Oriana. "I understand you have reservations, but it's my call. Comms, give me a broadcast to the ship."

"Ready, sir," Specialist Sansky said.

"Crew of the *Vigilant*, this is Colonel Quinn. Everyone is to go to their emergency stations. All nonessential personnel are to secure themselves in escape pods. We're about to try something that's never been done before. If we don't do this, the Krake warships will catch up to us before we can reach our space gate. It's a numbers game, and our point defense systems cannot stop all the attack drones heading for us. Set Condition Emergency."

They were making best speed to the space gate, and Sean ordered their braking thrusters to fire, allowing the *Babylon* to move ahead of them. Lieutenant Pitts followed his orders without question.

"Emitters are charging," Gabriel said.

"I've only tried this with a single emitter in a lab on the hangar deck," Oriana said.

Sean kept his eyes on the main holoscreen. The Krake warships had launched hundreds of attack drones that were speeding toward them. He imagined they looked like a swarm of bright fireflies flying in formation, streaking toward his ship with the promise of death and destruction.

"I know that. You had a brilliant idea, but I know this ship," Sean said. "Gabriel, you'll need to update the configuration of our inertia dampeners."

Everyone on the bridge returned to their seats and strapped themselves in. Condition Emergency required everyone on board the ship to secure themselves in such a fashion and go on personal life support.

Their point defense systems stopped as the power draw was redirected to the inertia dampeners and artificial gravity emitters used on the ship. They were essentially reversing the direction and projecting it to a point beyond the ship. This meant that they would lose artificial gravity inside. They'd be in a bubble.

The power requirements were such that all non-critical power was diverted and weapons systems went on standby. The calculations for the power adjustment to their artificial gravity emitters had to be done by Gabriel. Only the ship's AI could update the calculations based on available power and prevent them from overloading. A miscalculation with the emitters would tear the ship apart.

The lighting on the bridge dimmed as they went to

emergency power. Sean gripped the arms of his chair and glanced at Oriana.

"Projecting artificial gravity field around the ship, sir," Gabriel said.

Sean watched as the power spiked across all reactors aboard the ship. Sensor and video feeds didn't show them anything. Gravity was invisible, but its effects could be observed.

The nearest Krake attack drones experienced a deceleration a few kilometers from the ship. Several groups of attack drones tried to circle around the ship, but they were caught in the field and couldn't move.

"Gabriel, can you compress the field? Can you bunch them up together?"

"Calculating," Gabriel said. "Affirmative, but this will deplete our fusion reactor cores quickly."

"Understood," Sean said. "Tactical, have the point defense systems target the attack drones."

They weren't far from the space gate. However, the *Yorktown* hadn't gone through. It was maintaining the gateway. Sean frowned. "Comms, get me Major Shelton."

"Major, what are you doing?" Sean asked.

"We abandoned the ship, sir. Self-destruction has been set. I calculated your trajectory. Maintain speed and you'll get through the gateway," Major Shelton said.

Sean felt a surge of hope. "Major . . ." he began but stopped. They'd have to thread the needle one more time.

"Colonel," Lieutenant Scott said, "point defense systems are not responsive. Power draw has limited my access."

Sean opened a comlink to the *Babylon*. A moment later Lieutenant Pitts appeared on his personal holoscreen.

"Lieutenant, I need you to ready a salvo of Hornet B missiles. Target coordinates incoming."

"Aye, sir," Lieutenant Pitts said.

Within the next few minutes, midrange Hornet B missiles were fired, targeted at the globular cluster of Krake attack drones. Sean watched as the power draw on their fusion reactor drained much quicker than he'd thought was possible. The Hornet missiles flew toward the Krake attack drones and came to a stop as they were caught in the artificial gravity field.

"Colonel, reactors are reaching critical levels," Gabriel said.

"Maintain speed and heading," Sean replied.

There were three fusion reactors aboard the *Vigilant*, and each operated with emergency shutdown procedures that would automatically engage. One after the other, they began to shut down, and the gravity field outside the ship began to fail. The *Babylon* transitioned through the space gate and was quickly followed by the *Vigilant*. The globular cluster of Krake attack drones followed next. Then, the *Yorktown*'s self-destruct engaged and a cataclysmic explosion destroyed both the ship and the space gate in the alternate universe. Perhaps, if they were even luckier, the explosion would take out a few Krake ships with it. In any case, there would be nothing left for the Krake warships to find.

The artificial gravity field failed when the last of the reactors aboard the *Vigilant* went into emergency shutdown and the Hornets unleashed their fury into the tightly packed Krake attack drones. But the *Vigilant* was too close. Klaxon alarms blared on the bridge as the stern of the ship was impacted by the force of the detonating Hornet missiles. Damage reports came to prominence on the main holoscreen, and the *Vigilant* switched to emergency power systems as sensor feeds went offline. They were blind to the outside, and Sean didn't know if there were any attack drones left.

An emergency comlink came from Major Shelton. "Sir, the remaining attack drones have been taken out. What's your status?"

Sean swallowed hard, trying to loosen the tightness of his shoulders. "It seems we're out of fuel. Do you think you can give us a ride?"

This drew several chuckles from people on the bridge, and Sean felt a profound sense of relief. They'd survived.

"I'll see what I can do," Major Shelton said and smiled. "Comms have lit up across the board. We're home, sir."

Sean sagged into his chair and blew out a long, slow breath. Somehow, they had done it. He looked at Oriana. "I think you've found a way to nullify the advantage of those attack drones."

"I don't know if I'd go that far. Look what it did to the ship," Oriana said.

The damage reports continued to come in. The rear of the ship had taken most of the damage, but there hadn't been any casualties. They had drilled for scenarios involving a sudden loss of power from the reactor cores, but never all three cores at once. A complete loss of all power to a CDF warship usually meant the ship was no longer operable, but the *Vigilant* wasn't dead, at least not yet. They had to examine the reactor cores and shielding. They'd probably need to be repaired or even replaced, but at least they were in the right universe to get the help they needed.

# 25

CONNOR HEARD the landing gear deploy and the gentle whine of the engines spinning down as the ship landed. It wasn't a large ship, and Bradley's recon drone had explored most of the ventilation shafts. The Krake ship must have been remotely piloted under the control of a sophisticated guidance system. This made sense to Connor because of the Krake's affinity for using attack drones, which were remotely controlled and somewhat autonomously guided.

"Dash, enable the privacy mode of your MPS. I don't want them to have a look at your face, no matter what happens," Connor said.

Corporal Bradley and Private Marsters wore Nexstar combat suits and would already be in combat mode. They knew better than to show their faces to the Krake, but there was very little they could do about Cerot. The Krake would be able to tell right away that he was an Ovarrow, and covering his face wouldn't change that.

Minutes went by as they waited in the holding rooms. Since Connor and Bradley were the only ones armed, he told her to wait for his signal. He would look for an opportunity for them to escape.

An interior wall slid into itself, revealing a doorway. There was a light coming from each end of the passageway. Connor stepped out of the room and glanced to his left. A short distance away was a loading ramp that had opened to the outside. He opened the comlink to the others with him, and as he suspected, the suppression field had been turned off since the ship had landed. They'd be able to speak to each other undetected by the Krake. Amber lights flared overhead, and Connor saw Ovarrow symbols appear above the exit.

Connor walked toward the exit and down the loading ramp. The others followed. They were in a hangar bay, but they were still on the planet. He glanced to the outside where a wide door was open. The ship must have flown through it in order to have landed where they had. He saw a semi-translucent shield at the edge of the door and attempted to open a comlink to Samson, but he got no reply. So, their comms must have been limited to the immediate area.

Three rows of Krake soldiers were standing near the loading ramp, and upon seeing Connor and the others, they pointed their weapons at them. They all wore that living-tissue armor that blended with powered armor. The nearest soldier spoke. Connor thought it sounded similar to the Ovarrow language, but there were differences. The Krake repeated himself, his voice sounding authoritative, but Connor had no idea what he was saying. And he didn't seem to care that Connor held a weapon.

Several Krake soldiers stomped toward them and Cerot

began shouting, gesturing toward Connor and the others. Then Cerot beckoned Connor and the others to stand away from the loading ramp. The Krake soldiers seem to be waiting for someone as they kept careful watch.

"Corporal, pass control of your drone over to me," Connor said quietly.

A moment later, the drone interface appeared on Connor's internal heads-up display. He uploaded an Ovarrow interface and sent it flying off. He needed it to find the nearest terminal, which would allow the data exfiltration software to begin copying from Krake computer systems. The small recon drone didn't have much in the way of data storage, but it could relay the information to any one of their combat suits, which had more capacity. If they needed to, they could chunk it into pieces on their individual suit computers.

Another Krake entered the hangar bay. He wore similar armor to the other soldiers, but his face was exposed. There were certain similarities to the Ovarrow, but there were also significant differences, as if they were cousins on the same evolutionary tree. There was an air of deference afforded the newcomer, which indicated to Connor that this Krake was in charge.

The Krake leader strode over to Cerot and scrutinized him closely. He noted Cerot's wounded side and then his gaze flicked toward the wrist computer that included the Ovarrow translator. The Krake spoke to Cerot, but the Ovarrow remained silent. He stared defiantly at the ground as if refusing to acknowledge the Krake's presence. Several soldiers stormed over and grabbed Cerot by his arms, pulling him away from the others. They forced him to hold out his arm, and the leader jabbed his armored hand into Cerot's wounded side. The

Ovarrow let out a half-strangled cry and tried to move away, but the soldiers held him in place.

Connor glanced at the other soldiers, who watched them warily. There was no way he could take them by surprise, and as much as he hated what they were doing, he had to wait. There was a time to fight, and there was a time to wait. Connor clenched his teeth and watched. He heard Dash muttering something, but the others were silent.

The Krake leader attached a small, metallic box to Cerot's shoulder, and it shimmered as it activated. Metallic laces detached themselves from the box and plunged into Cerot's exposed neck, piercing his armor as if it provided no protection. Cerot's eyes went wide, and his body began to contort with pain.

Connor stepped forward. "Enough. It's for communications," he said and sent the signal to activate the Ovarrow translator on Cerot's wrist.

A personal holoscreen appeared over Cerot's wrist, and the Ovarrow symbols translated what Connor had said. The Krake leader peered at it and then looked at Connor. He spoke to Connor, but Connor couldn't understand him. Soldiers began stomping toward him, but before they could grab him, Connor stepped forward, moving away from the others. "I don't understand. This is how we communicate with the Ovarrow."

The Krake soldiers grabbed his arms and attempted to pull him back, but the Nexstar combat suit was capable of enormous feats of strength. Connor braced himself and refused to be moved. They struggled against his arms, trying to force him back. Power surged through his suit, and Connor tore free from their grasp. More soldiers moved forward, but the Krake leader shouted and they stopped their advance.

They hadn't fired their weapons, so it was clear that they didn't want to kill him, at least not yet. The Krake leader turned back toward Cerot and removed the colonial translator from his wrist. The interface remained active, and the Krake held a device up to it. The holoscreen began flickering as a library of Ovarrow symbols flashed across it.

"He's accessing the translator program," Dash said.

"I figured as much," Connor replied.

The Krake leader's gaze flicked toward Dash, and then, a few moments later, the Krake soldiers surrounded him and pulled him over to where Cerot was. The military-grade MPS couldn't produce the same amount of force that the Nexstar combat suit could. Connor inhaled deeply and looked at the Krake leader. Had he detected the comlink? Just then, a comlink opened from the personal recon drone and the data dump began. Connor watched the Krake for a reaction, but there wasn't any. So, he must've somehow heard the brief exchange between Connor and Dash.

The Krake leader produced another small, metallic box and placed it on Dash's shoulder. Again, the metallic laces burst forth from the box and attempted to penetrate the MPS. He heard Dash cry out in anticipation of pain, but then he suddenly stopped. The metallic laces couldn't penetrate the MPS, even though they tried several times on multiple parts of Dash's upper body.

The Krake leader held out his hand. The metallic laces lifted the box up, and it jumped like a spider into his outstretched hand. He turned toward Connor and flung the box toward him. Connor tried to swipe it away, but the metallic laces wrapped around his wrist and scurried up his arm, attempting to pierce his armor. Connor enabled his defensive countermeasures, and as power surged through his shoulder, the spider was flung off him in a charred wreck.

The holoscreen above Cerot's wrist computer went off and the Krake leader brought up several more of his own. Symbols Connor recognized from the Krake base flickered by. He must've been running some sort of analysis, and then that, too, finished.

The Krake leader gestured and one of the holoscreens flipped around. He tossed Cerot's wrist computer to the floor. The Krake soldiers let Cerot go, and he collapsed to the ground. He grabbed his wrist computer and slapped it back on. Connor's connection to Cerot's wrist computer was still active, and he noticed that there were differences now. The Krake leader spoke to Cerot again. This time, a translation appeared on Connor's internal heads-up display.

"Name of origin," the Krake leader said.

Connor's eyes widened, and he looked at the leader.

"You know better than to resist, Ovarrow. Answer me now, or you'll join the thousands of others we have participating in the trials," the Krake leader said.

Cerot regained his feet. "I'll never tell you!" he yelled and lunged for the Krake leader.

The Krake raised his hand and a burst of energy slammed into Cerot, throwing him back a dozen meters and slamming him into the wall. The Ovarrow collapsed into a heap.

Connor brought up his weapon and fired it at the Krake leader's unprotected head. Incendiary darts bounced off a personal shield, but the Krake leader flinched backward. Connor charged forward, but a soldier tried to block his path. He swung his AR-71 toward the soldier and squeezed the trigger. The incendiary darts ripped into the Krake armor and

Connor updated the ammo to high-impact rounds. It would chew through his ammunition quicker, but it would also provide more of a punch.

The Krake leader sent a blast of invisible force toward Dash, catching him by surprise.

"Suppressing fire," Connor shouted.

Together, he and Bradley sprayed suppressing fire against the Krake soldiers while Marsters ran toward Dash and got him to his feet. They were close to the wide-open door, and Connor shouted for them to head toward it. He and Bradley covered their flank. Krake soldiers raced toward them. Behind them, Connor saw that they had Cerot pinned to the ground. Connor cursed as the doors began to close. There was no way he could reach Cerot. Marsters picked Dash up and slung him over his shoulder. Engaging the combat suit, he quickly made it through the door.

"I'm out of ammo," Corporal Bradley said.

Connor's ammunition was nearly empty as well. They ran through the door as the Krake soldiers fired their weapons. Bolts of energy streaked past them and into another building.

Connor and the others ran along the building until they reached the end. There was an open area beyond, where they'd be picked off when the soldiers caught up to them.

"Take Dash and rendezvous with Samson," Connor said.

"General, I can't leave you here alone. We can't even reach Captain Samson," Bradley said.

"I'm sending you the rendezvous coordinates. Make your way there, best speed. Don't look back. That's an order," Connor said.

Marsters shifted Dash's weight onto his shoulder, but he was slowly regaining consciousness and moving on his own.

"General, I can help you," Bradley said.

"No. I'm going to lead them away from you, giving you a chance to get away. The uplink is still active. Get whatever data you can back to Captain Samson, and you're ordered to go back through the gateway ASAP. I'll follow you when I have Cerot," Connor said.

The Krake soldiers were nearly upon them, and Connor didn't wait for a reply. He engaged his suit's jets and launched himself to the top of the adjacent building. Running along the roof, he fired three-round bursts at the soldiers, drawing their attention. They quickly changed course and scrambled up the side of the wall. Connor fired his remaining grenade, and it hit a Krake soldier in the chest just as he was coming over the edge. Several Krake soldiers tumbled to the ground, and Connor engaged his Nexstar combat suit and ran. Combat suits enabled him to run at ultrafast speeds. In fact, he wasn't actually running but taking super long strides.

The helmet's rear video feed showed that the Krake soldiers had climbed onto the roof, but they couldn't catch up to him. Connor dropped down off the roof of the building and headed back toward the hangar, bringing up the tracker he'd placed on Cerot's armor. They'd placed them on all the Ovarrow's armor in case they got separated.

The words "Acquiring signal" appeared, but he had to get back into the building in order for the signal to connect. At first glance there seemed to be an endless number of walls. He could create his own doorway, but that would draw a lot of attention. Connor kept running until he saw a small hatch near the ground. He grabbed the handle and pulled it, forcing the hatch to open. Slipping inside, he found himself in a different part of the hangar.

Cerot's personal locator signal went active as soon as he entered the building. He was on the other side, and Connor headed toward him.

A loud noise echoed from across the hangar. There was minimal lighting in the area, but he saw several small ships in standby mode. He ran among them, going as quickly and quietly as he could.

Connor raced to the end of the row of ships and stopped, seeing Cerot sitting on the ground. The Krake leader stood nearby, and he was speaking to another soldier on his holoscreen. Connor's Ovarrow translation program was still active, and it began putting the words on his internal heads-up display.

"Alert Skywatch Base. Have invader ships been detected in the system?"

"None have been detected, Sector Chief," came the reply.

Connor frowned for a moment. Invader ships? What were they talking about?

"Be on full alert. Invader ships utilize misdirection tactics as recorded by their assault on our processing center. Their designation is Colonial Defense Force," the sector chief said.

*Trident Battle Group!* They were talking about Sean! Connor felt a rush of adrenaline. They hadn't received word from Sean for months. This was the first confirmation he had that they were even alive and had attacked a Krake processing center, whatever that meant. But the moment of relief soon left him as he refocused on getting to Cerot.

He squatted down and peered across the hangar bay but couldn't tell if Cerot was awake. He wasn't moving, and Connor hoped they hadn't killed him. He needed to get a closer look, but any second now, the soldiers that were chasing him would return. Connor was on borrowed time. Thinking of a way to distract them, he hit upon the reconnaissance drone that was broadcasting from the Krake terminal. Connor accessed the drone and brought up a secondary interface to access the terminal. He ran the interface through the updated translator and was able to understand more of the layout. There were power systems, communication systems, and maintenance systems. Connor selected the maintenance systems and engaged a diagnostic. A warning appeared, indicating the recycling of some kind of shield. Connor acknowledged the warning and engaged the maintenance protocol. The semi-translucent shield on the far side of the hangar flickered off, and the sector chief, as well as several other soldiers, glanced in the direction of the door. When they approached the shield to investigate, Connor burst from cover and raced toward Cerot. As he reached the Ovarrow, a group of soldiers who'd been hiding nearby rushed him. It was an ambush. A wall of living armor tackled Connor to the ground before he could react. They slapped some kind of suppressor cuffs on his wrists and he found that he couldn't move, even though the combat suit controls still worked.

The sector chief walked back over to him and leaned down. "Now, we can begin."

The words appeared on Connor's internal heads-up display in plain English. Normally, Ovarrow symbols accompanied the English text, but there weren't any this time.

The Krake sector chief regarded him for a few moments and then spoke. "We can now communicate directly. I have questions."

The sector chief stood up and a soldier handed him a metallic rod, which the Krake held in one hand while caressing it with the other. Connor thought it looked like a stun baton. The tip glowed in pale silver, and the suppressor cuffs glowed in response. He was on his hands and knees one moment, and the next, he was being lifted off the ground by the cuffs and hung in the air several feet above the ground. He tried to yank his arms down and only succeeded in swinging his legs and feet. He could still feel his hands down to the tips of his fingers. He was able to make a fist, but he just couldn't exert any force that would free him.

"I've analyzed your translator. It's an interesting approach to communicating with the Ovarrow but still a work in progress, I think. I've augmented it to speed this interaction along. Do you understand me?" the sector chief asked.

Connor clenched his teeth for a moment. The sector chief had been manipulating them the entire time. He must have been. Why else allow your prisoners to retain their weapons and leave the hangar bay doors open with just a force field to block communications?

"I can understand you," Connor replied.

The sector chief was silent for a few moments, and Connor wondered whether he had understood him. "You returned for this Ovarrow. Why would you do that?"

"I brought him here."

"But he's Ovarrow. You are something else."

"It's called loyalty. Maybe you've heard of it."

"We are familiar with this archaic concept. We haven't seen an Ovarrow wearing armor like this for a long time. You must be from a fringe universe, but which one?" the sector chief said and watched Connor for a few moments. "We'll get back to that question. Where are your ships?"

The sector chief must have thought he was with Trident

Battle Group. Whatever Sean was up to had garnered some attention. Connor considered whether Sean could actually be in this universe and decided the odds weren't in favor of that. He wouldn't wager anything, but it did give him some options.

"You don't expect me to answer that question," Connor said.

"Defiance is common in the beginning. You've traveled a long way. Why would you come here?"

The Krake was full of questions. They were exchanging blows, of a sort, and this encounter was no less dangerous than if they were firing their weapons at each other. The hangar was shielded again, and he couldn't get a signal out.

"Your reluctance to answer is anticipated, and I have you at a disadvantage—"

"I came here to learn about you," Connor said, cutting him off. Whoever steered the conversation controlled the outcome. "We're not from around here."

"That much is obvious and yet doesn't tell me anything I don't already know. This is a delaying tactic—a much different approach than brute force and too subtle for the Ovarrow, though there are some who step beyond the established confines of acceptable response."

"You're slaughtering them, manipulating them to play your game," Connor said.

The sector chief's alien gaze was filled with cold calculation and an energetic intelligence. Though the Krake held himself still, Connor wondered whether his mind was ever still or quiet.

"Why invade this planet? Your targets have had strategic importance, but I don't see the logic of the action."

"Who said anything about an invasion?" Connor replied.

"So, invasion isn't your goal?"

"Why experiment on the Ovarrow? What have they done to

deserve this?"

"All external efforts are experiments. I don't need to explain this to you. The fact that you're here in this capacity indicates that you are familiar with the concept."

Connor used his implants to adjust the speed of his comlink and sent out a broadcast. The signal failed as before.

The sector chief stepped closer to Connor. The suppressor cuffs flashed, and Connor was lowered to a few inches above the ground, which put him at eye level with the Krake. The alien extended his hand toward Connor's shoulder for a moment, and Connor thought he was going to touch the armor. He had his suit's countermeasures armed, and if the sector chief touched him, the Krake would receive quite a shock.

"Interesting protection you have. Much more capable than this Ovarrow," the sector chief said, gesturing down toward Cerot.

The Ovarrow had regained consciousness and slowly rose to his feet as the Krake soldiers watched him.

"Defiant to a fault," the sector chief said and then looked back at Connor. "They are easily manipulated. Though this is our first meeting, this isn't your first encounter with my kind."

"That's obvious. I'm sure you can figure out why I'm here," Connor said.

He was able to move his feet, which meant he was only being held by his wrists.

"Won't your companions come back for you? I would expect that they would since loyalty is a behavior your species has demonstrated."

"Some things are more important," Connor replied. They'd stolen data about the Krake, and it was more important for Dash and the others to get to Samson and escape than it was to rescue him. He had no intention of dying, but he had to admit that the odds of him leaving this hangar bay alive were dwindling.

More Krake soldiers entered the hangar.

"Loyalty and sacrifice. We've seen these behaviors before—inspiration for the feebleminded. You have given me much to ponder," the sector chief said.

"I'm glad you find me so interesting. If you know so much, why do you keep experimenting on the Ovarrow?" Connor asked.

"You mistake me, or perhaps we're having an issue with the translator. It was based on inferior attempts at communication. Me saying that you've given me much to ponder doesn't mean that I find you or your species merely interesting. In fact, the knowledge I'm going to extract from you will be fascinating. Entire factions will align themselves with what I will gain here. They'll yearn for more."

"You haven't answered my question. You force the Ovarrow prisoners to fight, herding them toward an arch with a gateway to where? Their homes?"

"We do not force the Ovarrow to do anything. We simply create conditions whereby a choice must be made, and we offer them a way to salvation," the sector chief said.

He turned away from Connor and a large holoscreen appeared, showing multiple vantage points of the battlefield. Each holoscreen had a combat HUD, and Connor found that the translator was able to interpret the Krake language. The Krake had complete control over the battlefield, and Connor saw where they had their heavy cannons fortified, their soldiers deployed, and their orbital platforms locked onto the area for the next bombardment.

Connor clenched his teeth. This wasn't an elaborate experiment. He jerked his body, trying to tear free from the suppressor cuffs, but they held him firmly. The sector chief regarded him for a few moments.

"Ah, an emotional response. These images anger you, which means you're intelligent enough to realize—at least on the surface—that there is futility in fighting what is inevitable," the sector chief said and stepped closer to Connor. "But tell me, would you still fight even for the slightest chance to return to your home?"

Connor knew he was being baited, and it was working. The sector chief was putting himself within reach to try to get a response from Connor. He clenched his fists from within the armored confines of the combat suit and glanced at the dozens of Krake soldiers that stood nearby. They waited with an almost practiced patience, as if they expected him to strike the sector chief and were ready to respond once he did. He couldn't do what they expected. As much as he wanted the moment's satisfaction of kicking the crap out of the Krake sector chief, he knew it wouldn't gain him anything.

"Would you?" Connor asked.

The sector chief didn't exactly look smug, but it was as close to smug as an alien could look. Instead of answering, he engaged a holo-interface below one of the holoscreens. Connor watched as heavy cannons atop mobile platforms swung around and a bright flash of orange burst from them, scorching the ground and decimating the Ovarrow lines. They kept firing in bursts, forcing thousands of Ovarrow prisoners toward the city where Krake soldiers waited.

The sector chief's cold gaze watched the holoscreen dispassionately. This experiment wasn't about whether the

Ovarrow could defeat the Krake. They couldn't. This was an experiment about what the Ovarrow would do in their last moments—how they reacted to death. Connor watched as the sector chief's gaze flicked toward the Krake soldiers. He was watching them as well. Was he measuring the reactions of the soldiers? A response to Connor's comlink broadcast appeared on his internal heads-up display. His reconnaissance drone was inside the hangar bay. It must have been close enough to detect his earlier broadcast.

The sector chief turned back toward Connor. "Are we everything you feared us to be? I know you don't like this. If we were able to measure your biometrics, then no doubt your system would be showing signs of increased stress."

"We're not afraid of you. So far, you're everything I thought you were."

The sector chief raised the rod that controlled the suppressor cuffs and thrust it above his head. Connor's body lurched into the air. Then he was flung to the side and dragged helplessly behind by the cuffs on his wrists. Connor gritted his teeth and exhaled forcefully. The cuffs changed direction and his body sped toward the floor. His armored body slammed onto the hard surface and bounced into the air. Sharp pain lanced down his back and legs, and pain suppressants and nanites entered his system. As the pain dulled, his MPS engaged from within his combat suit. Just when gravity was about to bring him down, the cuffs engaged again. Connor sent a concentrated burst of power to his wrists, intending to overload them, and as his velocity through the air slowed, he quickly sank toward the ground. He slammed his wrists together with all the force he could muster and then hit the ground, shoulder first. The combat suit absorbed most of the impact, but jarring pain still ignited down his arm. Connor regained his feet and looked down at his wrists where the suppressor cuffs were mangled and bent. He tore them off and looked around. The Krake soldiers were still gathered in an open area near the center of the hangar bay. He peered at them and saw the sector chief raise the rod into the air, making a slicing motion with it.

Connor felt his lips lift up in amusement, but then he heard the clang of something hitting the ground. He hastened to the side and saw Cerot dangling upside down. The box with metallic laces had shifted to his back, and it glowed like Connor's suppressor cuffs had.

The sector chief lifted the rod up into the air and Cerot's body rose in response. The Krake turned toward Connor. He was a hundred meters away, but the open hangar bay doors were between them. Connor could reach the door and get away if he chose. The sector chief flicked the rod and Cerot spun right-side up. The Ovarrow was bleeding from the wounds he'd sustained, but he was still conscious. He lifted his head and looked at Connor. After a few moments, he inhaled deeply and shouted.

"Leave!"

Cerot's shout was cut off by violent coughing.

The smart move was for Connor to leave, take what he'd learned about the Krake, and return to New Earth, return to his family. He closed his eyes for a moment and sneered.

"Leave!" Cerot screamed again.

Had their positions been reversed, Connor imagined that Cerot might have left, and he wouldn't have blamed him. There were so few Ovarrow on New Earth, and the intelligence gathered was worth more than one person's life. Cerot wouldn't hate Connor if he left, and Vitory probably wouldn't resent Connor when he learned of what had happened.

His personal recon drone had tapped into a Krake console, and Connor had given it more precise search parameters based on what he'd seen with the new translator program. He'd found gateway references for hundreds of universes, all accessible through the arch, but the number wasn't infinite. It wasn't even close, and Connor didn't know why that was. If he left now, he could take that knowledge with him and come up with a more effective strategy for defeating the Krake. He could make sure Cerot's sacrifice was known to everyone.

Connor watched as Cerot's body hung in the air. The Ovarrow was willing to die for this. Lenora had saved Cerot's life when they were trapped under a collapsed bridge, and Cerot must have seen this as a way to repay the debt, but that was only part of it. Cerot must've believed that Connor and the CDF were the only chance the Ovarrow had of defeating the Krake. Loyalty mixed with pragmatism.

The sector chief waited for Connor to make his choice. No matter what Connor did, the sector chief would learn something about him. He glanced at the open hangar bay doors and the path to freedom; then he looked at Cerot, waiting to die. The Ovarrow had sacrificed so much to be there. He'd been raised in a world of war, a world where sacrifice was required in order to survive. It was why the Ovarrow had gone into stasis, and it was why Cerot was willing to sacrifice himself so Connor could leave. But he wasn't going to leave. Connor decided that he was going to educate the Krake on what fighting a single human would be like. The Krake data dump would be lost, but Connor had something he wanted to teach the Krake, and Cerot.

# 26

CONNOR CRANKED up the combat suit's power systems to maximum. Then, with a running start, he leaped into the air and engaged the suit thrusters. The Krake soldiers all seemed to move at once. Connor pulled out a massive combat knife as he closed in on the nearest Krake soldier. The soldier tried to bring his weapon up, but Connor was already on him, ramming the knife through his side. The force of the blow was augmented through his suit thrusters, and it pierced the Krake armor. The soldier let out a mournful howl, and Connor lifted him up and threw him into the nearest soldier. He leaped into the air again and stepped off the nearest Krake soldier's shoulder to jump even higher. He'd managed to get his arm wrapped around Cerot's middle when the section leader slammed his arm down, and Connor felt Cerot's body begin to plunge back to the ground. Connor jabbed the tip of his knife into the metallic box on Cerot's back and pried it loose. He then clutched Cerot to him and twisted in the air to shield the

Ovarrow from harm as they landed on the ground. Pain blossomed down his side despite the pain-numbing meds already in his system. His combat suit status showed multiple damaged sections. Connor regained his feet just as another Krake soldier attacked. Connor fought him, driving him back, but more were coming. He engaged the suit thrusters near his elbow and struck a crippling blow at the oncoming soldier. Then he quickly spun around and grabbed Cerot, running toward the rows of small ships.

The Krake soldiers were quickly catching up to him. One grabbed hold of Cerot and pulled Connor off balance, so he dumped Cerot onto the ground and turned to face the soldiers. They didn't use their weapons but instead chose to fight him hand-to-hand. With the help of the combat suit, Connor was keeping his attackers at bay, but more soldiers were closing in and he was getting struck more often. If he stayed there, he'd be overwhelmed. A Krake soldier attempted to maneuver Connor toward another one who held suppression cuffs in his hand, and Connor quickly scrambled out of the way. He noticed Cerot stumbling toward some kind of small fighter that had an open seating area on top.

A Krake soldier struck Connor in the back and unleashed a burst of energy. The combat suit conducted the power as best it could, but his systems were being overloaded. Sensing he was vulnerable to the attack, the Krake soldiers banged their fists together so they were all glowing. Connor turned and ran, knocking into one of the soldiers before the rest closed in on him. He engaged the combat suit's self-destruct protocol and adjusted the timer. Then he engaged it and selected the quick-exit protocol. The combat suit split down the middle, allowing him to jump free. Connor's MPS became active and propelled him at speed away from them. He only had mere seconds before the suit exploded, and the force of it thrust him forward. He just barely kept his feet under him and stumbled into the ship Cerot was attempting to bring online. Glancing behind him, he saw that Krake bodies had been flung away from the scorched ground where his combat suit had been, but more were coming.

He hopped onto the front bench of the ship where Cerot had opened a holo-interface. Connor sat down next to him and took over. The translator enabled him to access the holo-interface, and the ship came online. It was more like a battle sled, and there was a cannon off the back. Connor activated the cannon and it swung around, priming for a few seconds before unleashing a bolt of molten fury that blasted through the hangar bay walls. There were several flashes off to the side where Krake soldiers were firing their weapons. Connor grabbed the controls and flew the Krake ship out of the hangar. He banked to the side and headed directly toward the battlefield where the battle was raging on.

"Take control of that cannon," Connor said.

Cerot brought up a secondary-weapons interface and the rear cannon responded to his commands. He looked at Connor, and Connor gestured to where the Krake weapons were herding the Ovarrow prisoners along. Cerot understood. The Ovarrow began firing on the Krake forces, taking their line of soldiers completely by surprise.

"Take out their cannons," Connor said.

Cerot began aiming for their cannons, which were unable to swing around in time to track the small ship. A proximity alert appeared on the ship's HUD, and Connor saw that there were multiple ships heading in his direction. He flew along the main thoroughfare, and Cerot was able to take out the Krake defenses there. The Ovarrow prisoners rushed down the street, heading for the arch. Connor hoped it actually led to their home world, or at least someplace that wasn't under Krake control, but he was afraid it was a lie. He couldn't be sure, but he didn't have time to worry about it because the Krake ships were firing on him.

Connor's ship dipped to the side, and Connor grabbed onto Cerot to keep them in the seat. He flew among the buildings, using them for cover, but the craft was sluggish to respond to his commands. The Krake fired on his ship again and took out his engine. They began to spin, and it took everything he had to hold on. The ship struck one of the buildings and crashed. Somehow, they landed right-side up, and Connor scrambled out of the seat, helping Cerot to his feet.

"Come on! We have to run!" Connor yelled over the din.

He engaged the comlink system of his MPS, but there was no reply and no acknowledgment of the message.

"They're going to catch us," Cerot said. "You should've left me behind."

Connor half dragged the Ovarrow down the street, hearing Krake ships flying overhead. They continued running close to the buildings, trying to stay out of sight. Cerot stumbled and nearly fell.

"Don't quit on me now," Connor said, helping him back to his feet.

Cerot held something out toward him, and he was stunned to see that it was his own personal recon drone. Connor didn't know how Cerot had gotten it, but it was the only thing that held the data they needed about the Krake.

"Hold onto it for me," Connor said. It wasn't as if he had a place to put it. The MPS didn't come with additional storage. It was his emergency protection, and he didn't have any weapons. All he had was a protective suit made of nanorobotic materials designed to protect the wearer from extreme harm.

Connor glanced at the sky, expecting more Krake ships to come flying over, but they didn't. He heard more ships nearby, and they sounded like they were hovering close, but then their engines went off. They were going to hunt them.

"Come on, we've got to move," Connor said.

Cerot clutched the recon drone to his middle and used his other hand to grab Connor's shoulder to help him stay upright. Connor glanced behind them as they made their way toward another row of buildings and saw bloody footsteps. Cerot was badly wounded. He'd have to stop soon or the Ovarrow would die.

He heard a Krake shout something in their language, and the translation appeared on Connor's internal heads-up display.

". . . trail to follow," came the partial translation.

Connor tried to hurry Cerot along and then lifted the Ovarrow over his shoulder. The MPS helped Connor bear the heavy load, but it wasn't as strong as his combat suit, and he felt the weight. Running forward, he stepped carefully so he didn't lose his balance. The dull ache in his back and legs flared intensely. Krake soldiers were closing in behind him. He reached the end of the street and hesitated for a moment, glancing back the way they'd come. Two soldiers were running toward them with their weapons, ready to shoot. Connor scrambled to the side and kept going.

Cerot's blood was dripping down his chest, and Connor realized that he was bleeding too much. Connor had to place a field dressing, but if he stopped, the Krake were going to find them. Granted, they were going to find them whether he stopped or not.

Connor saw a flash of something metallic moving among the buildings in front of him and muttered a curse. The Krake were already ahead of him. They were tightening the noose around them. Connor peered ahead and saw something out of place on top of the building. There were several shapes along the roof. Connor narrowed his gaze, seeing one of the shapes detach itself from the others. A CDF soldier waved to him and then readied his weapon. Gritting his teeth, Connor lunged forward, running as fast as he could. The Krake soldiers attempted to close in behind him, but the 7th fired their weapons, taking the Krake soldiers by surprise.

Connor ran for cover. Two CDF soldiers took Cerot from his shoulder and carried him away. He heard the CDF laying down suppressing fire, and then Samson stood in front of him.

"Your timing is almost impeccable, General," Samson said. "Come on, we only have a few minutes to reach the gateway."

Connor's breath was coming in gasps, so he didn't reply; he just followed his friend. They ran a short distance to an open part of the city. It must've been a park at some point, or perhaps a courtyard between buildings. Connor saw the semi-translucent shimmer in the air, denoting a gateway. The soldiers in front of him who were carrying Cerot ran right for it.

"Go! Don't stop!" Samson shouted.

Connor ran through the gateway and emerged into a forest glade surrounded by silence. One moment there'd been the sound of a battle being fought, and the next it was gone. Connor doubled over and rested his hands on his knees while he caught his breath. He was pulled to the side by a soldier who spoke a quick apology, but they had to keep the way clear for the rest of the 7th to come through. Samson was the last to emerge, and he ordered the gateway to shut down. The arch immediately went dead, and the platforms maintaining the alignment quickly separated.

Connor was still catching his breath when Samson walked over to him. "You crazy son of a—Did you intend to fight the Krake all by yourself? That was our final sweep. We almost left you."

Connor inhaled deeply, finally catching his breath. "I'm glad you didn't. Did you find Dash, Bradley, and Marsters?"

"Yeah, we found them. We need to talk about our secondary protocols for when our egress point is no longer a viable option," Samson said.

Connor couldn't argue with that. This whole thing had turned into something way too fast and loose for his liking. He saw Esteban and Felix kneeling by Cerot while a CDF medic tended to his wounds.

Samson glanced at all the blood covering Connor's chest. "What the hell happened over there?"

Connor looked at his friend. "We met the enemy."

---

THE KRAKE SECTOR chief had hunted the human. He knew what species it was, but he hadn't anticipated a connection to the Ovarrow. Some of his soldiers had been slain by this human. They weren't entirely predictable, at least not in all things. He retraced the human's path and found the Ovarrow's blood drying on the ground. Leaning down, he extracted a sample of it. It would help him identify the universe that the humans came from. It wasn't an exact measure, but it would help narrow the search. Once he reported this encounter to the overseers, things would change. The Krake had to change. The sector chief had a new project to propose to the overseers, one they couldn't afford to ignore.

A Krake soldier reported in that several hundred Ovarrow had breached the arch gateway before they'd been able to bring it down.

"Let them go. They're not important," the sector chief said.

The Krake soldier didn't question the orders he'd been given. He simply obeyed.

# 27

Connor had sustained significant impact trauma to his back from his fight with the Krake. He hadn't realized the extent of his injuries because his system had been flooded with pain-numbing agents so he could keep moving. The Nexstar combat suit would report the injuries detected, but he'd been fighting, and the self-destruct sequence he'd used to stop the Krake soldiers from killing him had also destroyed the report of his injuries. There was no link between his combat suit and the MPS he wore, which had a limited medical interface.

The injuries did register with his biochip, however, and when the medics checked it, they discovered that he had suffered a lot more than a few bumps and bruises. He'd sustained internal bleeding that could have happened either when he was fighting multiple Krake soldiers or when he'd crashed the ship during his escape. Connor had pushed the limits of what a Nexstar combat suit was even capable of, and now he was paying the price.

He lay in the bed at the hospital on base at Sanctuary and glanced at the time on his internal heads-up display, frowning. He'd been asleep for over ten hours.

*Ten hours!*

He quickly brought up the status of his ZX-64c implants, which were an upgraded version of what the NA Alliance military had given him all those years ago, but the controls for the implants were grayed out. He frowned, thinking that perhaps they'd been damaged, but a quick diagnostic showed they were working fine. He'd been locked out of his own implants! He hit the call button on the panel next to the bed and attempted to sit up but winced and gasped at the sharp pain from his back and quickly lay back down.

The door to his room opened and a short, young woman with dark hair walked in. Her name and rank appeared on his internal heads-up display. At least *that* was still working.

Dr. Monica Torres smiled as she walked over to him. "General Gates, you're awake right on schedule. I'll raise the bed for you so you can sit up."

"What's going on here? Did you lock me out of my implant control systems?"

"Yes, I did. We had to, but I had permission."

Connor knitted his eyebrows together and shook his head. "I didn't give permission—"

"Your wife, General. Your wife did," Dr. Torres said, coming over to his bedside. "You broke your back. You're lucky to be alive."

Connor's mouth opened, but the words wouldn't come. He glanced down at his feet for a second. "That's crazy. I know I got hurt, but if I'd broken my back, I wouldn't have been able to walk."

"That's right, you wouldn't have been able to, but you had an MPS on. It helped you keep moving and stay alive. Had you not had the MPS on, as soon as you stepped out of your combat suit, you would've collapsed to the floor," Dr. Torres said.

Connor looked away for a moment and then back down at his feet. He wiggled his toes, relieved that he could still do so. Swallowing hard, he looked up at her, and she waited for him with a knowing look.

"How bad is it?" he asked.

"Not nearly as bad as it could have been. We've been applying treatments to you all night, and now you'll just have to take it easy for a little while. You'll also have to wear a back brace while the nanites continue to heal your spine."

Connor nodded, feeling relieved. "Why are you inhibiting my implants?"

"Because you need to slow down a little bit. The medical journals all indicate that you *can* function with a mere two hours of sleep, and you've been doing it longer than anybody else, but such little downtime does take its toll on certain cognitive functions," Dr. Torres said, leaning toward him. "Signs of this include irritation and a certain level of anxiety. In your case," she said, smiling a little in understanding, "it's to be expected, given the extreme amount of stress, but it's been ongoing for a while. You need longer blocks of rest. This will help you heal."

"I know you're looking out for me, Dr. Torres, but I've been at this for a very long time. Irritation and anxiety are part of what I do. I want full access to my implants returned to me right now. I promise to get as much rest as I can and—" Connor said, suddenly stopping when Lenora walked in the room. Lauren stood next to her with her little hand held in her mother's. She looked up and saw Connor lying there, and her eyes widened. Lauren smiled and squealed, and everything Connor had been about to say vanished as his daughter hastened over to him.

Lenora picked Lauren up and deposited her onto Connor's lap. He hugged his daughter, feeling his throat become thick, and saw Lenora share a look with Dr. Torres. Lauren wrapped her arms around Connor's neck and snuggled into him. The tension drained out of him as if the floodgates had been opened, and he squeezed his eyes shut, holding his daughter in his arms and breathing in her scent. Her silky, soft hair smelled like lavender, and he loved the feel of it against his cheek.

After a few precious moments, Lauren sat back and scrutinized Connor with a look of childlike wonder and intensity. Her gaze went to the bruise on his neck. "Ouchy," she said.

Connor smiled. "That's right. I have an ouchy, but I'll be fine."

Lenora looked at him for a moment, and Connor could tell she was reining in her emotions. Then she glanced at Dr. Torres. "Would you please give us a few minutes?"

"Take all the time you need," Dr. Torres said and left the room.

Lenora inhaled deeply and sighed. Walking over to his bed, she grasped his hand. "You know, we first met in a hospital room."

Connor chuckled a little, remembering when he'd first woken up aboard the *Ark*.

"I spoke to Samson and Dash. They told me what happened," she said.

Connor had no doubt that Lenora had pulled every ounce

of information from both men. She had a way of getting what she wanted. Connor tried to think of a response that didn't make him sound foolish, but he couldn't. He'd almost died, and they both knew it.

"Connor, I know you. You did what you had to do. And I'm just so glad you're home. But we need to make some changes," Lenora said.

"All right," Connor answered.

"I just . . ." Lenora began to say and stopped. "First, the problem with the implants and . . . I've had those concerns since before you left."

"I've had them for years and have never had an issue."

"Yes, but you had check-ins, and even . . . They're not meant for long-term use."

"So what are you going to do? Lock me out of them?"

Lenora shook her head. "You know better than that. Do I need to lock you out of them? No, that's not who we are. All I'm saying is that we need more of a balance, and *you* need more of a balance. You can't be on the go for twenty-two hours a day every day for years and years and expect not to have any repercussions."

Connor was quiet for a few moments while he considered his thoughts. If there was one thing he'd learned over the years it was that there were times to think things through and then there were times to do what needed to be done. This was the latter. "All right, I'll talk to Dr. Torres and Ashley. We'll see if we can work something out."

Lenora seemed satisfied with that response. Over the years, they had learned to trust each other, but he knew she'd be watching him. He'd certainly given her enough cause to be worried about him.

They spent a few hours together, and the pain in his back lessened. He was able to sit up comfortably. Later, he received another treatment for his back, and they fitted him with a back brace to continue monitoring and administering healing nanites.

---

A FEW DAYS LATER, Connor was in his office. Dash had come to see him.

"Cerot is asking for you," Dash said.

The Ovarrow were staying in a barracks that had been designated for them. Colonial doctors had done what they could for Cerot, but his recovery would take much longer than Connor's.

They left his office and headed over to the barracks.

"About what you did," Dash said once they were outside. Connor looked at him. "I never got a chance to thank you."

"You're welcome."

Dash eyes widened for a moment. "You make it seem like there's nothing else to say."

"What else *is* there to say?"

"It mattered to me."

"It mattered to me too. That's why I did it. And it was important to get the data we recovered."

"Do you compartmentalize everything?"

"If saving your life is going to lead to a lot of questions, I may have to rethink it in the future," Connor replied.

Dash shook his head and grinned a little.

"Look at it this way: At the rate we're going, you'll be able to return the favor by this time next week," Connor said.

"I hope not," Dash said, his voice becoming serious.

Connor nodded. "Me too."

They entered the room where Cerot was being cared for. He looked much better than the last time Connor had seen him, which was when he'd almost bled out in the middle of a battle.

Cerot spoke. "Alone," he said.

The Ovarrow soldiers left the room and Dash joined them.

"Better translator now," Cerot said.

"It's better than typing everything we want to say to each other," Connor said in agreement.

"I have to return and report to Warlord Vitory and High Commissioner Senleon."

"I understand," Connor said. He was more than a little bit curious as to what Cerot would report to his superiors.

"It may take some time, but I will gather as many Ovarrow as I can and persuade them to help you," Cerot said.

"We'll appreciate any help you have to offer," Connor said.

"My words might not be correct. What I mean to say is that I will help you in your fight against the Krake."

Connor regarded the warlord's First for a moment. He'd begun to suspect what Cerot was implying, but he wanted no misunderstandings. "You mean you'll help the colony? All of us?"

"Your colony is important to you like our city is important to us, but they are not one and the same. I meant what I said, and I will help you fight the Krake. You are beginning to understand what it means to battle them. And if our leaders are too foolish to understand that, I will help you anyway with as many soldiers as I can bring," Cerot said.

Connor inhaled deeply. "Then I hope it doesn't come to that."

Divisions among the colonists and among the Ovarrow were a danger to them all. They didn't need to agree on everything, but they did need to focus on the Krake, together.

Connor and Dash went with the Ovarrow to the hangar where a troop carrier waited to take them home. Cerot was carried onto the troop carrier first. The rest of the soldiers that they'd named Esteban, Joe, Felix, Luca, and Wesley stood before the loading ramp and faced Connor. They each placed their hand on their own shoulder and pulled it across to their other shoulder, giving Connor the Ovarrow sign for gratitude.

Connor returned their salute, and the Ovarrow soldiers walked up the loading ramp. The troop carrier doors closed, and the ship left.

"I think you made a few friends," Dash said.

"I guess I did."

"I don't know what this means for an official alliance, but the Ovarrow seem to hold actions in higher esteem than they do intentions. This is something I've noticed with them," Dash said.

Connor nodded. "It's a start, at least. We'll have to take it from there."

A short while later, Connor and Dash entered a small conference room. Nathan and Samson were speaking quietly.

Nathan looked at Connor. "You're looking surprisingly agile for someone who broke his back just a few days ago."

"You know me; I get irritated when I sit still," Connor replied and leaned in toward Nathan. "Are you trying to recruit my captain?"

Nathan grinned. Pilfering each other's soldiers had become something of a joke between them. "I'm afraid not. Captain

Samson was just telling me that the Ovarrow you found have left that capital city."

Connor looked at Samson.

"The report just came in. They're gone. All traces of them, including the ryklars," Samson said.

"There isn't much we can do about that," Connor said. He'd hoped to be able to speak with Brashirker one more time with the improved translator. It might have changed the outcome.

"They worry me," Nathan said. "They don't have to work with us, but we can't let them work with the Krake."

"Agreed. We'll have to keep an eye out for them," Connor said, "but I don't think they would work with the Krake. They wouldn't have done what they've done to stay hidden for as long as they have and then decide to work with the very enemy they were hoping to avoid."

"Ordinarily I would agree with you, but I don't want to leave anything to chance. You said it before—we can't make any assumptions where the Ovarrow are concerned," Nathan said and looked at Dash. "Mr. DeWitt, I understand you had a role in all this."

"I did, sir, but I'm not sure what to do now."

"I'm sure we'll keep you busy," Connor said.

Dash looked at both Connor and Nathan. "I'm ready to help, but I have a request."

Connor arched an eyebrow. "I think you're entitled to one request."

Dash smiled a little. "I need weapons training. Things got out of control so fast, and I need to be able to do something so I'm not a liability."

"Are you saying you want to join the CDF?" Nathan asked.

Dash shook his head quickly. "No, and I don't mean any

disrespect either. I'm not a soldier like all of you, but I've been working with soldiers for a long time."

Dash looked at Connor, letting the thought go unfinished.

"I'll give it some thought," Connor said.

"I'd be happy to show the kid a few things," Samson said mildly and then looked at Dash with anticipation.

Dash swallowed hard. "I'm not sure that would be such a good idea," he said.

Connor grinned and the others joined in. "We'll see. I'm sure we can come up with something, especially if we need specialists in the field with us."

"We need to start thinking about the next steps. And . . ." Nathan began to say, pausing for a moment. "Would you two excuse us for a few minutes?" he said, looking at Samson and Dash.

Samson stood up. "Come on, kid, there's something you need to see."

Dash looked only slightly worried as they left the room.

"Next steps," Connor said. "We need to analyze everything we brought back."

"You're not wrong about that, but there are a couple of things I need to discuss with you," Nathan said.

"I bet I can guess what one or two of those things might be," Connor replied.

"You've got what you wanted. You looked the enemy in the eyes."

"I've looked *an* enemy in the eyes. I still don't feel like we have a handle on them as a whole."

"Fair enough. Do you intend to lead every mission that involves a team going through a gateway, whether it be here through an arch or a space gate?" Nathan asked.

Connor shook his head. "Of course not."

Nathan smiled. "You don't know how glad I am to hear that, because it seems to me and a few other people that you excel at putting yourself right in the thick of it."

"Maybe I'm just the lucky one."

Nathan chuckled. "Or you just have a natural talent for finding trouble." He paused for a moment and regarded Connor, pressing his lips together. "We have to figure this enemy out—you and me, and a whole lot of other people. We have to be able to trust other people to get the job done. Would you agree with that?"

"I would."

"Look, Connor, I haven't been a soldier as long as you have. But I do know that not every fight has to be personal."

"You think I'm making this personal?" Connor asked.

"Aren't you?"

Connor looked away for a moment and pursed his lips in thought. "This *is* personal, Nathan. I feel like we're a heartbeat away from fighting this war in our backyards. It's worse than the Vemus. We dodged a horrible fate with that, but this is different. I know we're supposed to be diplomatic when it comes to dealing with Governor Wolf and the other Security Council members, but make no mistake—this *is* personal. The Krake are going to test us beyond anything we've ever faced before. It's like they're hyper-logical to a fault. Extremely advanced. They toy with civilizations just to see if they can influence the outcome."

"Ovarrow civilizations," Nathan said, pointedly. "They haven't encountered ours before."

"And they've been at it for who knows how long. It has to be a few hundred years at least."

"So, what are you saying?"

"What I'm saying is that I don't know how we're going to defeat the Krake. Throughout every encounter we've had, we try to be better prepared for the next encounter, and then we find that they're capable of much more than we thought. This is personal for me because that's how I can effectively do my job. Our job is to stop the Krake."

"Yes, that's our job, and we'll need to sacrifice lives in order to attain victory. That means you and I can't lead every charge."

"You've seen the Security Council. Do you think they're ready to hear about sacrifice, especially where lives are concerned?"

Nathan twitched his head to the side in a slight nod. "They might surprise you. I think you've done an excellent job of making them aware of the risk. Just because they don't like to be reminded of what could happen doesn't mean we shouldn't remind them."

"Be careful. I bet they won't like to hear that."

Nathan chuckled. "I have a few ideas of my own for how to deal with the Krake, but I don't even want to entertain the thought of fighting this war without you. This colony needs you, Connor. I know the Krake surprised you," he said and then shook his head. "I don't think I would've survived if I'd been put in the same situation. I'm not you, and there's no one else like you."

Connor shifted in his seat, feeling a little uncomfortable. "We have Sean. They thought Trident Battle Group was there. It was the first confirmation we've received that they're still around, and the fact that Sean has got the Krake worried is a win in my book."

Connor refused to even consider that Sean and the rest of Trident Battle Group had been lost. They were still out there.

"We do have Sean, and Celeste Belonét, and half a dozen other outstanding young officers, but it seems to me that we're barely staying a step ahead of the Krake. One little misstep and everything changes," said Nathan.

"We don't do this because it's easy; we do this because it's necessary," Connor said.

The conference room was profoundly quiet while the two generals regarded each other.

"I might be the head of the CDF, but you will always be its heart. I saw it on the command deck of a warship, and I've seen it in a hundred different ways ever since."

Connor felt his throat thicken for a moment. Nathan was speaking as a friend who'd watched as someone close to them almost die. Connor just wanted to focus on the next thing. This wasn't the first time he'd risked his life, or even come close to losing it. But maybe this was someone telling him to take a few moments and seriously consider what he should do next.

The door to the conference room opened and Samson stuck his head in. "You're going to want to see this. Trident Battle Group has returned home."

# 28

THE FEW MOMENTS of elation didn't last long after they heard the news. Connor and Nathan headed to a briefing room where Colonel Belonét gave them a brief update. The battle group had emerged in an area of space that wasn't near anything—a void between New Earth and Sagan's orbit. Phoenix Station wasn't anywhere nearby, so salvage and rescue operations had to be coordinated from the lunar base near New Earth.

The *Vigilant* was completely without power, and the CDF soldiers and civilian personnel were being transferred over to the remaining ships in operation. Trident Battle Group now consisted of only six CDF destroyers, and there wasn't enough room on the destroyers for the people currently stranded. The battle group had lost two destroyers and the converted freighter that had been serving as a carrier. In addition to smaller ships, such as combat shuttles and Talon-V troop carriers, Sean had nonessential personnel in escape pods that were running under their own power. It was a temporary solution.

"The *Vigilant* needs to be refueled," Connor said. "If we transfer the reactor core from one of the ships in the lunar shipyards, we can at least restore critical power to the *Vigilant*, and that should be enough to get them back to New Earth."

Colonel Belonét shook her head, muttering a curse. "Yes, General, you're correct. I should've thought of that. I'm sorry."

"Don't worry about it, Colonel," Nathan said. "General Gates has been doing that to me for years."

"Yes, sir. We'll get to them in time," Colonel Belonét said as a soldier called her attention off-screen. She nodded and looked back at Connor and Nathan. "I have a priority mission report that is directed to both of you, for your immediate review. It's from Colonel Quinn. I've sent it along priority channels, and you should have it now."

"Thank you," Connor said as a priority mission update appeared on the sub-window of the main holoscreen in the briefing room. "Carry on, Colonel."

The comlink from the lunar base went dark. The briefing room at Sanctuary wasn't overly large, but there were quite a few people inside. The room quickly cleared out until only Connor and Nathan remained. Priority mission reports required additional authentication, and both Connor and Nathan had to provide that in order to access the report. The minutes flew by as Connor scanned the account. As he read, he felt his brows knit together.

"Holy shit," Connor said.

"That's putting it mildly."

Connor stood up and paced for a moment. "A mutiny," he said and paced some more. "A damn mutiny!" he repeated.

Nathan looked away from the report. None of the questions that were now bursting in both of their minds were going to be answered right then. "This is going to require an extensive investigation."

Connor nodded slowly. "I know. I just don't believe it."

"Neither do I, and I don't want to jump to any conclusions. Sean was giving us both a heads-up."

Connor shook his head, still coming to grips with what he'd just learned. "What the hell happened to them?"

"That's what we need to find out."

"First things first. We need to get them to Lunar Base. Then we'll need to debrief them all," Connor said.

"The investigation will be conducted out of Sierra," Nathan said.

Connor felt a momentary territorial response, but he squelched it in an instant. He just needed to know what the hell had happened. The briefing indicated that Major Lester Brody had attempted a coup in direct opposition to Sean.

"We'll need to brief Governor Wolf," Connor said.

When word of the mutiny spread throughout the colony, things were going to get tense. They needed to conduct this investigation and get it done as quickly and as thoroughly as possible so they could be prepared to answer the tough questions.

"I'll need you in Sierra for a few weeks but not for a day or two. You're still healing, and we have a little bit of time," Nathan said.

The back brace Connor wore caused an itch that he absently scratched. He looked at Nathan.

"I want to go just as badly as you do," Nathan said, as if reading Connor's thoughts.

Hearing Nathan admit that lessened Connor's desire to get on a shuttle and order it to take him to the lunar base right then. "After they reach the lunar shipyards, we'll bring him dirtside ASAP. We need to follow the protocols for debriefing; otherwise, someone might accuse us of meddling."

"We don't want that," Nathan replied.

"The debriefings will be classified until we can present an official report to the Security Council," Connor said.

Nathan nodded and then frowned for a moment. "Have you ever had to deal with anything like this?"

"No, not like this. Mutiny is different than insubordination. This is much worse, and we could speculate on it, but I think we need to wait and get more information."

"Agreed. I'm headed back to Sierra to meet with Governor Wolf. She's going to have a lot of questions that we won't have the answers to, but at least we'll be keeping her informed," Nathan said.

Connor watched as Nathan looked at the mission report on the holoscreen for another moment and sighed, then Connor walked Nathan out of the room and headed back to his office. Debriefing soldiers who returned from a mission had well-established protocols, but what Connor needed to do was to see if they had anything on the NA Alliance military record that dealt with a mutiny. He might find some historical reference, but he doubted he'd find anything like an official report.

Connor closed his office door so he had privacy and opened a comlink to Ashley. It didn't take long for her to be reached at the medical center in Sanctuary.

"Hello, Connor."

"Sean is back," Connor said.

Ashley frowned and peered intently at him. "What?" she asked, her voice sounding slightly hushed.

"Sean is back, Ashley. Your son is home. It'll be a few days before he gets to New Earth, but I wanted you to know first, and I wanted you to hear it from me," Connor said.

Ashley's eyes welled up and she covered her mouth with her hand. She closed her eyes and he heard a half-formed moan as she smiled. "Thank you. Thank you."

Connor smiled back, happy to be the bearer of good news, at least for now. The bad news was coming, but at this moment, Connor was happy to see the relief of a mother who'd learned that her son had returned home from a very dangerous place.

# 29

A WEEK LATER, Connor was at the CDF base in Sierra. As far as weeks went, it had been long and grueling, even with the extra sleep he was getting. He still needed to wear a back brace, but the doctors were pleased with the progression of his healing spine. One of the biggest adjustments Connor was making was the additional sleep required. He was now getting six hours of sleep each night and had been given control of his implants once again. He did feel less agitated, as if the additional sleep had taken some of the edge off his mood. Connor had to grudgingly admit that perhaps the doctors had been correct.

The remaining ships of Trident Battle Group were now at the lunar shipyards. The *Vigilant* had been brought back online with emergency power, and the mission reports had been extracted from the computer core. All the ships in the battle group would be examined from top to bottom before being returned to service.

News of Trident Battle Group's return had quickly garnered

the attention of the colony. What was supposed to have been an expeditionary mission had lasted almost a year, and they had the mission reports to prove it. It was going to take them a long time to go through everything. Of the 2,290 people who'd left with Trident Battle Group, 1,951 returned. There'd been 339 casualties, and among those casualties were 26 mutineers.

Both Connor and Nathan had been reviewing the mission reports from the senior officers of Trident Battle Group. Connor had a lot more to go, but he'd stopped because they were finally going to see Sean face to face. The crews of those ships had been brought back to New Earth, and the debriefing had begun.

Connor headed toward a small conference room where Sean was waiting. He had decided to head there early, and Nathan would join them later. He walked into the empty conference room and found Sean looking out the window. Upon hearing Connor enter, Sean turned around and saluted him. Connor returned the salute and took in the sight of his friend. Throughout his career, he'd seen soldiers age rapidly due to the stresses they'd been exposed to as part of the job. Sean had aged, and he had aged a lot. He was lean and his face was all sharp angles, but his dark eyes still had fight in them. They'd always had a brilliant intensity to them, even though they looked a bit strained. Connor remembered first seeing it when Sean had joined the original Search and Rescue platoon. That was when he'd seen what Sean was really made of.

Connor tried to think of the last time they'd been in each other's presence. So much had happened since then. Both men just stood there, silently regarding one another.

"Hello, Sean."

The edges of Sean's lips tugged slightly. "Sir."

"Welcome home," Connor said.

Sean's brows squished together for a moment and he sighed. "Thank you, sir."

"At ease. It's just the two of us in here. Nathan will be along shortly. You've had quite a journey," Connor said.

Sean was wound up as tight as a torsion spring.

"This isn't going to get any easier. There's a lot for us to talk about, but let's cut right to the chase. Tell me about the mutiny."

Sean did. When he first started speaking, it was only the facts—exactly what had happened and what he'd done—but the more he spoke, the more Connor could see some of the tension leaving him. Connor didn't offer any opinions or ask much in the way of questions. He just let Sean speak. Nathan had joined them part of the way through and told Sean to continue.

Sean broke down the entirety of the mission step by step from when they'd first left this universe to when they realized they had a problem with targeting and couldn't return home. The more Sean told them, the more Connor began to understand the amount of strain that had been put on the entire battle group. More than a few times, Connor and Nathan shared a glance.

"I know there will be a formal investigation," Sean said.

"You can count on it, but before we get to that, there's something I'd like to say," Connor began. "What you and your crew have gone through is beyond anything we could've imagined when you left. You've gone through hell and lived to come out the other side. I don't want you to discount the accomplishments you've achieved, especially in light of what's coming. And what's coming is going to challenge you in particular, but I want you to know that you're not alone. This is the part of the job no one likes, where every decision you made is scrutinized by people who weren't there. It's frustrating as all hell, but it makes us better. Try and remember that."

Sean gave a crisp nod. "I will, sir."

"I can only echo what Connor has said. This investigation is going to take some time to get through. It's not going to end in a few days," Nathan said.

"What happens now?" Sean asked.

"There are going to be long days ahead where you're going to be asked a lot of questions regarding your reports. This will involve all of the senior officers and probably everyone in Trident Battle Group," Connor said.

Sean swallowed and looked away for a moment.

"We need to get through this so we can continue our work building a strategy for the Krake," Nathan said.

"There's a lot you'll need to be brought up to speed on, but there will be time for all that," Connor said.

Sean's gaze hardened. "They're hunting for us. It's not a matter of *if*, it's a matter of *when*."

"Indeed," Nathan agreed. "We'll get to all that," he said and glanced at Connor. Connor wondered what Nathan had in mind but saved that question for later.

"Brody snapped," Sean said. "He snapped under my watch, and I didn't see it coming until it was too late."

Connor and Nathan were both quiet, waiting for Sean to continue.

"I've been going over everything that happened leading up to the mutiny—reviewing reports and going back through my meetings with Brody—trying to objectively look for some sign that would have given the slightest indication of where things were heading. And . . ." he said, pausing for a few seconds to collect his thoughts, ". . . now I don't know if I'm just seeing things because I know what happened. So, it's got this bias now . . . I trusted him. We had our differences, but we had an understanding. He raised good points during planning sessions. He was my XO. The mutiny shouldn't have happened," Sean said with a slight shake of his head. "I understand that there's going to be a lot of people angry about what happened to Brody and the other mutineers. There's going to be a lot of people questioning what I did. I've been questioning it myself since it all happened, and I don't know what I could've done differently to prevent the mutiny from happening in the first place."

"Maybe you couldn't have prevented it," Connor said. "Maybe in *that* situation with *those* soldiers, it was unavoidable. The purpose of the investigation is to reveal whether that was the case. The facts are pretty clear. You didn't give an unlawful command. That's not going to sit well with the civilians, but civilians aren't on the front lines. You're right, Sean. Brody cracked under the pressure. Everyone has a breaking point. We all do, but you didn't reach yours. You held everyone together, even after the mutiny, and got them home alive. Not only that, you brought home critical intel about our enemy."

Sean was quiet for a few moments and then nodded.

"Sean," Nathan said. "Why don't you get some rest and we'll continue to sort this out.

Sean left the conference room, and Connor and Nathan were alone.

"What a mess," Connor said.

"It's about to get worse. News of the mutineers' deaths has

spread. We'll need to assign a protective detail to Sean for the time being. Just until we sort this out."

Connor nodded. "All right, let's get the others in here and start piecing this together."

They needed to provide an official report to Governor Wolf and then deal with the inevitable fallout from that.

# 30

IN THE WEEKS following Sean's return, there had been long days of intensive debriefings that felt more like interrogations, like he was standing trial. Connor and Nathan weren't leaving anything to chance. Every after-action report was scrutinized closely.

Sean was prepared for news of the mutiny to make its way into the public eye. While military personnel could be instructed that events were classified, there was no such agreement with civilians. The CDF was getting pressure from the colonial government for an official report regarding its stance on Sean's actions.

Officially, he was still allowed to come and go as he pleased, but he simply hadn't had the time to leave the base. Sean was being called upon to relive some of the most intense moments of his life over and over again to be scrutinized by other people. Now that he wasn't on the *Vigilant* and in enemy territory, Sean and the other members of his team had had time to reflect on what happened. Major Vanessa Shelton had also endured grueling hours of questioning, which she'd taken in stride, and spent her evenings working out, punching a heavy bag. She'd recommended it to Sean, and he found it was a great way to blow off some steam.

It was early afternoon, and the days were starting to blur together. They were in the middle of a recess, but he knew they'd be sending somebody for him soon. Sean decided to take a walk. He needed to stretch his legs, so he left the main administration building on the CDF base. His two military escorts were an appropriate distance behind him.

The air outside was a bit humid and the skies were gray. It would probably rain later. He found that he kept looking up at the sky. He was still adjusting to not living on a ship. It was nice to be planetside again, but he'd spent too much time sitting in a chair these recent weeks, and he was becoming restless. He needed to move and be active again.

He heard someone call his name and turned to see Noah jogging toward him. Sean smiled and gave his friend a bear hug.

"I guess you hadn't heard, but I woke up," Noah said.

"They've been keeping me busy," Sean said. "It's really good to see you. I'm glad you're feeling better."

"I'm getting there. It took me a few days to even be able to get access to you. It's good to see you too."

They were both quiet for long enough that it was almost becoming an awkward silence. So much had happened to both of them.

"I'm not going to ask you about any of that stuff that's been on the news-net or anything like that."

"I heard about Lars," Sean said, switching the subject.

"Yeah, he's being detained at a facility in Delphi," Noah said. "I've been reviewing some of the research that's been done on the space gate. I'm trying to meet with the scientists involved."

"You should talk to Oriana. She came up with the foundation for the theory that we're working with. We're pretty close. I could introduce you to her. Her name is Oriana Evans," Sean said. He hadn't seen Oriana at all since they returned home. Civilians were undergoing their own debriefing, and he was getting worried.

Noah's eyes widened. "Evans? Her last name is Evans?"

Sean frowned. "Yes. Why?"

Noah looked away for a moment and then gave Sean a guilty look. "Does she have a brother?"

Sean nodded. "She does. His name is Colton—" Sean stopped at the look on Noah's face. "What's the matter?"

Noah swallowed hard. "I don't know how to tell you this. Colton Evans was working with Lars, and he was a terrorist. He's dead. Lars killed him. Colton Evans was responsible for killing both Ovarrow and colonists."

"Lars killed him?" Sean said in surprise.

"Colton almost killed Connor and a lot of soldiers, and Lars stopped him."

Sean frowned and looked away for a moment. Oriana's brother was dead. That could be why she hadn't contacted him. He needed to find her. Sean glanced back at his escorts for a moment. Then he turned back to Noah. "I need to know everything about this. And I need a ride."

Noah nodded, and at the same time, a young soldier ran over to Sean. "Colonel Quinn, they're ready for you to return."

Sean muttered a curse under his breath. “Private, tell them I had to leave. They’ll need to reschedule.”

The young soldier blinked rapidly. “Yes, sir,” he stammered.

Sean followed Noah, and his escorts followed him. Noah glanced at the soldiers questioningly.

“They're with me,” Sean said.

As they walked, Noah told Sean about what had happened with the rogue group Lars had been part of. Sean considered opening a comlink to Oriana, but if she was grieving, he needed to see her in person. She had her own apartment on the outskirts of Sierra, and it was a relatively short ride by C-cat. Noah flew them to the nearest landing area and Sean climbed out.

“Do you want me to wait for you?” Noah asked.

“No, I don’t want to keep you. I’ll find another way back. Thanks for coming to see me. I’ll get to Sanctuary as soon as I can,” Sean said.

He headed to the apartment building and was soon standing outside Oriana’s door. He glanced at the two soldiers behind him.

“We’ll wait outside, sir,” one of the soldiers said.

Sean knocked on the door, but there was no answer. He called out for Oriana, but there still wasn’t an answer. He was about to knock again when the door opened and he peered inside Oriana’s apartment. She was sitting on the couch with her arms wrapped around her legs, which were pulled up to her chest. He walked inside and the door shut behind him.

She didn’t look at him. She was staring at nothing in the general direction of the floor. Her eyes were puffy and red, and it was easy to see that she’d been crying.

Sean slowly walked into the room and couldn’t think of

anything to say to her. Maybe it would be better if he didn't say anything. He sat down next to her and rubbed her back. She squeezed her eyes shut and leaned toward him, and they sat like that for a few minutes.

"I just heard about your brother. I'm so sorry," Sean said.

Oriana lifted her head and looked at him. "I didn't . . ." she said, pausing for a moment, ". . . I didn't want to bother you."

Sean hugged her. "You . . . I'm here for you, no matter what. You know that."

Oriana nodded into his shoulder and he felt her tremble just a little bit. "I should have been here for him. I could've . . . I should have been here."

Sean didn't know what to say. What could he have said? His friend had killed her brother. They sat there together, holding each other on the couch, and eventually they fell asleep. It wasn't a fitful sleep, filled with nightmares, but a deep, dreamless sleep as if neither one of them had slept in months.

## 31

CONNOR WALKED into the Colonial Administration Building. Both he and Nathan were meeting with the Security Council to review the official Trident Battle Group report.

They entered the meeting room that was already occupied by Dana Wolf, Jean Larson, Damon Mills, Clinton Edwards, and Connor's favorite person, Bob Mullins.

"Gentlemen," Governor Wolf said, "thank you for coming. We understand that preparing this report has required a huge effort."

Connor and Nathan sat down.

"I want to go over some of the preliminaries so we're all on the same page," Dana said. "But before I begin, is there anything either of you would like to say?"

"Just that we'll cooperate in any way that we can to put this whole thing behind us," Nathan said.

Dana looked at Connor, but he didn't have anything to say

at the moment. It was probably better that he didn't say anything, at least right then.

"According to the CDF charter, Lester Brody was found guilty of sedition and mutiny. He was supported by twenty-six senior officers, which included the captains and XOs of three destroyer class vessels. No one here is going to argue that Lester Brody wasn't guilty of what he did and the situation he created. However, what we do have questions about is the handling of the mutineers who surrendered to the Spec Ops teams—those officers Colonel Sean Quinn executed by way of opening an airlock with them inside, exposing them to deep space."

Governor Wolf paused for a moment and Connor waited for her to continue.

"I think I speak for most people here by saying that these actions are highly disturbing."

"I agree," Connor said. "But Colonel Quinn did what he had to do to preserve the chain of command."

Bob Mullins leaned forward. "And this gives him the right to be judge, jury, and executioner?"

"In this case, it does," Connor said. "Without the chain of command in those conditions, you have anarchy. Colonel Quinn was establishing order."

"By murdering twenty-six people?" Mullins said.

Connor leaned forward. "Not twenty-six *people*. These were senior officers in command of military warships. They chose to disobey their commanding officer, and not only that, they tried to blockade them from the mobile space gate. They're not just twenty-six random people," Connor said, and his gaze swept across the Security Council. "These were officers who had access to the most destructive weapons in our arsenal. The equivalent would be if I were here and pointed a weapon at all of you. To go one step further, we'd be in enemy territory with the Krake breathing down our necks. So, you can try to compartmentalize what you think are the important points, but not taking the entire situation into context would be a disservice to everyone involved."

Mullins narrowed his gaze.

"Bob," Dana said.

Mullins leaned back. "I apologize, General Gates. I didn't mean to imply that the deaths of the mutineers should be considered out of context of the entire situation. However, I'd like to highlight the point that the mutineers had been taken into custody. They'd also taken the civilian mutineers, but Colonel Quinn didn't have *them* executed."

"No, he detained them."

"So detaining was an option. Why didn't Colonel Quinn choose that for those officers?" Mullins asked.

"It's in the report. We've questioned Colonel Quinn extensively on that point. In his own words, he'd decided that they were a threat. There was a significant risk that they couldn't be held in custody."

"He didn't think he could hold them, so he had them executed, and both you and General Hayes are okay with this. Do you condone these actions?" Mullins asked.

"This is pure speculation," Nathan said. "You can ask me and General Gates how we would've handled the situation, but we weren't in that situation. We might have an opinion that we can safely offer here, comfortable in this room, but would it have been the right call? We'll never know."

Mullins looked at Connor. "General Gates, I know you have strong opinions about this."

Connor clenched his teeth for a moment and inhaled

deeply. “You want to know if I'd have done the same thing if I'd been in command of Trident Battle Group. Despite wearing the same uniform, we’re not all the same, but I’m not afraid to answer the question. If I had been in Colonel Quinn’s position, I would’ve done the same damn thing. I would’ve executed the mutineers because it would have saved lives in the long run. Colonel Quinn was in an extremely hostile situation with an enemy who, in a lot of ways, is superior to our current capabilities, and that wasn't the time to allow the chain of command to unravel. We don’t make commands by popular vote, especially not on a warship. You cannot win a war that way. And make no mistake, this was a war scenario. Nathan is right. This is pure speculation, but I wanted to give you an answer because I’m not afraid to give you an answer. I’m not going to hide behind rules and regulations that I helped create. There are reasons why a commanding officer has that kind of power. I realize this is difficult for you to understand, and it might appear to be brutal, but you’re not out there.”

“You’re right. We're not,” Mullins said. “What we’re trying to determine is whether or not this was a grievous abuse of power.”

“You asked if I’m okay with the situation, and I want all of you to know that I’m not," Connor said. "I want to know where we failed. You seek to point a finger at Colonel Quinn, but I want to know how I let an officer like Brody command a warship. Colonel Quinn’s actions were within his rights as commanding officer of Trident Battle Group.”

Mullins regarded Connor for a few moments and then looked at Governor Wolf.

“General Hayes,” Dana said, “I understand your point about being speculative regarding the situation, but given your experience and the facts, how do you think you would have handled that situation?"

"I would've reasserted control to preserve the chain of command. I would've used deadly force, but what you really want to know is whether I would have executed the mutineers that had been taken into custody," Nathan said, and paused for a few seconds. "I've tried to put myself in that situation ever since I learned about it. What would I have done? And more importantly, did I believe Colonel Quinn had taken appropriate action?

"First, within the letter of the CDF charter, my opinion is that Colonel Quinn acted within his rights as a commanding officer. But to answer your other question, I would not have executed the mutineers that I had taken into custody. I would have detained them, and they would've been brought back here to be dishonorably discharged and put in prison." A flurry of comments began from Mullins and the others. "However," Nathan continued, and the room became quiet, "if detaining the mutineers became an issue, as in they once again attempted to take control of a ship or even the entire battle group, I would have done exactly as Colonel Quinn had done."

Connor looked at Nathan, and they regarded each other for a few seconds. Then Connor gave him a crisp nod.

Bob Mullins appeared smug. "Thank you for your answer, General Hayes. So, the situation we find ourselves in is that we have both of you, who are the most senior officers in the entire CDF, and each of you would have handled things differently."

"Congratulations," Connor said. "You just demonstrated that Nathan and I are different people who have fundamental differences in how we approach tough situations. This doesn't change anything."

"On the contrary, this could change everything."

Connor looked at Governor Wolf. "What's he talking about?"

"May I?" Mullins asked, and Governor Wolf nodded. "Our justice system doesn't have the death penalty. Those extreme measures of justice have been abolished for hundreds of years, but it still exists in the military. It's time that we put this under review."

Connor shook his head and looked at Governor Wolf. "The rules and regulations we have in the CDF charter weren't put there because we simply thought it was a good idea. These things were put there because they're built upon established military practices that have been in existence for hundreds of years. They've been proven. They work. At the end of the day, what we'll all need to accept is that this entire situation was an unfortunate consequence," he said and looked at Mullins. "You want to point a finger at Colonel Quinn, and as the commanding officer of Trident Battle Group, that might be appropriate. We, as leaders, are responsible for those under our command. But the fact of the matter is that Lester Brody created the conditions under which Colonel Quinn had to act."

"What other action could Brody have taken? He was a senior officer, and I presume he took the action he thought was necessary," Mullins replied.

"You mean what could Brody have done other than hold civilians as hostages and threaten to open fire on other CDF warships?" Connor asked, his voice like sandpaper rubbing on a bit of a snarl. "He could have recused himself from duty. That would've been a peaceful form of rebellion. Instead, he chose sedition and a grossly negligent act of mutiny," he said, his eyes glittering dangerously. He inhaled deeply and sighed. "In simple terms, he cracked under the pressure."

Governor Wolf regarded him for a few moments. Connor could tell she was conflicted. Some of these issues were hitting close to home. Meredith Cain and the rogue group's activities had occurred under her stewardship. Did this make her ultimately responsible for everything Meredith Cain had done?

"It's important that we review these things," Dana said. "It's how we improve. Maybe nothing will change, but maybe something will. We shouldn't be complacent with practices that have been around for hundreds of years. Sometimes things need to be questioned, reviewed, and considered as to whether those practices still make sense."

"I understand, Governor Wolf," Connor said.

She was doing what she felt she had to do, but what Connor knew was going to happen was that people were going to use these events to assert themselves. They were going to prop Sean up as a dark example. Sean was a war hero and deserved much better. Connor glanced at Bob Mullins and could guess where most of the mudslinging was going to come from.

As the rest of the Security Council meeting went on, Connor had to accept that there could have been no other outcome. Part of him even agreed with what Dana had said. Maybe they should review these policies, but he would never find fault with what Sean had had to do. Perhaps it was because he'd been a soldier longer than anyone here. This situation was a morally gray area, and it irritated Connor that there were going to be people who used that to gain an advantage in their political machinations. What he had to figure out now was how to prevent it from ruining Sean's life.

## 32

SEAN WENT with Oriana to visit her brother's grave—the place where his ashes had been buried. She wiped off the top of the headstone and placed some flowers native to the area on top. They had flaming orange petals that surrounded a purple center like a fan. He thought they looked nice.

Oriana felt extremely guilty, believing that if she'd been on New Earth she could have prevented her brother from committing his crimes. She was angry—at her brother, at herself, and even at Sean a little—but he understood. She didn't blame Sean. Not really. She was grieving. He knew what it was like to mourn the loss of someone close. Family. It'd taken him a long time to grieve the loss of his father. He'd never stopped missing his father, and there were times when he found himself wishing he could speak to his father again. How would his father have reacted to some of the things Sean had done? Would he approve? Sean didn't think his father would have, and he could live with that. It was more important that his father understood why Sean had made some of those tough decisions, even if they'd never agree. His understanding would have been enough.

He exhaled softly. Noah had been there for Sean when his father died. He was a good friend. Lars had been there for him too. They were like brothers to him. Sean winced a little.

*Lars . . . what happened to you?*

He shook his head slightly. He couldn't dwell on Lars right then—another time, but not now. Oriana needed him.

"He did such horrible things. That's what everyone is going to remember about him," Oriana said.

"What do *you* remember about him?"

Oriana shrugged a little. "He was my baby brother. He always had a temper, but he was sweet. He wanted to help people."

"Then remember that. Remember the good things he was and try not to hold onto the bad things he did," Sean said.

They stood there quietly. Sean would be there for as long as she needed him to be. He wished he could think of something else to say, something that would take away her pain, but he knew there wasn't anything. No one could ease her pain. She just needed time.

Later, they returned to the Colonial Administration Building where the Security Council was meeting. They had been meeting there for days, going over the Trident Battle Group report that contained the findings of the CDF investigation. Sean knew they were discussing his actions, and he felt that he should be in the room. Both Connor and Nathan agreed that he didn't need to be there, but Sean couldn't be anywhere else. If he wasn't allowed into the room to defend his actions, he could at least be nearby.

He and Oriana were sitting in the large atrium just inside the entranceway when he noticed somebody walking toward him and saw that it was his mother. She gave them both a hug.

"I'll give you two some time to talk," Oriana said and left them.

His mother looked at him with a bit of sympathy and then glanced in the direction Oriana had left. "Are you together now?"

Sean smiled. "Yes, we are, but I'm sure you don't want to talk about my love life."

"As long as she treats you right, that's all I really care about. Does she make you happy?"

Sean rolled his eyes. Of all the things that were going on right then, that question had caught him off guard. "Yes, she does. Thank you for asking."

They sat down on a nearby bench.

"You may not realize this, but I understand what you're going through," Ashley said.

Sean arched an eyebrow toward her.

"Don't give me that. You think because you're a soldier you're the only career field that deals with life-and-death decisions."

Sean considered it for a few moments. His mother was a medical doctor. "I guess I never really thought about it."

Ashley nodded. "Life-and-death decisions are my forte, and they sometimes get reviewed and scrutinized by everyone for years. So I understand what you're going through, at least in part. It's never easy."

"What I did is putting pressure on the entire CDF," Sean said.

"Sean, don't be foolish. The CDF is always under pressure.

You made your decisions based on the situation. You're no stranger to making difficult choices in situations that the best of us might freeze in. Remember, the people who got to come home did so *because* of your leadership and not in spite of it. No matter what happens, never forget that."

"Do you ever second-guess yourself? I keep thinking about whether I should've handled the situation differently."

"Of course I do. It's the tough choices we have to live with that make us do so. Honestly, I'd be worried if you weren't conflicted about what happened."

Sean exhaled deeply. "I regret the lives that were lost, but I still stand by my decision. Does this make me a bad person?"

"I'm not here to judge you, Sean. You're my son, so I'm a bit biased. You have to live with the decisions you've made, and it sounds like you are. You've already answered the question. You wouldn't change anything but you don't like it, and there's nothing wrong with that."

Sean nodded. "I've been thinking about whether I should resign from the CDF."

Ashley looked at him for a few seconds and then shrugged. "That's another question I can't really answer, but I will tell you this: You don't owe anyone anything. This colony survived because of your actions during the Vemus War. Time and time again you've risked your life for this colony. You've risen so far because people trust your leadership. The question is, do you still trust yourself? I trust you. I know Connor does. And your father did. He would've understood what you did."

"But would he have been able to look me in the eye afterward without seeing all the . . ." He'd been about to say "blood on my hands," but his mother knew what he meant.

"Yes," Ashley said. She reached out and took his hands in her own. "Without question. You are our son and we love you."

Sean felt some of the weight he'd been carrying lift just a little bit. "Thank you," he said. "I guess I just need some time to think about it."

"Well, whatever you decide, I'm sure it will be the right decision."

# 33

THE EARLY MORNING hours at the Colonial Administration Building were dark and quiet. Connor had gotten only a few hours of sleep, but he was restless. He could have remained at his quarters on the CDF base, but he knew he had to come here anyway for another meeting with the Security Council.

His footsteps echoed across the vast atrium just past the entrance of the building. Wallscreens were active, showing various scenes of the colony from when they'd first arrived to the sprawling cities they'd built. There were even several wallscreens showing CDF soldiers. Connor walked over to them and gazed at the various portrayals. He was about a quarter of the way around the atrium when Bob Mullins spotted him.

Connor glanced at the advisor. "I'm surprised you don't just sleep in one of the meeting rooms in the upper levels."

"It wouldn't be the first time," Mullins replied.

They were alone in the atrium and probably the whole building.

“Don’t let me interrupt you, General. I’ll leave you to it,” Mullins said and began walking away.

Connor watched him go for a few moments. “What do you really want from me?”

Mullins stopped and turned around, frowning.

“I might be guessing, or let’s call it careful speculation," Connor said. "You want to review the CDF charter. The mutiny. There isn’t a legal case there. Even if something changes, it won’t affect Sean. You can’t change the law and then retroactively prosecute someone.”

Mullins nodded. “You’re right; we can’t do that.”

“But you can ruin Sean’s reputation. What I can’t figure out is why. Is it because of me?”

“What he did was reprehensible,” Mullins said, but then his gaze softened. “But then again, so is war.”

“I respect that you want to improve things, but do it without riling the public into a frenzy. Those kinds of decisions should be based on good judgment rather than anxiety,” Connor said and closed the distance between them. “So, I figure there's something you’re angling for.”

“I work in the governor’s office. There is always something I’m angling for. You think you’re different than me, but you’re not. Otherwise, you wouldn’t be here.”

Connor snorted bitterly. “So, we both have a healthy work ethic.”

Mullins looked away, considering. “You’re convinced that the Krake are going to find us. They’re going to come to New Earth, and we need to be prepared.”

Connor frowned and then nodded.

"Well, it just so happens that I agree with you."

Connor's eyes widened a little. "Then why are you working against me?"

Mullins shook his head. "Not necessarily against you. We just have a different opinion on how to prepare for the threat."

Connor glanced at one of the wallscreens. It showed an image of the *Ark* in orbit around New Earth. He looked back at Mullins. "This is about setting up another colony, isn't it?"

Mullins twitched his head to the side in a small nod. "A backup site. Just in case. Continuity of the species and all that."

Connor pressed his lips together slightly. "What does this have to do with me?"

Mullins let out a small chuckle. "I need your support. I won't gain any traction for establishing a new colony if I don't have your support."

It was Connor's turn to chuckle. "I don't see—"

"There it is," Mullins interrupted. "Let me put it this way. If I were to get your support, then the new colony would stand a much better chance of getting off the ground."

"Why didn't you just ask me?"

"This *is* me asking."

Connor shook his head. He was finding it hard to believe what he was hearing.

"You don't believe me, I can tell," Mullins said. "Fine. I do believe the CDF charter needs to be reviewed and challenged. This will take time, and there will be people whose performance will be highlighted as examples of our core values and of what we should strive to improve."

Connor narrowed his gaze, knowing that Mullins was referring to Sean. "You're proposing a compromise."

Mullins nodded. "Yes, neither of us gets exactly what we

want, but we each get something. You get to save your protégé, and I get your support to establish a secondary colony. What do you say?"

Connor pursed his lips, thinking about all the possible outcomes of compromising with someone like Mullins. Alternatively, he could spend weeks or even months in meetings defending the CDF charter instead of devoting himself to the important task of defending the colony from the Krake. He looked at Mullins, who waited with all the patience of a spider. They clashed like water on flame. Connor thought about the work that would be involved in establishing a small colony on another world, but the request wasn't unreasonable.

"I think we can work something out," Connor said.

---

"I'M sorry for all the trouble this has caused," Sean said.

Connor and Sean were standing in Connor's office at the CDF base in Sierra. "That's the last time I want to hear that from you. Stop apologizing. I mean it."

Sean nodded. "What happens now?"

"We put all this behind us and focus on what's important. But I will say this: Over ninety percent of the soldiers that were part of Trident Battle Group would serve under you again."

Sean frowned and looked away for a moment.

"Brody was the minority, and sometimes the minority has the loudest voice. They don't represent what everyone is thinking. Remember that. You're a good soldier, a good leader. I'm proud of you. I don't think it's much of a stretch to say that one day you'll be a general."

Sean's eyes widened and he almost shook his head. "I

appreciate that, but I don't know . . . if staying in the CDF is what's best for me."

"I don't care; I need you."

Now Sean did shake his head, and he smiled a little.

"You're a soldier to your bones. It's part of you just like it's part of me. So we both got beat up a little bit. We can take it because that's who we are. We can make the tough choices, but we can also evaluate our decisions to make sure we're still on the right path. Do you understand what I mean?"

"Yes."

"Good," Connor said and used his implants to activate the nearby wallscreen.

The entire wall became active. The top showed the words of the Krake hierarchy. Just below them was a label that said "Overseers?" The lights dimmed in the office, showing the full breadth of the data they'd gathered about the Krake.

"This screen just shows us what's on the surface—what we know of the Krake and how they operate. This one includes the Ovarrow and contains all the interactions we've had with them so far," Connor said and gestured toward the adjacent wall, activating a third wallscreen. "And these are things the Ovarrow believe they know about the Krake. We've been trying to analyze what's fact and what's conjecture."

"That's difficult to say because the Krake control what the Ovarrow know about them," Sean said.

Connor nodded. "That's true. There's a lot more information we have to go through, but I figured you'd want to see this."

Connor watched as Sean took a good look at both wallscreens and all the data on them.

"Somewhere, buried amid all the evidence we've gathered

here on New Earth and possibly on some other world, is a way to stop the Krake. And don't doubt for a second that they can be stopped."

Sean frowned. "Aurang said the Krake had never encountered anyone like us on any of the other Ovarrow worlds. I think it's that kind of challenge that's going to draw them to us."

Connor nodded. "You're probably not wrong about that. Now, all we need to do is find out where they live and stop them from coming here."

"Just that?" Sean said. "So, you're saying this is going to take a while?"

Connor grinned. "Maybe a little."

# AUTHOR NOTE

Thank you for reading Harbinger, First Colony Book 9. I sincerely hope you enjoyed it and the rest of the books in the series. Telling Connor's story has been a privilege, along with Sean, Diaz, Lenora, Noah—Yeah, I know, we'll see a lot more of Noah in book 10. Head injuries can take a long time to heal. I have personal experience with this with one of my kids.

These days it seems like everyone is asking for a review for anything and everything. I get review requests when I go to stores, visit the doctor's office, and even the dentist. Enter for your chance to win...I bet you can guess what's coming next. I'd like for you to leave a review for Harbinger. I know. Not another one! I get it, but they are essential to help spread the word about the book to other readers. Your reviews also help Amazon decide whether to show my books to other readers. I also read all my reviews. Every single one of them. I don't respond to them, but I definitely read them all. If you've reviewed my other books, please accept my thanks and consider writing another one for Harbinger. If you don't want to leave a review, then don't worry about it. I get it. Telling a friend who might like the book also helps a lot.

Again, thank you for reading one of my books. I'm so grateful that I get to write these stories.

**If you're looking for another series to read consider reading the Ascension series. Learn more by visiting:**

**https://kenlozito.com/ascension-series/**

I do have a Facebook group called **Ken Lozito's SF readers**. If you're on Facebook and you'd like to stop by, please search for it on Facebook.

Not everyone is on Facebook. I get it, but I also have a blog if you'd like to stop by there. My blog is more of a monthly check-in as to the status of what I'm working on. Please stop by and say hello, I'd love to hear from you.

**Visit www.kenlozito.com**

THANK YOU FOR READING HARBINGER - FIRST COLONY - BOOK NINE.

If you loved this book, please consider leaving a review. Comments and reviews allow readers to discover authors, so if you want others to enjoy *Harbinger* as you have, please leave a short note.

**The series will continue with the 10th book.**

**If you're looking for something else to read, consider checking out the Ascension series by visiting:**

https://kenlozito.com/ascension-series/

If you would like to be notified when my next book is released please visit kenlozito.com and sign up to get a heads up.

I've created a special **Facebook Group** specifically for readers to come together and share their interests, especially regarding my books. Check it out and join the discussion by searching for **Ken Lozito's SF Worlds.**

To join the group, login to Facebook and search for **Ken Lozito's SF Worlds.** Answer two easy questions and you're in.

## ABOUT THE AUTHOR

Ken Lozito is the author of multiple science fiction and fantasy series. I've been reading both genres for a long time. Books were my way to escape everyday life of a teenager to my current ripe old(?) age. What started out as a love of stories has turned into a full-blown passion for writing them. My ultimate intent for writing stories is to provide fun escapism for readers. I write stories that I would like to read and I hope you enjoy them as well.

If you have questions or comments about any of my works I would love to hear from you, even if it's only to drop by to say hello at KenLozito.com

Thanks again for reading ***First Colony - Harbinger***

Don't be shy about emails, I love getting them, and try to respond to everyone.

## ALSO BY KEN LOZITO

**First Colony Series**

Genesis

Nemesis

Legacy

Sanctuary

Discovery

Emergence

Vigilance

Fracture

Harbinger

Insurgent

Invasion

**Federation Chronicles**

Acheron Inheritance

Acheron Salvation

Acheron Rising (Prequel Novella)

**Ascension Series**

Star Shroud

Star Divide

Star Alliance

Infinity's Edge

Rising Force

Ascension

**Safanarion Order Series**

Road to Shandara

Echoes of a Gloried Past

Amidst the Rising Shadows

Heir of Shandara

**Broken Crown Series**

Haven of Shadows

If you would like to be notified when my next book is released visit kenlozito.com

Made in the USA
Columbia, SC
20 May 2021

38254011R00195